Also by Jason Mott

THE CROSSING

THE WONDER OF ALL THINGS

THE RETURNED

THE FIRST

WE CALL THIS THING BETWEEN US LOVE

HIDE BEHIND ME

HELL OF A BOOK

or

The Altogether Factual, Wholly Bona Fide Story of a Big Dreams, Hard Luck, American-Made Mad Kid

Jason Mott

First published in the United States by Dutton,
an imprint of Penguin Random House LLC, New York

First published in Great Britain in 2021 by Trapeze,
an imprint of The Orion Publishing Group Ltd
Carmelite House, 50 Victoria Embankment,
London EC4Y 0DZ

An Hachette UK company

3 5 7 9 10 8 6 4

This book contains an excerpt from the poem
'Requiem for a Friend' by Rainer Maria Rilke.

This is a work of fiction. All the characters in this book are the
product of the author's imagination or are used fictitiously, and any
resemblance to actual persons, living or dead, is purely coincidental.

A CIP catalogue record for this book is
available from the British Library.

ISBN (Hardback) 9781398704640
ISBN (Trade Paperback) 9781398704657
ISBN (eBook) 9781398704671

Designed by Kristin Del Rosario
Interior art: Silhouettes by Vividfour/shutterstock.com;
Hat by LU_Designer/shutterstock.com

Printed in Great Britain by Clays, Elcograf, S.p.A

www.orionbooks.co.uk

For All the Other Mad Kids

HELL OF A BOOK

"When you see yourself in the mirror, do you like what you see?"

"I try not to look. I think a lot of people like me are like that."

"When you say 'people like me,' what do you mean?"

In the corner of the small living room of the small country house at the end of the dirt road beneath the blue Carolina sky, the dark-skinned five-year-old boy sat with his knees pulled to his chest and his small, dark arms wrapped around his legs and it took all that he had to contain the laughter inside the thrumming cage of his chest.

His mother, seated on the couch with her dark hands folded into her lap and her brow furrowed like Mr. Johnson's fields at the end of winter, pursed her lips and fidgeted with the fabric of the tattered gray dress she wore. It was a dress she'd bought before the boy even came into this world. It aged with him. Year upon year, the blue floral pattern faded, one shade of color at a time. The threads around the hem lost their grip on things. They broke apart and reached their dangling necks in every direction that might take them away. And now, after seven years of hard work, the dress looked as though it would not be able to hold its fraying fabric together much longer.

"Did you find him?" the boy's mother asked as her husband came into the room.

"No," the boy's father said. He was a tall man with large eyes and a long, gangly frame that had earned him the nickname "Skinniest Nigga Breathing" back when he was a boy. The name had stuck over the years, lashed across his back from childhood to manhood, and, having never found a cure for his almost mythological thinness, the man had taken to wearing long-sleeved clothes everywhere he went because the empty air held within the sleeves made him look larger than he was. At least, that was what he believed.

He was a man who had been afraid of the eyes of others for all of his life. How could he not want his child to learn the impossible trick of invisibility?

"It's okay," he said. "We'll find him soon. I know it. I'm sure that, wherever he is, he's fine. He can take care of himself. He's always going to be fine." He took a seat beside his wife on the tired brown couch and wrapped the spindly reeds of his fingers around the fidgeting doves that were her hands. He lifted them to his lips and kissed them. "He's a good kid," the father said. "He wouldn't just up and leave us. We'll find him."

"He's the best boy in the whole world," the mother said.

"Maybe he just went off into the woods to find some briarberries. I bet that's where he went."

"You think so?"

The father thought for a moment. "Not sure, but I'm hopeful, Dollface."

The boy's mother chuckled at "Dollface" and dabbed the corner of her eye. Was she crying?

The groundswell of laughter that had been tickling the boy's throat for so long finally—as he sat, invisible and unseen only an arm's length away—faded at the sight of his mother's tears. His arms tightened around his legs.

He shouldn't have done this. He shouldn't have made them worry like this. They were good parents and they hated worrying about him. A lead ball of regret formed in the boy's stomach. It rang and drummed through his entire body. He needed to stop this trick he was playing on them . . . but how?

What could he do? He was less than two feet from where his parents sat, but guilt over his mother's tears pushed down on the hands that would reach out and touch her and let her know he was there. It weighted down the tongue that would sing her name and free her from fear.

There was no way, his five-year-old mind figured, that he could let them know that it had all been a joke. He could never explain to them that this was all meant to be fun. Not just fun, a celebration! After all, he had done it! For three years now, his mother and father had been trying to teach him to become invisible, to become "The Unseen." That was the name the boy's father gave to it. He said the words with a fantastic tone. He spoke with his hands in the air, sweeping back and forth gently like he was playing some magical instrument. "You will become The Unseen," the boy's father said. He added an almost spooky "Ooooooo" to the end of it sometimes. "You'll be unseen and safe for as long as you live," his father said. ". . . Can you even imagine it?"

It was the words "unseen and safe" that made his father smile. It was the boy's favorite smile, like he was watching his father gain everything he had wanted out of his life.

Unseen and safe.

Sanctified words.

"What should we do?" his mother asked her husband.

"Should we just call it quits?" replied the boy's father. He put a spindly hand on his forehead and looked very dramatic all of a sudden, the way people in movies sometimes did. And, yet, the boy thought he saw the beginnings of a smile hiding in the shadows of his father's face. "I mean," the boy's father continued, "if he's gone, maybe we should make like a banana and split. We could pack it all up and head out west somewhere. I hear they got tons of kids out there who need a fine set of parents like us."

The boy's mother smiled as though her husband had told a joke. Humor was one of his gifts. His jokes painted the walls of his family's home in brushstrokes of laughter.

But, in spite of the fact that he knew his father was trying to be funny, the boy heard his words and imagined his parents leaving him and, once again, the sea of fear swelled up inside of him.

"No, no, no," said his mother.

And just like that, the fear ebbed.

"You're right," his father said. "We could never leave him. He's just too great. No other kid in this world like him. So what should we do?"

"I have an idea," the boy's mother declared. Excitement filled her voice and spilled over into the boy. His mother always had the best ideas.

"We'll cook everything he likes to eat. All of it. One big meal like they used to do back in the old days. And the smell of it will go out all over the world and find him. That'll bring him home!"

The boy almost cheered. A great dinner of all his favorite things. All of it spread out on the kitchen table, one dish after the other. The idea that the smell of the foods he loved could go out into the world and bring him home . . . it was like something from one of the books he read at bedtime: all myth, and dream, and splendor.

The boy's father leaned back for a moment and looked at the mother through squinted eyes. "His favorite foods?" he said, stroking his dark, narrow chin. "You reckon that'll work?"

"I know it will," his mother said. "He'll smell them. The chicken. The macaroni and cheese. Maybe even a sweet potato pie or two. He never could turn down sweet potato pie."

"Pie you say?" The boy's father licked his lips. "You could be onto something with this scheme of yours. It's got legs, I think. Just like you." He kissed his wife's neck and she laughed the light, lilting laugh that she sometimes did late at night when the two of them were alone in their bedroom with the door locked.

"Stop that," she giggled.

"I don't know," the father said, his mouth a wry grin. "I still think we might could go out west and find a new kid. I hear they make some out there that actually like to eat their vegetables."

The mother laughed and the boy almost laughed too. "No," she chuckled. "We'll cook and he'll come back to us. Just you watch."

She stood then and brushed off her old dress as she always did and she went into the kitchen. For a moment, the father stayed in the living room and stroked his chin again. "Well, kid," he mused, "wherever you are in this world I hope that you know that I would never move out west and try to find another son. You're the only ankle-biter I could ever want."

Then he stood and went into the kitchen and began helping his wife.

Before long, the house billowed with the smells and sounds of the boy's favorite food. The chicken fried in a heavy black skillet and the macaroni bubbled and baked in the oven. There were sugared strawberries, and muscadine grapes, and leftover pound cake that the boy had forgotten was still in the house. Even though he was still hidden, his stomach growled so loudly that he feared it would give him away. But his mother and father didn't seem to hear and so he was able to continue to sit—even with the hunger in the pit of his stomach—and close his eyes and smell all of the dancing aromas.

In that moment, invisible and buried in his parents' love, he was happier than he had ever been. And soon, in spite of his hunger, he was asleep.

He awoke to the feeling of his father lifting him in his arms.

"There you are," his father said.

He carried his son into the dining room, where the table was covered with all of the boy's favorite foods.

"There he is!" the boy's mother screamed at the sight of her son. Then she hugged him so tightly that he could hardly breathe. That was always his favorite type of hug. It was like melting into the summertime earth.

And when the hug was over, his mother kissed him and asked, "Where were you?"

"I did it," the boy exclaimed. "I really did it!"

"Did what?" his father asked.

"I was invisible!"

His parents' eyes went wide as star magnolias.

"No!" his father exclaimed with joy, looking very dramatic like TV people again.

"You really did it?" his mother asked, equally elated.

"Yep," the boy chirped, almost laughing. "I was in the living room this whole time. Unseen just like you said. It really worked, Mama!"

Then his mother hugged him and the three of them danced and laughed and smiled like they never had before. In that moment, the worries that had always hung over their heads were suddenly gone. It was as though all three of them might suddenly levitate off of the floor, float up into the blue sky that sprawled itself out long and wide above the small country house that the family called home.

The next day, the boy, still drunk on sweets and wonder, asked his father: “You really couldn’t see me, could you?”

“It doesn’t matter if I saw you or not,” his father said. “All that matters is that you felt safe.”

The thing to remember is this: above all else, this is a love story. Don't ever forget that.

But now that that's out of the way, let's get acquainted:

It's 3 a.m.

It's 3 a.m. and I'm somewhere in the Midwest—one of those flat states where everyone seems nicer than they should be. I'm in a hotel. In the hallway. I'm running. No, actually, I'm sprinting. I'm sprinting down this midwestern hotel hallway. Did I mention that I'm naked? Because I am.

Also: I'm being chased.

About fifteen feet behind me—also sprinting, but not naked—is a very large man wielding a very large wooden coat hanger. Sometimes he holds it like a baton. Other times he holds it above his head like a battle-axe. He's surprisingly fast for a man his size.

The very large man with the very large coat hanger is draped in Old Navy couture: beige straight-fit stain-resistant khakis, argyle sweater vest, brown twill boat shoes that may or may not be faux leather. He's a family man for sure. 2.3 kids. Dog named Max. Cat named Princess. Aquarium that's on its twelfth goldfish named "Lucky." He drives a Camry and lives on a cul-de-sac in a home surrounded by a picket fence. There's an in-ground pool in the backyard. He's got a healthy 401(k).

He's everything a responsible adult should be.

He looks to be about the same age as I am—leaving the decadent comfort of thirty and reluctantly knocking on the grizzled front door of forty. And for an instant, as the two of us sprint down this luxurious hotel hallway—feet thumping on the carpet, lungs burning, arms pumping like oil wells—I think about stopping and asking him how he built that life. How he made it all come together so perfectly. How he managed to do everything I've been unable to. I want to hear his secret.

But as I take a look back over my shoulder, I see him raise that coat hanger of his into a battle-axe position and shout, "My wife! That's my wife! We made babies together!"

No. This won't be the day I find out the secret of people like him. All I can do now is try to stay ahead of that coat hanger. So I put my head down and try to remember what my high school track coach told me: "High knees. High head. High speed."

It's in moments like this that I remember why I don't have encounters with married women. Inevitably, it leads to encounters with married men.

Anyhow, the angry man behind me has a damned good stride, but I've got better turnover. Being fast is all about turnover. That's another thing my old track coach told me. "Pick-'em-up, put-'em-down. Bam-bam-bam-bam! Hustle! Hustle!"

And that's what I do. I hustle.

I also like to think that being naked affords me some sort of advantage as well. Wearing no clothes means you're carrying less weight. That always makes you faster.

And, sure enough, I'm slowly pulling away from both him and his coat hanger. But the problem is, all hotel hallways, like all lives and stories, eventually lead to an end of some sort. Either an elevator or a fire door. In this case, it's an elevator. Those shiny sliding doors peek out from the distance as he and I round a bend in the hallway.

That's where he's going to catch me. At the elevator doors. I know it. He knows it. That large wooden hanger in his right hand knows it.

I'm not generally the praying type, but there are no atheists in foxholes or in the path of a cuckold's rage. So I send up a little prayer and try to focus on keeping my knees high.

I manage to open up a little more distance.

"Our daughter was almost in a Target commercial!" the angry husband behind me yells. "We're a family! You don't boink a man's family!"

In any other context I'd high-five the guy. That's a hell of an accomplishment. I mean, we're talking Target! To almost land that . . . man, that's something!

Just as I'm getting close enough to that dead end where the elevators stand and where I'll have to come to a stop and this angry, large man and his coat hanger will finally be able to have their way with me, just then, the elevator dings and the silver doors glide open just as smoothly as the gates of heaven.

My personal savior steps out of the elevator. She's eighty if she ever danced a jig. Short. Thin. Wispy blue hair crowning her head like dandelion spores. Makeup thick as stucco. Her arthritic back bent with the burden of two fistfuls of grocery bags and octogenarian existence itself.

Why she's out grocery shopping at 3 a.m. doesn't seem to be an important question just now.

"Ma'am!" I shout.

She looks up. Sees me—my high knees, my high head, my high speed, my nakedness. She sees the man behind me with his hanger battle-axe. She shrugs her shoulders, turns on her heel, turns and steps back into the elevator.

"Would you hold that elevator, ma'am?" I yell.

The angry man behind me shouts something about the high cost of two daughters with braces.

The elevator doors start to close and I kick it into a gear higher than I knew I had. I'm just a blur of knees, and elbows, and naked flesh. Even my genitals have pulled themselves into an aerodynamic tuck.

I'm just close enough to make a dive as the elevator doors begin to close. I take the leap.

It's all slow motion. I sail through the air for what seems like an hour. As I soar past the Blue Hair—just before my face meets the back of the elevator—I can see from the smirk on her face that this isn't her first late-night rodeo. She's been around. She's danced on water in life's late hours.

My face meets the elevator wall a split second before my body does. Momentum holds me there like a bug on a windshield, then gravity shows up again and I thud to the ground.

"Thirty-second floor, please," I say as soon as my naked body has come to rest on the floor of the elevator. The Blue Hair complies and pushes the elevator button.

The two of us watch the doors grind closed just as the husband with bloody murder in his eyes—who probably isn't a bad guy when you really get to know him—reaches the elevator a moment too late and can't do anything other than watch me leave. He shouts something indecipherable as the doors close in front of him. Something to do with responsibility. Something to do with family, and marriage, and love.

Then he's gone and there's just me and the Blue Hair. The two of us watch the elevator count off the hotel floors one by one. I imagine the silence is awkward for her. Most people don't like silences. I learned that at my old job. I used to answer phones for a living. All day long, that job was nothing but talking to people. I'm not what you might call a people person. I hated that job. But the irony is that by working there, I found out how to talk to people really well. One thing I know is how to make folks feel comfortable.

"Hell of a night," I say.

"I could tell you stories," the Blue Hair replies, quick as a whip.

"I'll bet you could. You've got that look about you."

"Life's chaos," the woman says, sounding suddenly like an oracle. "It's all just a runaway mule hell-bent on destruction."

"That's some mule."

"You bet it is."

I give a nod to indicate her grocery bags. "Good haul?"

"Capital," she says. "Just capital." She gives a nod to indicate my exposed genitals. "You wax?"

"No, ma'am. Razor."

"Gets that close?"

"Five blades. Pivoting head. Marvel of the modern age."

The woman nods in agreement. Then she clears her throat and

contorts the corners of her thin, old lips into a thin, old frown and says "Did you hear about that boy?"

"Which boy?"

"The one on the TV." She shakes her head and her blue hair sways gently like the hair of some sea nymph who's seen the tides rise and fall one too many times. "Terrible. Just terrible."

"Yes, ma'am," I say.

The truth is that I haven't heard about whatever boy on the TV she's suddenly so sad about, but I don't have to know about it to convey the appropriate amount of sadness and concern. I turn the corners of my mouth into a frown that matches the one the Blue Hair's got. I don't want to frown too much and make it look like I'm trying to make this terrible thing—whatever it is that happened—about me. But I also don't want to not frown enough and come off uncaring. There's an art to knowing how sad you're supposed to be at moments like this.

"A terrible shame," I say. "Just can't believe such a thing could happen in this world." I shake my head.

The old woman sucks her teeth in pointed disapproval. "So sad," she says. "Just so sad."

I don't say anything for a while. I let the air grow cold between us. A moment of silence for whatever boy's sad tale we're both grieving over right now. I want this wonderful stranger to know that I cared about this boy, because caring about people is what good people do. And more than anything, I want people to think of me as a good person.

The elevator chimes, breaking the silence. The doors open at my floor.

"Well," I say, stepping out into the soft, empty hallway that has no angry husbands or wooden coat hangers, "I guess this is goodbye. Thanks again for your help. And God bless that poor boy." I give one final nod. I feel like I should say something meaningful about chance meetings, the allure of strangers, serendipity . . . all those sorts of things. But nothing comes to mind so I turn on my heel and begin my naked walk back to my room.

After I'm a few steps down the hallway, I hear her call out: "Hey!"

"Yeah?"

"You look familiar. Have I seen you before? Are you famous?"

"Aren't we all?" I say.

She nods and retreats into the elevator. The doors close and I'll never see her again. Not because I don't want to. But just because that's how it goes. Life decides.

I walk the rest of the way back to my room feeling pretty good about life. Tonight's been an adventure. Met a lovely woman. Met her husband—who I'm sure is just as lovely when you get to know him. Even met a sweet old lady with a flair for conversation. I've got fresh air on my naked skin.

What more can a person ask for in this life?

It's only when I get to my hotel door that I realize I've left my key in my pants back in the bedroom of the angry husband's wife.

WITH IT BEING AS LATE AS IT IS, THE HOTEL LOBBY IS NEARLY EMPTY. It's one of those big hotels where the floor is overly polished and the ceiling is so high you can hear yourself breathing if you really stop and listen. It's an eerie place, especially when it's crowded. The whole room sounds like some grand train station. Voices blend together into that familiar assonant murmur, suddenly sounding like every conversation you've ever had has come rushing back to you and, in spite of yourself, you can almost believe that at any moment a train might come rumbling up right in front of you, right behind the concierge's desk, carrying every person you've ever known. It's strange, but I get that particular feeling six days out of seven in my life.

"How can I help you?" the woman working the front desk asks. From the calmness in her tone, you'd think she's spent every day of her life dealing with naked hotel guests.

"I seem to be locked out of my room," I say.

"Well, I'm sorry to hear that," she replies brightly, her voice almost in a singsong. "I'll definitely help get that straightened out for you. Which room?"

"3218."

She clicks on her keyboard.

"Do you get a lot of naked people in your hotel lobby at this hour?" I ask.

"Define 'a lot,'" she says, smiling a toothy, slightly crooked smile that's as warm as sunlight in August. After a few more keystrokes, she says, "Now, I'll just need some type of identification."

I reach past her and into the nearby magazine rack. I pick up a copy of *Entertainment Weekly.* My beautiful mug is right there on the cover, larger than life, even overshadowing the headline about Nic Cage's newest Cagetacular film, beneath the looming demi-Helvetica headline: **AMERICA'S HOTTEST NEW AUTHOR.** I hold the magazine up next to my face and say, "How's this?"

BECAUSE MY FACE AND A COPY OF *ENTERTAINMENT WEEKLY* don't qualify as "acceptable identification," the receptionist and I are in the elevator together. I'm still naked. She still doesn't seem to mind. Hotel policy says she needs to see a driver's license, which, luckily, wasn't in my pants—which are still in the room of a certain married woman and a coat-hanger-wielding husband. So she's riding up to let me into my room so I can show her that I am who I and *Entertainment Weekly* say I am.

She smells of vanilla.

"You smell like apples, Sport," she says, maybe reading my mind, maybe not, and she glances at me with a grin—being sure to keep her eyes above the waist. It's the kind of grin that I sometimes don't know what to do with. The kind of grin that says maybe she likes me. And, believe it or not, I'm never really sure how to act when a woman throws me that kind of attention. So I just stand there, thinking about what a random thing what she said is to say to someone. "I know that's a pretty random thing to say," she continues, continuing to be uncanny. "But I think it's a pretty random thing to experience. You know?"

"I do know," I say. I want to tell her that "a pretty random thing to experience" would make for a fitting send-off on my tombstone one day, but I think that might come around as a bit morbid, and I don't think morbid is what this moment calls for. So, instead of the headstone remark, I just say something along the lines of "It's amazing the things we notice sometimes. Makes us wonder if they've always been there."

"I know what you mean," she says. "Also, I read that if you meet someone and they smell like apples, what you're really smelling are pheromones. You know what pheromones are, don't you, Sport?"

"Pheromones, huh?" I spend a second just thinking about the word "pheromones." A good word, that one. Looks sharp on the page and feels good on the tongue. "Why do you keep calling me Sport?" I ask.

"What's the matter?" she replies. "Aren't you a sporting kind of guy?"

Somewhere around the sixteenth floor I start to figure out that maybe she's flirting with me and even before the sixteenth floor I knew that she was beautiful in that managerial way and so I think it's time I let her know that, hell, I think she's pretty swell too. So I put on my best Bogart brogue and I give it to her right down the middle:

"Nice set of pillars you're standing on."

"They hold me up," she says, not missing a beat. She says it like she's read the same script as me. She's a caricature and so am I and right now in my life that's, well, that's pretty aces in my book.

"I always knew heaven had to stand on something," I say.

"Is that a quote or something?"

"Or something."

This is one of those times when I can't tell how much of this moment—or almost any moment of my life, honestly—is real and how much is imagined. I've got a condition. I've got several conditions, actually. The most interesting one is this thing I got where my mind runs away with itself. It's like daydreaming except it doesn't really go away when I want it to. It lingers. Sometimes people call it a disorder, but I'm a glass-half-full kind of guy so I don't go in on that dime-store wordage.

Basically, I'm a daydreamer. But my daydreams tend to persist longer and more intensely than most people's do. At least, that's what I've been told by every doctor I've ever seen. The end result of it is that reality is a very fluid thing in my world. It's probably the reason I got into this whole writing thing to begin with.

Another thing you should know about me, beyond my tendency

to have an overactive imagination, is that I'm a sucker for old black-and-white movies. You know the type. The ones with fast-talking men and even faster-talking women.

Right now, my imagination and I could easily change the lighting in this elevator and it would be a scene fit for *Double Indemnity.* The same hard-shadowed lighting and machine-gun dialogue. Nobody today talks the way those characters talked in that movie. Maybe they never really did. So maybe this isn't exactly how the exchange between her and me went. Or maybe it is. Like I said, I get the sense that she's read the same script as me. I rarely worry about the facts, only about the reality that my imagination and I choose to see.

"You're confident," the receptionist who smells like vanilla says.

"And a confidant to those who need it. You got something you wanna share with me?"

"You always drive this fast?"

"You should see me in the curves."

And then she smiles.

WE TUMBLE THROUGH THE BEDROOM DOOR. IT'S HARD TO TELL where my body ends and hers begins. It's all just skin, and nerves, and warmth, and those little butterflies that come bubbling up in the pit of your stomach when you know—I mean really KNOW—that you've met someone special. Someone who will endure. Someone whose face you'll see again and again for years and live a life all the richer for it.

She could be *the one.* This could be love.

That's how alive all this feels. But love happens like this sometimes, doesn't it? A lightning strike rather than a rising tide. You meet someone and everything goes warm inside you and when they put their hand in yours, you can feel every inch of their body, like dipping your finger into a river and being able to feel the whole ocean.

And I feel that with this woman. At least, that's what my imagination tells me.

THE MORNING COMES AND I WAKE UP AND STILL DON'T KNOW WHAT midwestern city I'm in and the receptionist is already up and gone and she's left a little note behind on her pillow that reads, "You're a good sport, Sport!" And in the light of this new day I don't feel like last night was love at all, but it was a hell of a fun way to interact with another soul. Think about it: it took over 4 billion years for her life and mine to come together in that elevator. If that ain't special, I don't know what is.

So right now I'm feeling pretty good about fate and kismet and being a good sport, and I'm also feeling pretty hungry. I want pancakes, and orange juice, and maybe a little bit of vodka to get the aforementioned orange juice up on its legs.

I put on my clothes and ease out the door.

DOWNSTAIRS, BREAKFAST IS IN FULL SWING. THE HOTEL IS A BIT ON the swanky side but when it comes to feeding people they aren't much better than the usual Holiday Inn—a fine establishment, by the way; I'm just saying that for $300 a night—even when the publisher's footing the bill—I expected a little more than what's presented to me. But since I'm not the picky sort, I move through the

buffet breakfast line and grab my plate and take a seat in the far corner and I look out into the city—whatever city this is—and I wonder what the day will bring.

It's about this time that I feel myself being watched. It's one of those animalistic feelings. Something that rings of alarm and worry in the softest of ways. Like standing in the shade of an oak tree and getting the feeling that it's all about to come crashing down on your head.

"Hey," a voice says.

I turn to find a kid standing beside my table.

I peg him at about ten years old. A little gangly, meek, and nerdy-looking, you might say. Like the kind of kid who's spent too much time in books and not enough time grabbing life by the short and curlies. Sometimes you see kids and you just know. You can just see their entire future in their eyes. That's who this kid is: he's his entire future seen at a glance.

But all of that is secondary to his skin. It's black. But not just black, he's impossibly dark-skinned. The darkest skin I've ever seen. It's like a clouded ocean sky in the dead of night. It's like burrowing into old caves where sunlight has never set foot. It's the kind of black that makes me think he's got to be wearing some sort of makeup. The kind of black that makes me question if what I'm seeing is real or if I'm in the beginning stages of some kind of ocular or neurological crisis.

His lips are moving but I'm so startled by the color of his skin that I can't hear a word he's saying. "What was that?" I say.

"Can I sit here?" He points to my chair and begins seating himself before I have time to give him permission.

The kid has a plate of pancakes and sausage that's so much like my own I've got to respect it. As he starts eating, I look around, trying to lay eyes on whoever it is among the rest of these fine breakfast goers that might be his parents. The last thing I want is to have some terrified parent come up to my table screaming at me about why I'm having breakfast with her son. That kind of publicity can kill a book tour.

When I can't find anybody that looks like they might be the progenitor of this dark-skinned splendor, I resign myself to having met a new friend and I jump into the same type of banter I would offer anyone else in this world. "You look like someone who's had his fair share of adventures, Kid."

"Yeah, I guess," The Kid says. He keeps his eyes on breakfast as he talks, which I'm glad about because it allows me to look at the inky depths of his skin without making him feel awkward. It's hypnotic, The Kid's blackness. The kind of thing that has to be seen to be believed. Staring at this kid's skin makes me feel like I'm falling. Like it's pulling me into him. Like I was never separate from him to begin with and his skin—all shadow and shade—is only trying to take me back where I belong so that it can keep me safe.

"It's cool," The Kid says.

"What's cool?"

"Staring like that. It's cool. Everybody does it." He shovels another forkful of pancakes into his mouth and I imagine that they taste like embarrassment.

"Nonsense," I say. "I shouldn't be staring at anyone. I've got no grounds for it. Why, just last night I was down here in this very lobby naked for the world to see. Naked as a jaybird, as my dear, departed father might say. If anyone deserves to be stared at, Kid, it's me."

The Kid nods but continues to keep his eyes aimed at breakfast. I know shame when I see it. A twinge of guilt runs down my spine.

"So, to what do I owe the honor of this breakfast?"

As I talk, I look up at the television on the far wall just in time to catch the tail end of a report about some dead boy. Got himself shot by somebody but I don't know who because the television switches to ESPN and suddenly there are grown men slamming their heads into one another and shouting about first downs. "Tired of hearing about that shit," says the gentleman apparently responsible for the channel change. From the reaction of the others in the dining room, they're all a little tired of hearing about that shit too. So I turn my attention back to The Kid, who still hasn't answered my question.

"Well?" I say.

"Just thought it was time we met," The Kid says. "That's all."

"Well, that sounds ominous," I reply with a smile.

"Nah," The Kid says, flashing a smile full of marble-white teeth. Contrasted against the darkness of his skin, it just might be the most beautiful smile I've ever seen. "It's not like that," The Kid says. I begin to hear a drawl in his words. Something southern Black. He's offered up more than a few "y'alls" and "my neck of the woods" in his short-lived life. He sounds like old Cadillacs and boiled peanuts, sweet tea and home. It's as beautiful as his skin and his smile. "I've wanted to talk to you for a while now," The Kid says.

I smile my best "Always good to meet a fan" smile and I say, "Do you want me to sign a copy of your book?"

The Kid grins. "Nah," he says. "Not a fan. Just wanted to meet you."

"Alright," I say. I've met a few fans like this since starting this book tour. I'm learning to roll with it. "Well, it's great to meet you too."

As interesting as this kid is to look at, there's something unsettling about him too. As I watch him eat, I'm filled with the urge to get away from him. I want to go back to my room. I want to go back to my room, and curl up in my bed, and fall asleep and not see him in my dreams.

I realize that I can't just sit here with this kid anymore. My mind won't stand for it. I keep staring at his skin and I keep telling myself not to do it. I want to stare at him as much as I want to never look at him again. Something about him fills me with an immediate sense of love and hate. I want to hug him and push him away at the same time. And I know that all of this stems from the impossible color of his skin.

I wonder what growing up with skin like that must have been like. Going to school looking like that? Must have been hell. Pure fucking hell.

"Well," I say, "it's been good meeting you and I hope you enjoyed meeting me. I would love to say something about fate and the power of chance meetings, the allure of strangers, serendipity . . . all those sorts of things."

"It's cool," The Kid says. "You ain't gotta stay. I just wanted you to see me. That's all."

"Well, consider yourself seen," I say. I aim a pair of finger guns at him and "Pew-pew!"

I offer one last smile at The Kid in honor of his gentle yet eloquent phrasing. "I just wanted you to see me." That's a beautiful thing to say to someone. I mean, don't we all want to be seen?

Before I leave, I lean in close and say, in my sincerest voice, "I see you."

Then I head back to my hotel room.

I STRETCH OUT ON THE BED AND TRY TO GET SOME REST BEFORE THE next leg of the book tour. The last thing I see in the darkness before sleep takes me is the darkness of The Kid. I see his skin. It's darker than the darkness of sleep. And then he grins and his pearly whites shine like snow on dogwoods.

Then The Kid fades away. His smile lingers, but then it's gone too.

As sleep finally gets its fishhooks into me, I offer up a heartfelt "Poor kid" for the pitch-black boy I met today. Living a life looking like that in a world that works the way this one does? . . . I wouldn't hang that noose around anybody's neck.

The boy was ten now. Five years older than he was when his parents made him believe that he could turn invisible. And in those five years, he had learned that none of it was true. And nowhere else was the truth of his parents' lie more evident than on the morning school bus ride.

More than anything else in this world, he hated that ride. It was where they had named him "Soot."

Soot. Four little letters that hung around his neck like a lodestone. So every day as he watched the school bus come rumbling along the dirt road toward him, he shuffled his feet and chanted a mantra over and over again: "Don't let them see you. Don't let them see you." Even though he knew all the talk of The Unseen wasn't true, he was still child enough to want to believe that it was true.

So each morning, he tried to be Unseen.

He climbed onto the bus quietly—without laughter or hello—and he kept his eyes aimed at the floor as he made his way to his seat. Then he slid in against the window, and placed his bookbag in his lap, and pulled his hoodie over his head, and faced the window, and breathed slow and even, like a gazelle hiding among lions.

And sometimes it worked. Sometimes he was invisible. Or, at least, that was how it felt. But it was a tentative invisibility, full of tense nerves and anxiety. It was time spent listening to the conversations of the other kids, listening for his name, listening for the four-letter word that he had become: "Soot." It was a terrible type of hiding, not the safe and happy place his father and mother had described when they'd told him about The Unseen. But it was the best he had and so he took what he could from it.

And on the days it didn't work, when he hid as best he could but it didn't work, it always failed in the same way, all because of the same person.

When the bus pulled up in front of Tyrone Greene's house, Soot trembled. He pressed himself even more tightly against his window seat and held his breath as the eighth-grader climbed aboard the bus and stomped down the aisle to the back where the other eighth-graders sat.

Tyrone Greene was the biggest eighth-grader on the planet. His father owned a farm and kept Tyrone out in the field all through the summer and, because of it, he had the muscles and angles of a grown man even though he had barely broken the seal on being thirteen. He was the kind of kid who knew his body gave him power over others. He was the kind of kid who wasn't afraid to use that power. He was the kind of kid who had nicknamed the boy "Soot."

For the next twenty minutes, Soot didn't move. He stared out of the window, watching the old trailers, and magnolias, and sprawling fields pass him by. He counted the moments, hoping all the time that the school would suddenly appear and he could exhale and race off of the bus before catching Tyrone's attention.

"Hey!" a baritone voice called out from the back of the bus. Soot flinched. "Hey, Soot?" Tyrone called. "Soot? Hey, nigga, you hear me! Answer me!"

Soot's jaw tightened like grapevines and he closed his eyes as hard as he could. His entire body tightened. He whispered to himself: "You're unseen and safe. You're unseen and safe. You're—"

His mantra was broken by the thud of Tyrone's heavy bulk flopping into the seat beside him. "Soot?" Tyrone growled. "Don't ignore me, blerd nigga. That shit pisses me off."

"What?" Soot finally replied. He kept his face to the window because he knew that the tears were not far away and, if he had a choice, he would keep them to himself.

"Hey, man," Tyrone said, his voice soft all of a sudden. "Hey, turn around, my nigga. I'm trying to talk to you, you know?"

Soot pulled off his hood and turned to face Tyrone. He was as broad as any man, with a sharp nose, and light-brown skin, and a slightly crooked smile. "Why you be trying to ignore me, Soot? You know you my nigga." Tyrone's smile widened, like always. "We cool, ain't we?" He held up a large, callused hand offering a shake.

Soot watched the hand hang in the air for a moment. This too was a part of the way this dance with Tyrone always went. It was a terrible ceremony that resurrected itself over and over again, day upon day, through the years like the hope we all have of being truly loved.

"You ain't gonna shake my hand?" Tyrone asked. The hardness had returned to his voice. "Don't leave me hanging, Soot."

Because he had no other choice, Soot shook Tyrone's hand.

"There we go," Tyrone cheered. "That's my nigga."

The other kids on the bus watched and listened. They too, willing or unwilling, were a part of the ceremony. Up front, they turned and leaned over the backs of their seats, watching. Some of them grinned. Others did not grin, but neither did they look away. Soot wondered about those kids the most. He wondered how they could watch and say nothing. But he also knew that he would do the same.

The eighth-graders in the back all migrated up to the center of the bus, all of them sitting and leaning in a semicircle around Soot and Tyrone, pulled by the persistent gravity of cruelty.

"So how you doing, Soot? You good, man? Family good? All that?"

"Yeah," Soot replied. He said the word as hard as he could, trying to force the one syllable to make him sound bigger than he was.

"Yeah? That's real good to hear. Your daddy still skinny as fuck, I bet." Tyrone glanced around at the other kids, then turned back to Soot. "Hey . . . can I ask you a question, man?"

A lump swelled in the boy's throat. He tried to choke it down—the shame, the fear, the tears that were on their way—but it got stuck and he nearly vomited. He cleared his throat and turned his face to the window again, wishing for something to come along and take him away from all of this.

He wished that he could disappear again, become completely unseen like he had done that day. For years now, his mother and father had made him close his eyes and say, over and over again, "I am unseen and safe. I am unseen and safe." But it never worked. Sometimes his father would sigh heavily when the boy failed to become invisible again. Soot's mother was more patient, if not sadder, when her son failed to find the magic. "It's okay," she told him. "You'll get it."

"Is this for real?" Soot asked. "Darryl at school said people can't turn invisible. He said you're tricking me."

"Don't worry about what Darryl at school said," his mother

warned. "Just because nobody else can do it doesn't mean you can't make it happen."

"Have you ever done it? Or Dad?"

"No," his mother said, her voice suddenly a soft apology. "But you will," she said. "The only thing that matters is that you learn to do it."

"Why?" Soot asked.

"Because you have to" was the only answer she ever gave him.

"Hey," Tyrone said, pulling Soot out of his hope that some sort of salvation would come for him. "I said can I ask you a question? You not ignoring me again, are you, nigga?"

"Nah," Soot said. He took a deep breath and wiped the first tear from the corner of his eye. He couldn't stop what was coming. Now he just hoped to bear it out with as little crying as possible. "I'm not ignoring you. What you want to ask me?"

"Cool. Hey, you know you my nigga, right?" Tyrone began.

"Yeah," Soot said. "I know."

"So I gotta ask you, dude . . . you know you black, right?"

Soot hesitated. Again he wished to be invisible. Again, shamefully and persistently, he continued to not be invisible but to only be his impossibly dark-skinned self. Of course he knew he was black. Not dark-skinned, but black. Black as shut eyes. Black as starless nights. Black as stovepipe soot.

He wore hoodies and long pants all year round in the hopes that the kids would see less of his dark skin and find fewer reasons to pick on him. But none of it helped. He was the boy named Soot, and no one would ever let him forget it. Nothing he ever did would change that.

"Answer me, Soot," Tyrone prodded. "You know you black, right?"

Tyrone had the perfect skin. High yellow. Light as butter. The holiest of blessings. Light skin got you girls. Light skin made teachers like you. Light skin made you a star in Hollywood. Light skin was everything. And almost all skin was lighter than his, so what did that say about what the future held for him?

"Yeah," Soot said, "I know." He smiled, as though a smile could deflect the pain.

"Yeah. But you ain't just black, nigga. You extra black. Like, I bet you sweat coffee." The first snicker rippled through the kids on the bus. "I mean, why you steal *all* the darkness? Why you so stingy?" More laughter. A few rows away, a girl yelped out a high-pitched laugh. "Nigga, your mama must have been blind and she wanted you to look like what she saw. Nigga, I bet when you get out of the car your daddy's oil light come on." The snickers turned to giggles turned to belly laughs. The entire bus was in on the fun now.

"Why you gotta be so black?" Tyrone asked. "I mean, not just why, but how? How you come out so black? Is it the sun? Is that what it is? I mean, damn, nigga, you extra black. You black with a side of black. You my nigga and all, but damn . . . You got all the black!"

Every time Tyrone said the word "black," Soot flinched and the tide of laughter around him swelled a little higher. Soot swallowed again and tried to find somewhere to turn his eyes away from Tyrone but there was nowhere else that he could look. Tyrone was the mirror that reflected the blackness Soot wanted to be and could never be. Tyrone was blackness that didn't have to be black. His hair was soft and had a curl to it that didn't need chemicals, and his nose was straight and thin, and his lips were equally thin, and yet he could be black when he wanted and he could be something else when that mood suited him too.

What else could a person want?

"I mean, really, though," Tyrone continued, "what makes you so dark, nigga? Why you so black?"

Soot shook his head and laughed a nervous laugh. "You crazy."

"I'm not joking. Why you so black?"

"Man . . ."

"Why you so black?"

"Just . . . stop. Okay?"

"Nah. Not until you answer me. Why you so goddamn black?"

"Why are you doing this?"

"Why you so black?"

"Leave me alone."

"Make me. Why you so black?"

"Please . . ."

"Why you so black?"

"Please, Tyrone."

"Why you so black?"

"Stop!"

"Why you so black?"

Soot's cheeks were wet with tears. Laughter echoed around the narrow metal frame of the bus until the whole thing shook like the floor of a Baptist church at revival. The laugher continued until Soot sobbed in the corner and the bus driver finally yelled something back at all of them about getting back in their seats.

Tyrone stood. "What you crying for, nigga? Damn. You know I'm just fucking with you." Then he disappeared into the back of the bus, followed by the other eighth-graders, all of them grinning like angels.

Later that night, as the rest of the house lay sleeping, Soot sat up in his bedroom doing his best not to cry and failing at it. The sound of his intermittent sobs woke his father, who came and sat on the end of Soot's bed and said, simply, "Don't listen to what people say. Fuck them. You're beautiful, son."

"Why do I have to look like this?" Soot asked. His broken sobs became a steady stream.

"One day, you're going to have to learn to love who you are," his father said, but Soot could not hear him over the sound of his grief. And so, Soot's father climbed into bed with his son, and held him, and shushed him as the boy wept while, outside, stars shined and the ebony night wrapped the singing earth.

I'm sorry. I haven't introduced myself. I'm an author. My name is ———. Maybe you've heard of me and maybe you haven't, but you've probably heard of my book. It seems to be selling pretty well. It's called *Hell of a Book.* And, according to the reviews, it's a hell of a book.

It's in brick & mortar stores. It's online. It's been Kindled and Kobo'd, iPadded and Audible'd. It's been optioned so that it can be movie'd—Joseph Gordon-Levitt and Donald Glover are both said to be interested. We're even in talks to have it comic book'd. My publisher is happy. My editor is happy. The company I pay my student loans to is happy. My agent and publicist is . . . well . . . she's involved, and I think that's as close to happy as publicists get.

But I'm not here to talk about my book. Not just yet. Everything has to begin somewhere first.

I grew up in a small house in a small North Carolina town you've never heard of because it's never produced anything of value or done anything other than stand as a stagnant tide pool as the course of time rushed past.

I had parents whose names you don't know but I'm sure you can imagine. Picture my father, tall and lean. He worked at a sawmill all his life. Picture my mother, short and round. She worked as a mother all her life. Somewhere in the middle of that common equation, I grew into a skinny kid who read a lot of books. I was dead center of the bell curve in school. I was a prodigy of mediocrity.

I was fourteen when I decided I wanted to be a writer. Back then it was simpler. I started by writing alternate endings to my favorite books and myths. In my version of the *Odyssey*, Athena never shows up and Odysseus takes on the suitors in a battle royale. He loses an arm in the fight but is henceforth known as Odysseus the Severed which, obviously, is a much better name.

Even when I started writing, it wasn't anything impressive. My characters were flat. I couldn't write a decent scene to save my life. Every sentence ended in an adverb. The crowning achievement of my early attempts at creative description is summarized in the time when I once described a tree as "a tall, wooden growth with limbs like a tree."

But I liked telling stories. And that was really the only requirement to be a writer back then, back when I was still trying to be a writer. The irony is that, once I actually became a writer, my life wasn't really about writing anymore. Funny, that.

In high school, I was the skinny kid with bad acne that didn't talk and that no one talked to. I never fell in love. Or, rather, I fell in love but it was never returned. Friday and Saturday nights were spent in my bedroom with a bowl of Cheetos and a plot so complicated, I needed three dry-erase boards just to keep up with it. On senior prom night, while everyone else my age was out learning the geometry of the opposite sex in the back seats of cars and the bedrooms of parentless homes, I was lying on the floor of my living room with an ink pen between my teeth and a Boyz II Men cassette crooning at a low roar while I tried to figure out why the main character in my third novel—a detective named "D.T."—was a man who had never gotten a fair shake in life and had suffered because of it and, oddly, could never remember how to tie his shoes. I wanted it to be an endearing personality quirk, but it just wound up reading like he had Alzheimer's. Later in life, as I kept writing him, D.T. the Detective would come to remind me of my father, but for different reasons.

When I was fourteen, I was diagnosed with my daydreaming problem. I saw things. I saw dragons in sunsets and rainbow skies at midnight. I had friends that only I could see and my dog spoke to me. It was a wild time. And it was a bit too much for the small life my country upbringing had room for. I think I scared my parents pretty well in those first few months. We tried doctors and medicines but, in the end, I just learned to keep my mouth shut and, eventually, I began to get a sense of what was real and what was mine alone to see and experience.

Learning that difference made my parents feel like their son was sane again—being the Baptists that they were, they promptly offered up the glory to God—and it wound up being the greatest gift I ever had. Entire worlds were mine and mine alone. People, creatures, and sights unimagined by most people were a place where I lived.

It went this way for years. Just an era of dreams, delusions, and the usual social awkwardness mantled on the shoulders of all teenagers.

Before I wrote *Hell of a Book*, I worked in Customer Service Hell. I've ridden cash registers at Walmart, peddled pots and pans at Bed Bath & Beyond, slung soggy spaghetti noodles and endless breadsticks at Olive Garden. The list goes on. If there's a customer out there in need, chances are I've serviced them. But the job I held just before my life changed was at a certain internationally known cell phone provider that, for the sake of litigation avoidance, we'll just call "Major Cell Phone Company." As Sharon, my agent, likes to say: "Don't get sued unless you can guarantee it'll be good publicity for your book."

Let's take a little moment to backtrack a bit. Bask in a few memories of the way things used to be. In this context, the rules dictate that when memory is put on a page it's called backstory.

So picture me in a cubicle on the second floor of a three-floor call center in the sweaty underarm of southeastern North Carolina. I'm sitting there at my desk with a pair of headphones on, chatting with someone I'll never meet but who, in her own way, was a damned fine dame.

"Yes, ma'am," I tell the woman on the phone. She's in Brooklyn and I'm in North Carolina. She's got one of those splendid New York accents—all demand and immediacy—but she seems swell enough. She laughs at my jokes and she's one of the saner customers I've had today.

"So what do you think?" she asks.

"Well, I don't think he's cheating," I say. Which is only a partial lie. The truth is that I *don't* think her husband's cheating on her, but the fact that she felt the need to call in and have me sift through six months of phone records shows me that there's definitely some issue with their marriage.

"What do you think it is?" she asks.

"I just think maybe the two of you need to learn to communicate a little better," I say. "The fact is, you're pretty great—at least, from this side of the phone—and, from what I've heard, he seems like the type of Joe who's doing right by you. So I think the two of you should get a room somewhere for the weekend. You know, trip the light fantastic until nobody can breathe and all you can do is feel. When's the last time you did that?"

"Nineteen ninety-four," she says.

"Ninety-four was a good year," I say.

"It was a wonderful year," she replies.

"Jean-Claude Van Damme was king of the world back then."

"And let's not forget Seagal."

"Let's never forget Seagal."

Then she sighs and it's one of those long, relaxing sighs that says she's finally letting go of whatever she's been holding on to. She's finally clawing her way out of her relationship and back to herself. We all get lost in one another. And sometimes it takes a total stranger who just happens to work at our cell phone company to help us find our way out of that kind of forest. It's nobody's fault.

So the woman from New York and I don't forget Seagal for the rest of that conversation—which doesn't last much longer. She's gotten what she came for. I've applied a tourniquet to her marriage and saved her fifteen bucks on her monthly cell phone plan. A win for me. A win for her. A loss for Major Cell Phone Company.

I let her go with one of my classic lines: "Here's looking at you, kid."

She starts to say something but my finger is already on the End Call button. The last thing I hear is something along the lines of "Did you hear about the shoot—"

And then she's gone.

That's essentially what the job is: meet someone, form a bond, help them, let them go when the time comes.

Immediately after Ms. 1994 is gone, my buddy Sean comes walking over from his cubicle to mine. Sean's a good guy. The type of guy you'd be proud to go off to war with if the opportunity arose. He's a straight shooter, as some people are apt to say.

"So how goes the morning?" Sean asks.

"Met a woman who was in love back in ninety-four," I say.

"Ninety-four was a good year."

"That's what I told her."

"I could go for someone cool like that. I just spent the last hour talking to a pilot."

"Fuck."

For the record: pilots are horrible people. Just horrible, horrible people—at least, when it comes to the world of customer service. Maybe it's all that flight school bravado they get from watching reruns of *Top Gun* just before they take to the skies in what's basically a giant steel elephant. I think they imagine being pursued by Russian MiGs and all that.

Whatever the reason, when pilots become customers, they show up on the other end of the phone line barking orders. You always know a pilot when they call in because they always tell you they're pilots. "I'm a pilot!" they shout. And then they say: "If I make mistakes, people can die! Do you understand what that means?"

Apparently, it means that they're allowed to yell at you and call you a stupid buffoon, an idiot, a moron, a pussy, a bitch, a cunt, and whatever else comes to mind.

"Pilots," I say to Sean. "Goddamn pilots."

"Tell me about it."

"How many fuck yous did he lay on you?"

"I lost count at seventeen." Sean shakes his head. "Hey, did you hear about that boy?"

"What boy?" I ask.

"The boy who—"

Just then, an alarm goes off nearby. It's one of those rapid, irritating buzzers that makes you think of electricity arcing through fingertips.

"Hell," Sean says, pinching his nose in frustration.

"Surprised we made it this long before it happened," I say.

From somewhere in the sea of cubicles, like a tidal wave of obnoxiousness, they come . . . the Culture Crew. The Culture Crew are the people Major Cell Phone Company tasks with saving our sanity at a job steeped in insanity.

Working in customer service sucks. And working customer service at Major Cell Phone Company—or any cell phone company—sucks even more. The fact is, no one calls their cell provider's customer service number because they're happy. Nobody calls to say "Hey, guy or gal. I'm having a great day. Just wanted to let you know."

Oh no.

They call in with problems. And nine times out of ten, the problem is something that I or my coworkers had absolutely nothing to do with.

Your call got dropped? The cell tower did that. Not me.

Your kids ran up your phone bill? Little Johnny or Little Susie did that. Not me.

Your phone fell in a puddle of water? Gravity did that. Not me.

Your phone got eaten by your pet raccoon? Randy the Raccoon did that—true story. Not me.

You were traveling in Europe and your phone told you that you were roaming but you still used it anyway and now you've got a five-thousand-dollar phone bill? You and whatever network you were roaming on did that. Not me.

But when you called in, I'm the guy who got the call. I or one of my beloved coworkers. Eight hours a day, seven days a week, 365 days a year: we're the people you blame.

Try sitting through that for four years and not going off the deep end. Few people are built for it. Fewer and fewer each and every day. Half the people working at Major Cell Phone Company are on antianxiety pills or antidepressants. And a significant number of them are gun owners.

So with that going on, people got in the habit of quitting the job. They quit it frequently and in style. Our office had the highest turnover rate in the whole damn city. More than the police force. More than the local paper mill where at least twice a year somebody lost an extremity on a saw blade. So once the higher-ups got wind of how everyone was quitting the job, they came up with the Culture Crew.

The Culture Crew smiles too much. The Culture Crew laughs too much. The Culture Crew is too damned excited about any and every thing that happens in the course of an average day. But that's their job. They exist to keep you from quitting, to keep you from yelling at Mr. Asshole who has just called in and reminded you that he's not the kind of loser to ever work a job like yours. They exist to keep you from coming into the building one day with an anger that could get you in trouble.

So when the buzzer goes off, we know they're coming. It's like the blowing of some ancient war horn. You gird your loins and await the horde.

Sean and I watch as the Culture Crew emerges from the wasteland of corporate inculcation. Their smiles fly ahead of them like military banners. They carry baskets filled with miniature candies that sometimes spill out onto the floor, leaving behind a trail of sugary goodness, marking their sacred path for others to follow.

After a quick look around, I see where they're headed. A few rows over in Cubicle Hell, a young blonde woman—too young and too optimistic-looking to have been working here very long—has just bolted up from her desk with a grin on her face. She puts a hand over her headset and declares, "I just saved a customer!"

Major Cell Phone Company loves it when you keep people from disconnecting lines of service. They love it more than anything else in the world.

She looks around for someone to high-five her. She gets one taker. It's a pretty limp endorsement. Only new people who have yet to have their spirit broken actually care about saving customers. Veterans just want to survive.

But the Culture Crew more than makes up for that when they finally reach her. They pull the cover off of one of their baskets to reveal an assortment of doughnuts. They reach in and pull out two chocolate-covered ones and place them on the desk in front of her. Then they grab a fistful of miniature candies and toss them at her like confetti.

"Congratulations!" the Culture Crew leader shouts. She is a tall blonde woman who is perpetually too thin and perpetually wearing too much makeup. She looks like Barbie came to life and couldn't find anything better to do with her time. So she aged a little and married someone other than Ken and came to work for the corporate machine.

Having buried the excited, line-saving woman in doughnuts and candies, the Culture Crew disappears into the hive of cubicles like steam. One moment they're there, the next moment they're gone.

So, in my imagination, they are everywhere. Always ready to pounce. Always ready to smile at me, and cheer, and give me doughnuts because I saved the company thirty-two cents or something.

"Just wait for it," Sean says.

"I know," I reply.

"So, the boy," Sean begins. "He—"

But no sooner do the words leave his mouth than the Culture Crew buzzer crackles the air again. It sounds like a duck being electrocuted. They emerge, once again, from the places unseen and from time immemorial. Already, I can smell fire and brimstone and confectionary treats.

Another glance around Cubicle Hell shows me where they're going. Not far away from the woman who just stood up and shouted with pride about how she had saved a customer, there sits another woman. He eyes are puffy, and her hand is trembling, and, if I listen closely, I can hear the customer on the other end of the line yelling at her. He ends the phone call by calling her a "home-stealing cunt."

Whose home he blames her for stealing, I doubt any of us will ever know.

The woman is about to break down. About to cry and maybe even walk out of the building—finally quit this job and become the hero we all long to be. But the Culture Crew is there.

They swarm her desk: same smiles, same laughter, same trail of miniature candies spilling out onto the floor in their wake. Without a word, they place a chocolate-covered doughnut on her desk and a handful of candies.

"But I'm diabetic," the woman sobs, tears streaming down her face.

Then a tall, not-unattractive woman looks over at the two of us. She smiles and waves, aiming the smile at the both of us, but clearly aiming the wave at Sean. He returns the wave like sending back a Christmas fruitcake.

"How's that going?" I ask.

"The fact that it's still going is the issue," Sean replies.

"I don't see it," I say. "She looks like a fine dame. Maybe the kind a person settles down with."

"She does look that way, doesn't she?"

"So what's the problem?"

"Jesus."

"Ah," I say.

"She's just a little bit too . . . too . . ."

"For Christ!" I shout, throwing a salute at the same time.

"Yeah," Sean says. "That's it. We can't get through appetizers without talking about the Second Coming and the fate of my immoral soul."

"*Immortal* soul."

"That's not what she calls it."

"Did you tell her you're an atheist?"

"I did."

"And what did she say?"

"I forgive you."

"Gotta respect that."

Sean takes a look over my desk. Lying there in tatters is my latest manuscript. It's still a train wreck at this stage. Not yet blossomed into *Hell of a Book.* Right now, none of the characters know what they want. And since they don't know what they want, they don't know why they're doing anything. They're just billiard balls banging against one another. And nobody wants to read anything about that—even if that's just how people go through life sometimes. Naturalism is dead—at least in the marketplace.

"So how's that thing coming along?" Sean asks.

"It's a train wreck," I say.

"But what kind of a train wreck?"

"Vietnam."

"You know," Sean says, "I read an article the other day about how fewer people actually get the Vietnam reference when you use it that way. When you use it that way, you're dating yourself. It's better to say Afghanistan."

"So if I say Afghanistan, I sound younger?"

"Exactly."

"Hell of a world," I say.

"Tell me about it," Sean says. "It's like what happened to that boy."

Even though I have no idea what boy he's talking about, I say: "Yeah . . . damn shame."

Because like I told you before, that's what you say.

MOST OF THIS ISN'T OVERLY IMPORTANT. NOT IN THE GREATER scheme of things. This is just to talk a little bit about where I was before I got to where I am now. Because where I am now is a pretty surreal place and my therapist said that one of the best things I can do to help me deal with my depression is to keep my feet firmly planted in reality by writing down things from the past. "The past is the root from which the present grows," she said. And that's a true enough thing, I suppose. "Do you like what you see when you look in the mirror?" she asked. I try not to think about the past or the mirror much if I can help it. Hell, I try to think about the present the least amount I can. Reality as a whole—past or present—just isn't a good place to hang out, in my opinion. There are better ways and places to spend your time.

Reality is full of bad news. Pick up your phone and check out whatever news sites you frequent and I can guarantee that you're going to see a laundry list of atrocities. The planet's melting. People are getting trafficked, and murdered, and molested. It's just all too much. I figured that particular fact out a long time ago. My therapist says that my condition is related to some sort of trauma of my own, that I've experienced myself, but I don't buy that. I haven't had any traumas that I know of. Sure, I've had my fair share of bad luck, but that's different from trauma. My therapist said that I might not even know what the trauma is. It could be that bad or it could be that subtle. She talks about trauma in relation to that "root from which things grow" metaphor from before. She says that something made me break the boundaries between reality and imagination. She says it's not good for me.

I say it's gotten me this far, so why stop now?

She says it'll tear me apart eventually.

"You remember how good you were at drawing, Willie?" Daddy Henry asked with a cough. "Do you remember that at all?" He smiled and leaned back in the chair that his failing health would not let him leave.

"Parts of it," Soot's father said.

Daddy Henry was Soot's grandfather. He lived in a rest home on the far side of Whiteville, a sleepy, small southern town in a sleepy, small southern county with a long history of strawberry production and lynchings. Every few months, Soot and his father made the three-hour drive that only ever concluded in an hour-long visit. For the entire drive, Soot watched his father's body tighten, mile by mile. He sat behind the wheel of his pickup truck, thin and lanky like a plucked heron. He sawed the wheel back and forth, his spindly hands clutching so hard that veins rose up on the back of them.

"He's your grandfather," Soot's father told him, staring ahead as he spoke, as if he were driving into a gray-bellied storm. "That's the reason we're going. That's all."

"Yes, sir."

Soot never understood why his father got so knotted up when they went to visit Daddy Henry. From his perspective, Daddy Henry was a nice enough collection of wrinkles. He smiled a lot—curling his wide, dark lips into plum slice smiles—and his eyes shined like sea glass when he saw Soot. Most people didn't smile when they saw Soot. They stared. They stared into the impossible darkness of his skin as if the night itself had come to meet them. Or, if they didn't stare, they looked away, which was almost worse. But not Daddy Henry. Every time Soot entered the room, Daddy Henry reached out his arthritic hands and wrapped his grandson in the tightest hug his ancient frame could manage and said, "There's my boy. There he is."

Daddy Henry was a creature of magic. He was filled with stories of the way things used to be. People and places that used to exist in this world but that had long since faded away into little more than story and myth. He talked of muscadine grape vines that grew where now there was only highway and pavement. He talked of pear trees—reaching up like rockets to touch the heel of the sky—that used to live in places where now there were only housing developments and the clutter of traffic. Sometimes he even talked of the wife who had not lived long enough and he would try, and fail, at not hating the God who took her away from him.

He was, from everything that Soot knew, a good man. And the fact that he was dying made it all the more sad. That's why Soot never understood the anger his father had for the old man. Not until the time Daddy Henry asked about his son's drawings.

Daddy Henry turned to Soot and smiled, and whistled in amazement, and said, "When he was a boy about your age, he could do it all. Could draw folks so real you could almost reach out and catch 'em by the ankles. You could run your fingers through their hair. Stroke their faces. Smell their breath so clear you always knew what they'd ate for breakfast that morning. Ain't that right, Willie?"

"I don't remember," Soot's father replied.

"Well, I do," Daddy Henry barked. Then he waved his hand and pointed off in the direction of a small box that sat in the far corner of the room. "Get that for me," he told Soot, whispering a little in the way that people do when they want to spark a child's curiosity.

"Don't do that," his father said. His jaw was a tight, dark line framing his brown face.

"Don't tell me what to do," replied Daddy Henry. Then he turned his attention back to Soot. "Now go ahead and get that box like I told you."

"Yes, sir," said Soot.

He went over slowly, glancing at his father now and again, waiting for a firm "no" that would stop him in his tracks. But it never came. His father was just as much a victim of his parents as he was. So the man only stood there, clenching and releasing his jaw, wishing he could say something more.

The box was a small, leftover packaging box crisscrossed with used tape. The whole thing yielded like soft bread when Soot picked it up.

"Do we really have to do this?" his father asked.

"Hush up," Daddy Henry said. He motioned at Soot with his thin arms. "Come on. Bring it on over. Open it up!"

Soot kneeled and, after pausing once more, giving his father another chance to tell him to stop, finally did as his grandfather told him. He opened the small, mildewed box.

The first thing he saw was a family. A small Black family stood in faded Polaroid glory. The man was Daddy Henry, vibrant and young. A familiar stranger to Soot's eyes. He stood tall and lean beneath a bright summer sun, a wisp of a smile perched on his face. At his side was a stocky woman with dark skin and long hair. She wore a dark blouse and flowered skirt and a smile that looked as though it had never seen a cloudy day in its entire life. And between the pair was a boy, little more than five years old. He had a small Afro and wore a full suit with flecks of red and blue and his smile was even wider than his mother's.

Soot lifted the photo and stared at the boy. Then he looked at his father. He had never seen his father smile like that, and yet he knew that the man he knew and the boy in the photo were one and the same.

He placed the photo to the side along with a handful of others. Each picture was a flash of happiness. In one, Daddy Henry stood before a long record player, smiling back at the camera and holding up a Marvin Gaye album. In another, he sat on an old brown couch with his son on his knee, both of them looking at the camera with a wild mixture of confusion and joy.

The rest of the photos came and went and, finally, Soot found the drawings his grandfather had wanted him to find. The first one took his breath away. Buried, dusty, and wilting, was a woman. She sat at a desk, leaning on one hand, staring solemnly back at him. Around her, real enough that it made him worry about her drowning, was the ocean, lorded over by an evening sun. Soot stared at the picture, mouth agape. He could almost hear the waves crashing around the woman. He could see her hair dancing in the salt air.

He wondered how she had wound up in the middle of the ocean. He marveled at the expression she wore that looked so real it hid her feelings about where her life had taken her. Whether she was sad, happy, or afraid about floating through this beautiful ocean, Soot couldn't tell. All he knew for certain was that she knew how she felt, and her truth was left for him to guess.

There were more drawings in the box. Dozens of them. All of them beautiful. All of them real enough to spring to life at any moment. Meteoric and mundane, they all existed here. Men with swords stood at the base of long, ominous mountains punching up through purple clouds. Women walked through grocery stores, leaning over freezers, deciding on dinner. A bird took flight, feathers straining over treetops. A child leapt from a springboard, barreling downward at the shimmering surface below.

"Now, ain't that something?" Daddy Henry asked, a resonance of wonder in his voice.

"Wow," Soot whispered. He looked up at his father as though seeing him for the first time.

"I'm going outside," he said. Folded over his chest like saplings, his arms fidgeted.

"Why?" Soot asked.

"He's ashamed," Daddy Henry said.

"That's enough," Soot's father said.

"No," said Daddy Henry. "I might be on my goddamn deathbed, but I can still say what happens in my own tomb." He punctuated his sentence with a wet, rattling cough. "Not my fault you're ashamed of them. Don't aim that at me!" More coughing. The old man gripped the arms of his chair until the coughing was gone and he was almost slumped over in exhaustion. He spat something red into the trashcan beside his chair and gathered his breath. "Don't aim that at me," he repeated.

For a moment, no one spoke. The three of them only listened to the labored breathing of a dying man. All three of them listened. All three of them heard something different in the sound.

"You want to know what he's ashamed of?" Daddy Henry asked Soot finally. "He's ashamed because they're all White."

Soot's father cleared his throat as though he were about to speak, but nothing came out. He only turned his head away and looked out the window. As the sunlight poured in through the window, Soot's father looked skinnier and smaller than he had only a moment ago. Nothing more than a dark reed jutting up from the ground, aiming itself at a world it could not reach because this place was where its roots were buried, whether it liked it or not.

"All he ever drew was White people," Daddy Henry continued. "Never did draw no niggers. That was the best thing about it." He reached into the box and pulled out one of the drawings—the drawing of a blonde woman leaning on her hand—and he smiled at it. "Look at that," he said. "You ever seen a more beautiful White woman? You ever seen one drawn anywhere that looked that good? He tried to draw niggers a couple of times, but I put a stop to that. Wasn't no future in that. Still ain't." Daddy Henry shook his head and gripped his chest. His face tightened in pain. Eventually, it passed, like a cloud promising that rain was not far off. "I was trying to secure a future for him in that. He could'a been a rich man drawing White people. But he quit. He goddamn quit. Then he grew up and started hating me for it. Said it was all my fault. Said I made him hate Black people." Daddy Henry managed a laugh. "Can you imagine that? Like I could make him hate black skin." He looked at Soot. "If I hated black skin, could I love you the way I do, boy?"

"We're done here," Soot's father said.

Daddy Henry shook his head. "You're still acting like a goddamn nigger, huh? Ain't I teach you no better than that?" His hands curled into fists. "You're a goddamn shame."

"Let's go," Soot's father said.

"No!" Daddy Henry said. His tone shifted. Gone was the anger and bitterness, replaced by terror and something akin to pleading. "Don't go," he said slowly. "I'm sorry, okay? Please. Don't take the boy. I'm sorry."

But Soot's father did not listen. He walked over and grabbed his son by the arm and pulled him toward the door.

"Listen," Daddy Henry said, his voice trembling. "Don't do this. Don't take him away. Don't spend your life blaming me. I helped you. You shouldn't have quit. All I ever did was help you! I ain't make you hate Black people. I ain't make you hate yourself! You did that all on your own!" Daddy Henry licked his lips and looked up at his son. His face was frantic. There was something else that he wanted to say, something else that he wanted to put into words, but whatever that thing was, his mouth failed him and so he wrung his fists and looked even more panicked as he watched his son and grandson on their way out of his life. "I didn't mean that," Daddy Henry said. There was fear in his voice. The fear of a man who knows that he has pushed too far, too hard, and no matter what he does from here on out, that which he once held in his hands is forever broken. "I'll let it go. I promise. Just don't take the boy. Leave him here with me. Let me talk to him. There are things that he needs to know. There are things that I need to teach him about the way the world works. I can't let him come out like you came out. I can't let him come out hating people that didn't have anything to do with who he is. I can't do that.

"White people didn't do nothing to you. You ain't never been a slave. They didn't sell you and whip you. You can't hate a whole group of people for something their ancestors did. But that's the thing that niggers can't never understand. That's the thing that I need *him* to know. I need him to not be angry like you." He looked at Soot. "I need you to be happy the way your daddy used to be, boy. I need to know that you won't fall apart and give up on things like he did." Daddy Henry's eyes flitted from his son to his grandson. "I'm trying to help," he said, staring at Soot. "I hear you like stories," Daddy Henry said. "That's good. There's a future in that. You should take up writing. But you gotta tell the right stories. You gotta tell them the right way. No nigger stories, okay? You gotta do it right!" His face contorted with each word, it transformed from worried, to angered, to pleading, until it finally settled on a type of sad resignation. "Please," he said. "Let me help him. . . . Please."

"Say goodbye," Soot's father said.

"Goodbye, Daddy Henry," Soot said.

With tears running down his face, Daddy Henry made a move to get up out of the chair but his legs failed him. He pulled with his arms at the edges of the chair, trying to pull himself free of the prison that was his body, but that failed as well.

As he left, Soot watched the old man continue to struggle against the weight of his infirmity. He raged and fought, but remained pinned by gravity to his chair. His breath quickened and that was the only thing that kept him from screaming in rage.

But, in the end, his rage only left him trapped in his chair, as if he had always been there—in that chair, in that rage—and he always would be.

It was the last time Soot ever saw his grandfather.

The drive home was three hours of silence. Soot wanted to ask his father about why Daddy Henry said those things. He wanted to ask his father about the drawings. He wanted to ask about all the other parts of his father that he did not know because they did not get to survive the journey from child to father. He wanted to ask about the way Daddy Henry had pleaded with him to stay. He wanted to ask about the way the old man cried. He wanted to ask about forgiveness. He wanted to ask about love. He wanted to ask about telling stories. He wanted to ask if his father loved or hated what he saw in the mirror each day.

He wanted to ask.

But he only listened to the low grumble of the old truck's engine as it chugged its way beneath a freshly starred sky and, at one point, he reached over and took his father's hand and squeezed it and that gentle touch was all he said.

H*ell of a Book* book tour takes me out of the Midwest—with its flat earth and angry husbands—and deposits me somewhere on the West Coast this time. I haven't eaten since I don't know when. Not since meeting that kid, I guess. But I'm not really sure.

All I know for sure is that since then I've been to two cities in Florida—I remember sweaty armpits and air humid enough to drink—three book festivals in New Orleans—I remember some woman named Gladys and lots of shrimp—a Barnes & Noble in New Mexico—more heat—and a booksellers' conference somewhere in the upper Northwest—the woman I met there was named Kim. She was nice.

The plane landing here out west is a little bumpier than expected. I almost get some sleep on the flight and when I come out of my half-slumber, everything—from fuselage to fun-sized pretzel bag—is shaking. So, naturally, I assume we're in a freefall and death is imminent. I reach out and grab the hand of the man sitting next to me and I tell him I love him, I'm proud of him, and that I hope there are Nic Cage movie marathons in the afterlife.

Then the announcement comes on that we've landed wherever we are and everything between me and the gentleman next to me feels odd and out of place all of a sudden.

So it goes.

I STEP OFF OF THE PLANE LOOKING LIKE A MILLION EUROS AND FEELing like about two pesos. I smell like jet fuel, pretzels, and exhaustion. My eyes burn and I'm still more than a little hungover from a wild night with a woman from Colorado and some brownies that may, or may not, have contained certain illicit, mind-altering additives. It's hard to say, really. My mind is usually pretty altered all on its own so fringe drugs, oddly enough, tend to counter that effect and leave me stuck in reality.

I don't have much use for reality in my line of work.

I come down the escalator of Unknown Airport looking like a statue, which is appropriate because I'm asleep on my feet. When I get to the bottom, it's the near fall that wakes me up. I come to my senses just in time to keep myself from face-planting. I look up to see an older gentleman—who reminds me of James Hong, one of the unsung heroes of the modern era of acting—standing among the crowd of people waiting for their loved ones. He wears a well-cut gray suit and what look like two-thousand-dollar Italian shoes. The sign he's holding reads: HELL OF A BOOK.

"According to the sign you've got there," I say, "I think I'm the Joe you're looking for."

"I'm Renny," the man who is not James Hong says as we shake hands.

"Nice to meet ya, Lenny."

"Renny."

"Lenny."

"Renny."

"Lenny."

"Ren-ny!"

"Len-ny!"

"There's no *L*, you racist bastard! It's R-E-N-N-Y! I went to Harvard."

The airport travelers stop and look at us. In spite of myself, I can't deny Renny's position. "Well then," I say. "Renny it is."

Baggage claim is a sea of misanthropic souls. Everyone looks worn-out. Nobody looks happy to have arrived here in whatever city we're in. They're all staring blankly at the luggage carousel like a pack of Pavlov's dogs, waiting for the buzzer to sound. Everyone is strangely quiet, as if there's something going on that I don't know about.

You probably can't tell this about me, but I'm actually a pretty quiet guy. Few things make me happier than to just sit and not talk. Or stand and not talk. Or lie down and not talk. Or go swimming and not talk. I think you get the idea. Silence is a golden thing. Maybe it's yet another by-product of working for Major Cell Phone Company for all those years. Spend forty hours a week talking to people and you might come away from it not wanting to talk to anyone at all.

As we're waiting for the luggage to come, I can't get away from Renny's excitement. He's a ball of energy, the sweet old man. He rocks back and forth on his heels and he can't seem to figure out what to do with his hands. They flit about at the ends of his sleeves like trained doves. He looks at me the way a proud father looks at his son—his eyes slick with the beginnings of tears, his chest swelling to the point of bursting.

"I'm not going to hassle you," Renny begins. He's doing his best to keep his hands still. His hands want to reach out and touch me. To pat me on my head. To shake my hand. Something. He swallows and smiles: "It really is an honor to meet you."

I give him my best Author-On-Book-Tour-Meets-A-Fan smile. It's the smile that says: "You know more about me than I know about myself because reading my book is like reading my diary and I'm afraid that you'll say something that cuts me to the bone and makes me break down into tears . . . but let's not make this awkward."

"That book of yours," Renny continues, "you wouldn't believe how much it . . . well . . . the amount of impact it had on . . ." He swallows and wipes the corner of his eye. "It's . . . it's just something," he says.

"It's a hell of a book," I say.

"A hell of a book," Renny confirms.

Then we shake hands and Renny turns the handshake into a hug and, for a moment, I don't really mind. Maybe it's residual mood enhancement left over from the special brownies I had the night before in whatever town that was, or maybe it just feels good sometimes to be hugged by a stranger. Whatever the reason, I don't pull away from it. I realize right then, right there, in the arms of this strange old man, that I'm alone and have been for years and probably will be for the rest of my life and if he holds me for a second longer, I'm going to break down into tears right here in the middle of this airport and there isn't anything anyone will be able to do to stop me.

OUTSIDE THE AIRPORT, RENNY LEADS ME TO A LONG, BLACK LIMOUSINE. He opens the door and I get in the back and find the little Black boy from breakfast several cities ago sitting on the other side of the seat, flashing that impossibly dark skin and that impossibly bright grin of his.

"Uh . . . hello," I say, offering up a smile of my own.

"Hey," The Kid says, waving that dark hand of his. "What's up?"

"Not much," I say. "Would you excuse me for a moment?"

The Kid nods. "Yeah. Do your thing."

I turn my attention to Renny. "Renny?"

"Yeah?" Renny says. He looks worried. He looks confused. Maybe even a little afraid. Like he's just watched a grown man talking to someone who wasn't there. I've seen this look before over the course of my life.

"So it's just me and you for this trip, right, Renny?"

"What?"

"It's silly, I know. But just play along, if you don't mind. It's just you and me making the rounds today, right? Nobody else riding along on this ride?" I very gently tilt my head in the direction of the back seat of the limousine. I've done this before. It's an old trick. The key to it is to tilt my head just enough that it makes him look at the person or thing that could be a figment of my imagination, and yet, I don't want to commit too hard to the tilt. That way, if the boy in the back seat is real, he'll let me know and we can move forward without me seeming like too much of a weirdo. And if the boy is just something my imagination has produced, I can deny the nod and he'll spend the rest of the night wondering if he's crazy instead of wondering if I'm crazy.

It's an elaborate system, but it works.

Renny leans down and looks inside the car, then lifts his head again. "It's just you and me," he says slowly, evenly. It's the tone one takes around dogs you don't know and people who have taken too much medication.

I stick my head back inside the car and close my eyes once. The Kid is still there with that dark skin and he waves with a hint of mischievousness.

"You okay?" Renny asks.

"Fine," I say. "Just fine. This limo have a partition?"

"It does," Renny answers.

"Good," I say. "I'm probably going to ride with it up for a while. I usually don't do that because I think it makes me feel like a snob or something. But it's been a long flight and—"

Renny waves me away. "Don't bother explaining," he says. "I understand. I've been driving this car for ten years. I know how it goes. I used to ride in limos and I've been there."

I want to ask how Renny went from riding in limos to driving them. There's a backstory there, and backstories are where the real stuff is. But Renny's backstory will have to wait a little while.

I get in the car, shut the door, raise the partition, and I lean into the adventure that lies ahead.

"OKAY, KID," I BEGIN.

"I've been waiting for you."

"I don't doubt that at all, Kid. So you want to go ahead and tell me a little bit about yourself?"

The Kid clucks a laugh. "Man, don't you want to know why that other guy couldn't see me?" There's a clear note of pride in The Kid's voice, like he's fooled the whole world but can't stand not letting somebody in on his secret. Luckily for him, I already know his secret.

"I already know why he couldn't see you."

"Really?"

"Of course, Kid. I'm not new to this. I been around the block a few times in my life. I've set fire to the starlight before."

"You talk weird."

"You're not the first person to tell me that." I lay my head back on the headrest and close my eyes. Sometimes that makes my daydreams recede. Sometimes it doesn't. "That's a nice accent you got there. Sounds like the South. North Carolina, even."

"How'd you know?" he says. He's trying to hide the lilt all of a sudden, but failing at it.

"Because I know my own. I'm from North Cakalak."

"You don't sound like it."

"Trained it out of myself."

"Why?"

I open my eyes and take a long look at the kid. His smile has dimmed a bit, as if there's something on his mind, something to do with why I talk the way I talk. But I'm not going there now.

"Well," The Kid says, "don't feel bad about that guy not being able to see me. It's just that—"

"I know."

"You know what?"

"I already know why he couldn't see you."

"Think so?"

"Yeah. You're not real."

The Kid's eyebrows take a confused dive. Then he laughs. Long and hard. The laughter pours out of his dark neck and washes over his bright teeth and it is the sound of every good thing I've ever heard in my life. I wish this kid could laugh forever. "I'm not real?" he asks when he finally stops laughing long enough to speak.

"It's okay," I say. "You don't have to be real to matter. I mean, it helps, but it's not a requirement."

Again The Kid laughs. "Why am I not real?"

"Because I have a condition. I see things. People too. They say it's a sort of escape valve for pressure on the mind, probably caused by some sort of trauma. But I don't go in on that. I haven't had any type of trauma in my life. I mean, yeah, I've had my fair share of bad luck, but nothing big. Nothing worthy of a Lifetime network movie or anything like that. Know what I mean?"

"Haha! Nah. That ain't it. Seeing stuff that's not there . . . that's what crazy people do. And you ain't crazy."

"It's always good when a figment of your own imagination reassures you that you're not crazy."

"Nah, that's not what I mean," The Kid says. He reaches over and drives his knuckle into my arm. "I mean I'm real. So you ain't crazy. If I thought I was seeing things that weren't really there, it would probably freak me out. No, it would definitely freak me out."

I sigh. I've got a headache and my mouth feels like cotton ass. I'm not hydrated enough for this particular daydream. "Okay, Kid. I'll bite. You're real. Sure. So why couldn't Renny see you? That's what you want me to ask you, right?"

"Because I can be invisible when I want to."

Now it's my turn to laugh. "Oh. Okay. That makes a lot more sense. That really puts the cheese on the burger."

"No, really," The Kid replies gently. "I have this gift. If I want somebody to see me, they can. And if I don't want somebody to see me, they can't. Pretty cool, right?"

"Yeah. Real cool."

I wish I had a drink right now. It always makes me want to drink when my daydreams try to convince me that they're real. It's always simpler when a person who doesn't exist just admits that they don't exist. "So, you're some new kind of superhero, I guess. The Invisible Kid—here to save the invisible day!"

"Yeah," the boy says brightly. "I never really thought about it like that, but I think that's pretty dope. Like I can be here one moment, and then not here the next. Whenever I want. Nobody can see, or hear, or even touch me if I don't want them to." Something akin to pride creeps into his voice, but it's a hollow sort of pride. It's the pride of someone who's rarely proud of anything. It's the type of pride that can be knocked over with a feather, and so it rarely gets to shine in the face of the world. The little Black kid flashes those impossibly white teeth at me and he laughs and then he covers his smile and quells the laughter like Miss Celie used to do, and I know that he's spent his entire life being afraid to be happy.

"I'm sorry, Kid," I say, leaning back.

"What are you sorry for?" The Kid asks.

"For whatever trauma of mine led you here," I reply. And before I know it, everything and all of it hits, and I'm asleep.

"YOU KNOW, YOU SEEM PRETTY ODD, EVEN FOR A FICTION AUTHOR." Renny carves the car through the highway traffic like a hot knife. "Most of the fiction authors I meet are fairly ridiculous. Pure weirdos. But you're on a different level. Where did you go to school?"

"Actually I went to the University of—"

"Wait! A state college?"

"Yep."

"I'm sorry," Renny says. "I'll use smaller words," he says with a small grin.

I sit up and look out of the window, watching the city slide by around me. "I don't think I've been to San Francisco before, Renny." I sit back and close my eyes. "It looks beautiful, though. A marvel of the civilized world." I burp, and it tastes like airline bourbon.

"You look pretty drunk," Renny says.

"Drunk's a moving target," I reply. "Just a state of being, like water, or steam, or financial solvency. To be drunk is simply to define a moment. And since every moment has already passed by the time we're able to actually register its existence, can a person ever truly be drunk? I'm pretty sure that's in the Bible, Renny."

"Must be one of those state college Bibles."

"That's neither here nor there," I say. Then: "What's on the itinerary, Renny?"

Renny reaches into the passenger seat beside him and looks it over. "Five radio spots. Two television interviews. And then the bookstore event this evening."

I sit forward and peek into the small minibar in the back of Renny's car. "We're gonna need a bigger bar."

THE RADIO INTERVIEWS COME AND GO WITH THE SAME CADENCE OF questions and answers. "So," they say, "what's your book about?"

And then I lay it all on them. Give them the same beautiful narrative that I give every other interviewer I ever speak to. And then they smile and ask a few solid follow-up questions. And then

I smile and give a few solid follow-up answers. And all the while, Renny is right there with me like a faithful sidekick. Getting a media escort when you're out on tour isn't a groundbreaking affair. In fact, it's a tried-and-true tradition. The media escort's job is to herd the cat—you—from one location to the other and to make sure that you're everywhere you need to be whenever you need to be there.

But Renny is the type of guy who goes the extra mile. Case in point:

We make it to the television studio after all of the radio interviews are done. The studio is a large, sprawling maze of cubicles, and floors, and desks, and stairs, and the fact that I've already nearly cleaned out Renny's minibar did nothing to help make Daedalus's maze any more navigable.

But there is Renny. Right there beside me the whole way.

At one point, we walk into the room just before you go into the interview room and we sit and wait for our turn to go on while a receptionist sits at her desk and plasters the wall behind her with Post-it notes. Only these aren't the random, odd assembly of Post-it notes like you might expect. Not at all. It takes me a while to notice, but the woman is actually creating something on the wall behind her. She has three different colors of Post-it notes and is positioning them with the most meticulous precision I have ever seen.

And the longer I stare at the wall of Post-it notes, the more I begin to understand that I'm not just staring at a wall of notes, I'm staring at something greater than that.

The Post-its blend and bleed into one another, slicing out the silhouette of a castle—Gothic and grand—perched upon a cliff, dangling over a breaking sea. Violet sky. Ebon stone. A salty sea of paper and dye fluttering in the blow of an approaching storm.

It's a glorious thing. An honest-to-God work of art. And I wonder if anyone else can see it. These kinds of things go unnoticed by too much of the world, in my opinion.

I sit there with Renny at my side and all of Renny's alcohol in my bloodstream and I stare at the Post-its. How many hours it must have taken to create such a thing, I can't honestly say. Anything worthwhile takes time. Maybe that's what time is for: to give meaning to the things we do; to create a context in which we can linger in something until, finally, we have given it something invaluable, something that we can never get back: time. And once we've invested the most precious commodity that we will ever have, it suddenly has meaning and importance. So maybe time is just how we measure meaning. Maybe time is how we best measure love.

Finally, someone sticks their head out of the back of the TV studio and calls my name. Renny and I stand and make our way toward the studio door and, without really trying, I manage to walk directly into the wall. Maybe I'm more intoxicated than I thought. Luckily, Renny's a good man. He catches me before I hit the ground and props me up and steers me into the studio without so much as a hint of judgment.

After the television interview has come and gone—more of the usual question-and-answer periods—we're back in Renny's limousine headed to the next destination. But I can feel Renny's eyes watching me in the rearview mirror.

"You making it okay, State College?" Renny asks.

Even though I'm awake, I'm not really able to answer. The words are in my head but they don't seem to be able to make it to my mouth.

Renny stares at me for another second in the mirror. Then,

without ever taking his eyes away from the mirror, snatches the steering wheel so that the back of the car whips for a second. I'm thrown across the back seat and bang my head against the door. A shocking experience, but at least I'm able to speak now.

"It's a wonderful book!" I exclaim. "I had a terrific time writing it. It's about . . ." I'm reflexively in interview mode, answering questions about my book that even I don't fully know the answers to.

But before I can finish the sentence, my stomach makes a sound like a hell beast and I'm not completely sure there isn't one tucked down inside there.

"You okay?" Renny asks.

But I've got no time for queries just now. I'm able to get the rear window down just in time to vomit all over the expressway. I manage to keep it off of Renny's car—thanks to my profound understanding of aerodynamics—but the brand-new Ford Fusion zooming along behind us is at the right place at the right time to get the full brunt of it. As the spray hits their windshield, the old couple inside the car look aghast—but maybe also a little understanding. They seem like nice people as their pearl-white automobile is plastered with 98.6-degree, salmon-colored bile.

They take it like a pair of heroes.

Not to be outdone by their magnanimous nature, I tuck my head back inside the car—after the eruption has ended, of course—and I grab a copy of my book. I sign it and stick my head back out the window just as our two cars pull up to a stoplight. I toss the freshly autographed *Hell of a Book* at their windshield. Then I offer a hearty thumbs-up and mouth the words "You're welcome."

The couple in the bile-splattered Ford Fusion smile. The old man gives me a salute.

NEXT THING I KNOW, WE'RE AT THE BOOKSTORE FOR THE EVENING'S reading. Renny parks the car and I can feel him watching me in the mirror again. Renny reminds me of my mother. All that affection and worry. To be honest, it's not a bad feeling. Just one I haven't felt in so long that I've forgotten what it honestly feels like.

The door suddenly opens and Renny is there. Exactly how he got from the front seat to my door without my noticing, I can't exactly say. But I'm also not in my most sober and knowledgeable state of being right now. So I'm in no position to explain such things.

Renny helps me out of the car and props me up against the rear of it. As he reaches inside to grab one of my books, my legs go all rubbery and I slide down the side of the car. Quick as a flash, Renny's there. He grabs me around the waist and props me up again.

"State College," Renny begins, "are you going to be okay?"

"Swell," I answer. "Just swell. I'm a professional, dammit."

Renny reaches into the car again, making another try at grabbing one of my books so that when I walk into the venue I look like somebody who's not a wasted heap of intoxication. And as soon as he does, I slide down the car again.

But Renny catches me again. "Jesus, State College!"

"Don't worry about me," I say. "Those badgers will never make it through our defenses!"

For the record, I wasn't trying to say "badgers." I was trying to say "hamsters." And I wasn't trying to say "defenses," I was trying to say "tunnels."

For the further record, I wasn't trying to say "those hamsters." I was trying to say "my mother." And I wasn't trying to say "our tunnels." I was trying to say "that stroke."

For the even further record, you can leave off that part about the stroke and just say, "My mother will never make it." But the words we say never seem to live up to the ones inside our head.

To ease the gibberish, Renny slaps me square across the face.

I immediately slap him back.

"Son of a bitch!" Renny says.

He slaps me again.

I slap him again.

"Dammit, State College!"

We both take a deep breath.

The fog around me is starting to clear. I take a look down at my clothes.

"I didn't vomit on my suit," I reassure Renny. "Bogart would have never vomited on himself." Then, without really meaning to, I keep talking: "If my mother were here, she'd be appalled, Renny. She'd still love me . . . but she'd be appalled." Suddenly, there's something in my throat. I swallow to keep it there.

"Was your mother a kind woman?" Renny asks.

"I don't even remember anymore," I reply. Which, believe it or not, is the truth. "I've all but forgotten my mother. I can tell you the facts about her. I can tell you that she existed—that much is inherently provable by the fact that I exist. I can tell you that she was short. That she had long hair which she almost always wore in a ponytail. But that's about the extent of what I remember about her. All those years that she spent loving me and taking care of me have been reduced down to nothing more than a few simple cosmetic facts. Shrunk down to even less than a photograph in my mind. My mother is, more or less, a myth I carry around inside of me. She exists only because I can't conceive of a world in which she did not exist.

But how much of it do I believe?

I wish I knew.

There are no closing quotation marks there, because I'm not sure how much of that I say to Renny or how much of it I'm just thinking now. Maybe I say it all. Maybe I say none of it. Maybe I just talk more about hamsters and invisible boys.

As we've finished slapping each other around and are just about ready to head inside whatever bookstore we've come to tonight so that I can read from *Hell of a Book*, our own slapstick chaos is broken up by a chaos of another sort.

Down the street, Renny and I both hear a maelstrom of voices rising and falling in rhythm. The air around us suddenly feels ten degrees warmer, as if whatever's coming is sending energy out in front of itself. It's the type of thing that you wouldn't think could be real, but it is. I know it's real because I can see it in Renny's face. He's looking in the direction of the sound with just as much confusion as I feel. And not only is he confused, my friend Renny looks a little scared.

Something's coming. Something epic, and important, and potentially terrifying, potentially life-changing. I can feel it in my stomach.

. . . Or that could just be the vodka.

But, no, turns out it's not the alcohol.

Little more than a block away, a wall of people suddenly emerges from a neighboring street. They carry signs and banners. They shout, and chant, and punch fists at the overcast sky as though it's done something to offend or condemn them. They're all kids. Not a single adult mixed in among the bunch. The oldest among the mass looks like he just walked away from sixteen last week. The youngest is in diapers and still sucking on an insulated bottle.

But regardless of their age or wardrobe, they're a force to be reckoned with. At the front of the mass they look like they just got in from working in the garden. Earth-soiled pants and long-sleeved shirts caked with mud and God only knows what else. Their hair is kinky and unkempt like they didn't have time to get squared away before they had to go off and start singing their parts of "Amazing Grace." Hot on the heels of that bunch come the well-dressed whippersnappers in suits and ties and Sunday dresses belting out verses of "We Shall Not Be Moved" and "We Shall Overcome." They make a fuss about nonviolence even as "NO JUSTICE! NO PEACE!" tumbles from the throats of some of those around them.

It's a type of organized chaos, but at least it's consistent in its effort.

Then come the boom box boys dressed in red, black, and green. Four of them. Late teen, muscle-bound fellows with radios on their shoulders and "Fight the Power" blaring from their boom box speakers. All of them wearing four-finger gold rings across their fists. L-O-V-E and H-A-T-E on one pair of Black hands. G-E-T-M and O-N-E-Y on another. And the third, somehow, impossibly, reads SEE-ME-AS-HUMAN, NIGGA! I have no idea how all of that fits across his fingers, but there it is.

When the boom box boys pass by, Chuck D. fades away and the newest crowd comes with their pants low. BLACK LIVES MATTER, their signs, banners, t-shirts claim and voices proclaim. The ground quakes beneath their crisp-sneakered and Timberland-booted feet. Kendrick Lamar gets quoted. "WE GON' BE ALRIGHT," they all sing as one, and I hope to God it's the truth. They hold up poster board photographs of Emmett Till and Tamir Rice, Michael Brown, Philando Castile, George Floyd, and all the other names that will be added to America's list between the time I write this and the time you read this. I lose track and count around the seventeenth You-Will-Not-Be-Forgotten face. It's an ocean of protest songs and Rest-In-Power names hanging over our heads like that famous strange fruit borne by southern trees.

With the weight of generations bearing down on us, Renny and I have no choice but to move aside. We take our game of slapping each other in the face farther onto the sidewalk so as not to disrupt the wall of youth marching in our direction. We're both awestruck by it. Or, at least, Renny seems to be. I'm still trying to remember whose turn it is to slap who. I refuse to be one-upped.

"It's a damn shame," Renny says. His brow is furrowed in worry so that his eyebrows hang below his forehead like gray, geriatric caterpillars.

"A damn shame," I say, "that's exactly what it is." I say the words, but the truth is I have no idea what he's talking about. My stomach is still a little queasy and so I'm doing the best I can to appear engaged and invested in both Renny's moment of empathy and the kids' moment of shouting into deaf ears, but the truth of the matter is that I'd much rather be on my knees depositing my sins into the nearest toilet right now.

"Have you heard about that boy?"

"I have," I say. That's not a lie. I've heard volumes about that boy lately. I just have no idea what boy or what happened to him. Hopefully, it was something good, but I doubt it. There are so many kids that bad things happen to.

Renny shakes his head. "I hear that there's a video out there of how it happened. Can you even imagine it? A video of something like that and they turn around and put it right on the internet for everybody to see. That's the kind of world we live in, State College. You can pick up your phone right now and watch a ten-year-old boy come to the end of his life. Just think about that." Renny shakes his old head on his old neck.

"Signs and wonders, my mother used to say."

"It's the state of the world, State College."

Renny stares off somberly at the Black kids passing in front of the store and so I do the same. It's often in my life that I find myself doing things others are doing out of pure reluctance to break some sort of social contract about what's proper and right to do. And, for now, it seems proper and right to stare—with no small amount of solemnity—at the kids along with Renny and indicate through that stare that I am appropriately shocked and moved. I feel your pain, my stare says. I hear your anger, my stare says. I stand with you, my stare says—figuratively, of course.

"God bless those kids," Renny says.

"God bless them all," I say. I steal a quick glance at Renny to be sure that he's reading my concern and worry. Sure enough, he seems to be, which makes me feel good about myself. Maybe I actually am feeling something for these kids and their plight. Maybe I'm not just caught up in myself. Maybe the outside world is actually getting through. Maybe someone else's pain is actually crossing through my lead-based wall of narcissism and self-obsession. Maybe I'm empathizing. Maybe I'm being a good person!

"This must all be even more powerful for you."

"Indeed, it must!" I say.

"Such a tragedy."

"Yes . . . tragedy. One that is even more powerful for me."

"Are you just repeating what I say?" Renny asks, his eyes squinted in suspicion.

"Scoff!" I say. I literally say the word. "Of course not. I'm not the type of person to just repeat what someone else says with something this powerful and tragic." My legs are a little shaky again and I think I could use another good slap across the face, but I don't want to ask. So I stand there, unslapped and wobbly.

"Well?" Renny says, turning his attention from the youth who believe their lives matter and back to me.

"Well what?"

"Well, what do you think?"

"I think it's a tragedy," I say with confidence.

"And?"

"And what?"

"And what do you think about it, State College? You're a writer. You're supposed to say something about these things. And you're Black!"

"Am I?" I ask. I look down at my arm and, sure enough, it turns out that Renny is right. I'm Black!

A startling discovery to make this far along!

"Well now," I say, staring at the black hand at the end of my black arm and the black fingers adorning it. "That's very, very interesting. I wonder if my readers know that?"

"So what do you think about it?" Renny asks. "What do you have to say about it all?"

I really do want to answer Renny's question, but I'm still processing my sudden Blackness. How long have I been Black? When did it happen? Was I born that way? If so, why don't I remember it? Or maybe this is all just another part of my condition. Maybe I'm not Black and I'm imagining it. Or maybe I've been Black my whole life and my condition showed me something other than that?

I try to look back on my life and find my Blackness. Were my parents Black? My cousins? Come to think of it, I feel like I remember having a Black uncle. I think. It's all so fuzzy. It's all so much to think about. And what about my agent? Does she know I'm Black? My readers? Do they know? And what if Renny's right? What if my being Black is something that means I'm supposed to do everything differently?

"You're not supposed to just stand there," Renny barks, shaking a fist. "You're supposed to say something. You're supposed to speak about the Black condition! You're supposed to be a voice!"

"A voice? What voice? The voice of my people? Always? Every second of every day of my life? That's what Black people are always supposed to be? And the Black condition? What kind of condition is that? You mean as in an existing state of being? Or a condition as in a state of health—like an illness?"

Renny shakes his head. "I just can't believe you," he says in a tone that reminds me of my disappointed father. "Here you are, a famous writer, and a wonderful writer. Your book . . . it's just a hell of a book."

"Thank you."

"Shut up."

"Sorry."

"It's a hell of a book. You've got a gift for words. You've got the ability to say things that others can't say. You can pull out the things that other people have all trapped up inside of them. And it's clear that you can do it. Your book hit me in my heart!" He thumps his small fist against his narrow chest. "But there wasn't anything about the Black condition in it. There wasn't anything about *being* Black."

I consider Renny's words and I look down at my black hands. "Do I have to write about being Black? What if I were an artist that only drew White characters? What would that say about me?"

"What?"

"I mean, White writers don't have to write about being White.

They can just write whatever books they want. But because I'm Black . . ." I pause to look at my hands and reaffirm that, yes, I really am Black. The story checks out. ". . . does that mean that I can only ever write about Blackness? Am I allowed to write about other things? Am I allowed to be something other than simply the color of my skin? I mean, I can't quote it word for word, but isn't that what the whole 'I Have a Dream' speech was about?"

Renny's as quiet as an empty bourbon barrel.

"I mean, I'm not saying you're wrong, Renny. I'm just saying that I don't know. This is all new to me. This is all fresh and, if I'm honest, maybe even a little exciting?" Renny's left eyebrow arches toward the heavens. "No, hear me out," I continue. "Every day of a person's life they live it in the same way, over and over again. There's a pattern, a routine to it. A way of doing things that all boils down to a type of white noise hissing in the background of their minds every day. They know everything about themselves. When they go to look in the mirror, they know exactly what they're signing up for.

"But here I am, today, in this moment, finding out I'm Black. A Negro! A bona fide African American! Hell of a discovery. And if I've always been Black—which, as I'm thinking about my life, I think might be the case—then I wonder what it's done to me. I wonder how it's guided my life. Like, what decisions have I made that I wouldn't have made if I wasn't Black? And what's about the rest of the world? What has everyone seen in me and thought about me because I'm Black that I didn't see and think about myself?"

I rub my chin in contemplation.

"It's a hell of an enigma, Renny, my man. The kind of thing that doesn't come along often. A puzzle wrapped in a riddle wrapped in chewy nougat. I've got to savor the taste of it. Savor the moment.

I've got to let it sink in. Got to let it really become a part of me. Gotta steep in it like tea in water."

Renny responds by slapping me squarely across the face. Those formerly wobbly legs of mine straighten up. "Jesus Christ, State College. You're more fucked-up than I ever imagined."

"A day of discovery for both of us, then."

Renny's face is full of worry. Worry, confusion, and pity. He's looking at me the way I looked at Old Yeller just before the gunshot rang out. "Just get me to the door, Renny," I say, trying to muster my most comforting voice. I point toward the bookstore. "If you just get me to the door, I'll thrive. You'll see, brother. You'll see."

"Okay," Renny says.

He places an arm around me and guides me in the direction of the door as the sea of toddler-to-teenage protesters flows slowly past. "Black lives matter!" they continue to exclaim in unison. It's difficult to drown out, but I manage.

Renny and I stumble together like partiers after the bars have all shut down. I can see the bookstore clearly ahead. Stacks of my book line the display window. *Hell of a Book* is there in droves, looking back at me. The cover is black and the words are white. The publisher called it a "simple, yet impactful" design. They figured it would spark curiosity and imply a sense of gravitas when readers came across it.

I'm not sure if that's the effect it has on readers, but that's damn sure the effect it has on me. Sometimes when I look at the cover of that book, I have no idea what's inside of it. It's like looking at some mysterious and ancient monolith, something that's come forth from the seeping bowels of the abyss itself solely to vex me, to defy me. Put me in front of a crowd and ask me what my book's about and you'll get one of the greatest, most eloquent answers the marketing team can come up with.

But get me alone and ask me what my book's about and I'm never able to say. Much like my mother, my book has become nothing more than a ghost inside my head.

"Can I ask you another question?" Renny says.

"Of course you can, Renny. We're family now."

"In your book . . ."

"It's a hell of a book, Renny!"

"It is," he says. "One hell of a book. But when it comes to the part where the mother dies . . . and then, after she's gone, the way her son falls apart . . ."

I didn't know that Renny was telepathic. But that's something I'll have to focus on later. I'm still trying to get my mind around my Blackness and what it means, I can't afford to stumble backwards into some discussion about my mother and whether or not she's dead and how Renny seems to know what I'm thinking even before I do. One thing I pride myself on is my professionalism as an author. I've worked hard at it. Honed it. Went to a media trainer to get better at it—Sharon's idea. My professionalism and my imaginative condition are all I've got these days. I can't have Renny getting me off track.

"Just get me to the door, Renny," I say. "Let's stay on task."

"Sure thing," Renny replies.

An electronic door chime sounds as Renny opens the door. Dozens of white faces turn to greet me. And, speaking of faces, there's my face plastered all over the store. My author photo hangs from the rafters, sits on the walls, looks back at me from the cover of my own book. I have no idea who that person in the photo is. Whoever the person is, he's Black. Around the age of forty. Average-looking enough to walk through an airport and not get noticed, but also Black enough in skin tone to have a cop tell him that he "fits the description."

So I guess I really am Black. Always have been.

Signs and wonders, as my mother used to say.

The saving grace of this new discovery is the thankfulness that, at least, I'm not as dark-skinned as The Kid. Yeah, I'm not as light-skinned as I might want to be, but at least I'm not the walking ebony sculpture that The Kid is. If there's one thing I know about being Black—and I know it immediately even though I've known about my Blackness for only a few minutes—it's that dark skin is a sin. Hell of an affliction. The last thing you want. Just ask anyone.

As soon as the doorbell chimes, the fans who have come out to hear me read and talk about my book get the full package. I'm cleaned up. My suit is perfect and vomit-free. My hair is straight. My smile is toothy and sincere. Everything about me says, "I'm a healthy, happy, functioning individual who has come here tonight in joy and love to be with you and I hope all of you are living the lives you dreamed of when you were children and still willing to dream unfettered."

"Good evening, everyone!" I shout, my voice as bright as a Juneteenth fireworks show.

A geyser of applause and cheering erupts and spills out into the world.

Meanwhile, just as the door closes, in the streets behind Renny, the sempiternal line of children marches in the streets, carrying their signs, and pumping their fists, and shouting chants about justice, and police violence, and racism, and Black lives mattering—it's every generation of Black children that get burdened with this particular American work—and I cannot hear any of them over the sound of my pending book sales. I focus on the people who have come out to give me their money.

I am, after all, not an activist, not the kind of writer who ever actually says anything that might ruffle feathers. One thing my business has taught me: that stuff's murder on book sales. No. I'm none of those things . . . I'm a professional.

William could see what was happening to his son. The boy's smile faded a little more each day that he came home from school. It wasn't the history lessons that were to blame, though they were difficult and intense. History still was always one of those things that could be partially compressed, pushed down into the recesses of logic, barred from feelings. No, it wasn't the history but the current events that were slowly weighing on his son. Each day, there was a new news report about someone who looked like him being shot and killed. Each day, his son saw someone arrested, locked into prison. Each day, the tide of bad things swelled up a little more around him, clutching at his lungs, threatening to pull him under.

Each day, William wanted to talk to his son about it. Each day, he wanted to sit down with the boy and tell him, "This is how the world is . . ." And then, with that modest introduction, he would start into the reality of his son's life. He would talk about his son's skin color and what it meant. He would talk about all of the people who had come before and looked like him and all of the things that had happened to him. He would talk about how the rules were different. He would talk about reality instead of the fiction that had been sold to him. He would say to his son: "Treat people as people. Be color-blind. Love openly. Love everyone." And then, in the same breath, he would have to say to his son: "You will be treated differently because of your skin. The rules are different for you. This is how you act when you meet the police. This is how you act growing up in the South. This is the reality of your world."

William would one day have to say all of these things to his son and many, many more. And with each word, his son's heart would break. With each word, his son would be capable of a little less love, capable of a little less imagination, capable of a little less life. It was the bonsai of a child. His own child.

And because William couldn't bring himself to take away his son's optimism any faster than the world was already taking it away, he did not have The Talk with his son. He only preached love and equality and the idea that the world could be a fair place. And when his son asked him about why a boy his age had been shot and killed by a policeman somewhere halfway across the country, William did the best that he could with answering by not answering.

"It's hard to say why that type of thing happens," William replied. He and Soot were in the living room, weighting down the old couch and trembling in the glow of the television as the news rattled off the grisly details of the boy's shooting. He had been out for a walk when the police stopped him. Then, somehow, events conspired that ended with the boy lying dead on the sidewalk. The news showed the sidewalk where the boy's body fell. It was unremarkable concrete that now wore a rather unremarkable stain, as if someone spilled a bottle of syrup and walked away without cleaning up behind themselves. "It's not something that happens all the time," William said. He rubbed his thumb and forefinger together as he spoke, a habit that went back to his childhood. Something about the motion calmed him and, right now as he spoke to his son about the boy on the television's death, he wanted to be calm.

"What was the boy doing wrong?" Soot asked.

"Nothing," William replied. He cleared his throat. "I mean, from everything that they've said so far, he wasn't doing anything wrong. There'll be an investigation, I'm sure. So let's try not to make too much of a call on this until we find out more about what happened." William nodded in affirmation to himself. It was important to teach his son not to jump to conclusions, especially when faced with something like this. A person had to take news like this slow. They had to measure it out, moment by moment, and not let it get the better of them. That was the only way to survive the tide in the long run. You couldn't just drink in all of this and let it take control of the way you were thinking. That was how you lost your optimism. That was how you lost your hope.

And William wanted his son to have hope for as long as he could.

Soot would not take his eyes off of the television as a picture appeared on-screen. He was about Soot's age, lighter-skinned, of course. Everyone was lighter than Soot. In the photograph, the dead boy wore a blue baseball cap and t-shirt. His smile was wide and bright, like a winter's morning after snow has slipped in silently in the late of the night.

"What's his name?" Soot asked.

"I don't know," William said. "They're keeping the name private for now."

"I want to know his name."

"Why?"

"So that I don't forget him," Soot said, staring at the picture on the television screen. He gazed as though he were trying to memorize all that the dead boy was. "I can't forget him," Soot said.

William's thumb and forefinger rubbed together faster. He swallowed, trying to keep back the tears and trying to find the words to tell his son, "You will forget him." He tried to find the words to say, "This boy is only the first of many that you will meet over your life. They will stack upon one another, week by week. You'll try to keep them in your head but, eventually, you'll become too full and they'll spill out and be left behind. And then, one day, you'll grow older and you'll realize that you've forgotten his name—the name of the first dead Black boy that you promised yourself you wouldn't forget—and you'll hate yourself. You'll hate your memory. You'll hate the world. You'll hate the way you've failed to stop the flow of dead bodies that have piled up in your mind. You'll try to fix it, and fail, and you'll drown in rage. You'll turn on yourself for not fixing everything and you'll drown in sadness. And you'll do it over, and over, and over again for years and, one day, you'll have a son and you'll see him staring down the same road that you've been on and you'll want to say something that fixes him, something that saves him from it all . . . and you won't know what to say."

William wanted to say all of the correct words to Soot, but they were not in his mind. All that was in William's mind was the image of his son lying on the concrete, dead, just like all the boys that came and went on television.

Okay. Let's pause for a minute. Let's go back a few months. I think there's something there that I might have forgotten:

PROFESSIONALISM.

The word is painted on the wall of the office in midtown Manhattan in foot-tall lettering that's bolder and darker than any lettering I've ever seen before, like it's been etched there since the beginning of time and will continue to be long after I and everyone else on this planet have crumbled to dust. This word will remain. PROFESSIONALISM. Both a decree and a dare.

"What is this place again?" I ask.

"Media training," Sharon says. She's typing an email to someone with her thin, fast fingers. Like all publicists and agents, Sharon is always contacting unseen people.

"What exactly is media training?"

"Training you for media," Sharon replies.

At this point, I'm still new to the authoring machine. Still cow-eyed and optimistic about everything. *Hell of a Book* is still a full six months from being published and I'm learning the ropes as quickly as I can. Sharon's the agent who accepted my query letter and then accepted my manuscript for *Hell of a Book.* In fact, she's the one who came up with the title. She did the legwork of helping me revise it—she always said it was never personal enough—and then she helped me find a publisher. So when Sharon says I need media training, I take her word as gospel.

"Could you define 'media' for me?" I ask.

Sharon only focuses on her phone and her emails.

"And why did you insist that I wear a sport coat? It's ninety degrees outside."

"You're a professional now," Sharon says. "A professional author. Authors wear sport coats. Readers love authors who wear sport coats. Don't ever forget that."

I don't ask any more questions for the next half hour while waiting for the media trainer to show up. His secretary, a thin blonde woman named Carrie, offers me something to drink at exactly ten-minute intervals. Her hair is slicked back, giving her a lean, athletic look. But when she smiles, it's soft and full of light, like someone who, in the middle of a heat wave, has discovered ice for the very first time.

Her smile reminds me of my mother's.

It's almost 10 a.m. when the media trainer finally shows up. His name is Jack. Jack looks like he stepped out of a Christian Dior ad once upon a time and decided never to go back. He's too handsome to be real, so I start to think that maybe he isn't. You know how that happens to me sometimes.

But Carrie sees him and Sharon does too. "I'm Jack," he shouts as soon as the elevator doors open. "I'm Jack the media trainer. It's so great to meet you!" he says, stepping out of the elevator at a lope so fast you'd think he was being chased by someone threatening to return him to that Christian Dior ad.

He's got his hand extended for a handshake while he's still fifteen feet away. He steers his hand toward me like a torpedo. I barely manage to catch it in time, fearful that it might spear me through the breadbasket if I don't. Even though we're in midtown Manhattan, Jack smells like the ocean.

He shakes my hand like a pit bull. "I've been waiting all week to shake this hand of yours. I finished reading your book and immediately thought: I can't wait to shake the hand that made this happen! It's just an amazing creation. One pure, throbbing, screaming, convulsing, hell of a goddamn book!"

"Thanks," I say, trembling as the handshake persists. He squeezes tight enough that I think that, when this greeting finally ends, I might find a raw diamond where my hand once was.

"You're as welcome as hell," he says, finally giving me my hand back. No diamond. Just bruised flesh. ". . . You're Black?"

"I am."

Proof, in memory, that I've been Black this entire time, apparently.

"You didn't tell me he was Black," Jack says to Sharon.

"I wanted to see if you could tell from his writing."

"I couldn't."

"Good."

"Good indeed," Jack says enthusiastically.

"What does my being Black have to do with anything? And what do you mean it's good that you couldn't tell I was Black?"

"You see what I'm dealing with here?" Sharon asks, rolling her eyes.

"Not a problem," Jack says.

"I didn't know it could be," I say.

"We can work with anything here," Jack continues. "Anything. Had a client once who was a Russian spy. Murdered seventeen Americans over the course of his life. I still made him a bestseller. If I can handle that, I can handle this."

"I knew you could," says Sharon.

"Right this way," Jack replies.

Jack the Media Trainer leads Sharon and me into a small conference room with a large oval table and a handful of chairs placed around it. There's a small video camera on the center of the table and a few microphones. At the far end of the room, there's another camera, and a lectern, and even more microphones, as if the President of the United States might soon be coming by for a press conference.

"So this is it," Jack says proudly, opening his arms like a game show host. "This is the room where I'm going to train you to become you."

"Train me to become me?"

"Yep."

"Aren't I already me?"

"Nope," Jack says. "Right now, you're you. But I'm going to really help you really become you. I'm going to help you become the best version of you that you've ever seen. You won't even recognize yourself when you're done here."

"So, I'll look different?"

"That couldn't hurt," Sharon says, taking a seat at the table. She still hasn't looked up from her phone. "This 'Aww shucks' country chic wardrobe of yours will never cut it in Chicago."

Jack the Media Trainer laughs. "Sharon's right, as always. Would you believe me if I said that, yes, you're going to look physically different when this is all over?"

"No," I answer. "I wouldn't believe you."

"Of course you wouldn't," Jack says. "But facts exist objectively, regardless of whether or not you believe them. That's what makes them facts. The world is still round no matter how flat the horizon looks." He lets out another game-show-host laugh and slaps me on the shoulder and leads me to one of the seats at the table. "It's going to be a downright metamorphosis."

"Like Kafka?" I ask.

"Is that a rapper?"

He takes a seat on the other side, so that he's squarely in front of me as he talks, like a perfectly groomed and manicured army recruiter. "So here's what we're going to do," he begins. "I'm going to help you get to know yourself. I'm going to help you get to know your book."

"I know my book. I wrote it."

"Again, do you see what I'm dealing with here?" Sharon interjects. She looks up from her email long enough to shake her head in disappointment.

"It's okay," Jack says to me, smiling like a parent with a child who's had a potty-training accident. "You only think you know your novel. But you don't. Not really. A writer doesn't know their work any better than they know themselves. And let's face it: when you get right down to it, we're all strangers to ourselves."

"What?"

This is the point where I decide that Jack the Media Trainer isn't a real person. Or, at the very least, he's real but the things that he's saying are figments of my imagination. The way he talks reminds me of the character of John in *Hell of a Book*. John was a good guy that I based on my father. He spoke quickly and in full paragraphs, always aware of what he wanted to say long before he got down to the business of saying it. He was a mixture of Fred MacMurray, and Humphrey Bogart, and every time my father and I sat together and watched a movie about men who spoke fast, and wore hats, and lived in fuzzy black-and-white worlds.

"Think about it," Jack the Media Trainer says. "Have you ever felt some emotion that you didn't know why you felt it? Maybe you see some television commercial for a long-distance carrier and you start crying. Or you read some passage somewhere and, all of a sudden, you're angry, even though you've read the exact same sentiment and idea of that passage a thousand times before. But something about that specific way it's worded this time just sends you into a fury. That's happened to you, hasn't it?"

I don't want to answer any of Jack's questions. Even if he is just a figment of my imagination, he's steering me, guiding the conversation like GPS to some destination that he's been planning to make since long before he ever met me. He's media training me, one word at a time. All I want to do is sit back and let him talk. Offer no answers. Give him no ammunition to use against me, to train me with. But I'm still too new at being an author to not answer someone when they ask me a question.

So I find a compromise and decide to offer only the smallest answers I can. "I suppose," I say.

"Of course it has. It's happened to everyone. And then we sit there like idiots, angry or sad, not even knowing why." He shakes his head in contemplation. "We're complicated creatures, each and every one of us. We all contain mazes inside ourselves, and it's easy to become lost in that maze."

"So I'm a maze now?"

"Damn right you are!" Jack slams his fist on the table. "You're in that maze of yourself. That wild, chaotic world of wants and desires, solipsism, and egomania. You're only able to see the world through your eyes and that's what leads you into the heart of the maze itself, into the—"

"Please don't say 'Heart of Darkness.'"

"—into the Heart of Darkness! And you wouldn't want to drag others into a dark maze, would you?"

"I guess not."

"You're damn right you guess not," Jack says. He bolts up from his chair. "That's a terrible thing to do to someone. To lead them into a maze and . . ." Jack pauses for a second. "You know something, I've said the word 'maze' far too many times. What's another word for 'maze'?"

"Um . . ." I'm too busy trying to come to grips with the fact that I've got a maze inside of me to think of anything.

"Carrie!" Jack shouts.

"Yeah?" the receptionist answers from the other room.

"What's another word for 'maze'?"

"Corn."

"No, not 'maize.' 'Maze.'"

"Oh. Gimme a second."

We sit and wait and listen to the sound of Carrie's fingers flying over the keyboard of her computer. "'Labyrinth,'" she calls out finally.

"What?" Jack answers.

"'Labyrinth.'"

"That David Bowie movie? What about it?"

"It's another word for 'maze.'"

Jack considers this for a moment.

"She's right," I say, finally able to contribute to the conversation.

"So be it," Jack says. "Now . . . where was I?"

"You were saying that I shouldn't be leading other people into the labyrinth of myself."

"Exactly!" Jack says. "You're a labyrinth! And your book is a labyrinth. *Hell of a Book* is a labyrinth! And it's my job to teach you to help other people find a way to navigate both of those labyrinths. We can't have people getting inside of you, the author, and getting themselves turned around. We want all of them to make it home safely once they've entered you and, by proxy, your book. After all, the author is the book and the book is the author."

"I'm not sure I'm comfortable with the phrasing here," I say. I suddenly feel small and confused.

"You mean about having people enter you?"

"Yes."

"You're not homophobic, are you? Because I won't stand for that type of thing!"

"Homophobia doesn't sell books," Sharon adds, suddenly no longer looking at her phone but glaring at me instead. "On the average, we're talking a twenty-two percent decrease in sales compared to non-homophobic authors."

"I'm not homophobic. This has nothing to do with homosexuality! It's just the phrasing."

"Are you sure?" Sharon asks. "I don't really care if you are, but, if so, it's the kind of thing that I need to get in front of."

"I'm not homophobic!"

"Then why do you not like talking about people entering you?"

"Because I'm not a tunnel, or a house, or a mall, or any other structure that can be entered. I'm a person."

"A homophobic person?" Carrie asks from the other room.

"No," I shout into the air. "I'm just a writer. I'm just someone who loved books and wanted to write one. So I did. That's all I did. I just wrote a book!"

"That's right," Jack the Media Trainer says proudly. "You wrote a hell of a book! And now here you are. You're an author, not a writer, not a reader, not a plumber, or mathematician, or virology researcher. You're an author, something you've never been before. Something that few people actually are and even fewer people know how to be. And make no mistake about it, there's definitely a right way and a wrong way to be an author. I've seen it get the better of people. I've seen it drive them mad. I've seen—"

"You're about to quote Ginsberg now, aren't you?"

"—I've seen the best minds of my generation destroyed by authoring! Starving, hysterical . . ."

Jack goes on like this for another ten minutes or so.

ONCE THEY'VE BEEN CONVINCED—MOSTLY—THAT I'M NOT HOMOPHO-bic and once I've been convinced—mostly—that I've got a literal maze inside myself, we finally start talking about *Hell of a Book.*

"So I've got good news for you," Jack says.

"Good," I say, finally glad to have stopped talking about labyrinths and people entering me.

"You've written a good book."

"Thank you," I say.

"Don't thank me," Jack says. "I'm just glad that you've done it. Most people that come in here have written terrible books. And there's nothing wrong with writing a terrible book. Fact of the matter is, most books are pretty terrible when you get right down to it. Just like how most people are terrible."

"That's cynical."

"You're changing the subject."

"You brought it up."

"That's beside the point."

Talking to Jack is beginning to make my head hurt.

"I'm paying you a compliment," Jack continues. "It makes my job easier when I've got a quality product to work with. And your book . . ." He takes a deep breath. His eyes water a little. I think he's about to cry. "Well . . . your book is just something special."

"Thanks," I say.

Just then Sharon looks up from her phone and sucks her teeth. "Can you even believe it?"

"No," Jack says immediately. "He's pretty unbelievable, isn't he? But I've done more with less so don't you worry."

"No," Sharon corrects. "I'm talking about this." She holds up her phone and shows it to us. On the small screen we see the image of a grief-laden Black man and woman standing in front of a lectern, crying and trying to speak. It's a still image so there are no words coming out, only a picture of sadness and outrage and tragedy.

"That's so sad," Jack says, looking away from the phone and back to me.

"No," Sharon says. There's an edge to her voice that I haven't heard before. It's almost bitterness caused by concern. I didn't know that she was the type of woman who was ever concerned about anything.

"You're not looking," Sharon demands. And Jack and I both lean across the table, squinting to see what she's staring at. But all either of us sees is a picture of a couple standing at the lectern weeping. There isn't even a headline to describe the cause of the sadness that we're seeing.

"Okay," Jack says.

Sharon slams a manicured fist on the table. "You're not looking!" she shouts.

For a full minute and a half, Jack and I stare at the picture she is trying to show us. We stare so long that the screen times out and Sharon has to re-enter her pin code in order to light it up again. "They shot him," Sharon says. There are tears pooling in the corners of her eyes.

And it's now that Jack and I both understand what's happening. Somewhere a boy has been shot and the parents are grieving. Jack and I give one another a nod of affirmation.

"Oh no," I say.

"That's terrible," Jack says.

"God," I say. "When is it going to end?"

"You can't turn on the news nowadays without seeing something like this." Jack shakes his head. "When I was a kid, nothing like this ever happened. And now it's everywhere. It's just become this thing that doesn't ever go away. It's like a plague."

"Yeah," I add, "a plague." I want to say something better than this, but I'm afraid of saying the wrong thing. I'm notorious for saying the wrong thing on account of how often I have trouble distinguishing between what's real and what's imagined. And when you spend enough time in a world that's likely just your imagination, you tend to not care as much about the anomalies that you see. When you question whether or not people are actually real, you can't help but feel a little stoic at the news that someone has died. And it's not that you're a bad person, it's just that you have trouble getting emotionally involved in the life of someone who may or may not be real.

And let's face it: in this world that we live in, the fact of the matter is that it's hard to think of anyone as being real. Everyone is just an image on a screen somewhere. Even the people that we meet and come across in the flesh eventually get reduced down to an image on a screen as we interact with them and their social media. So when Sharon shows Jack and me the grieving family on the screen, I can only offer up the normal amount of concern for these people who I have never met and will never meet. And that's okay. That's what people are. Science has proven that there's a limited number of people that we can ever actually care about. It's just a limitation of our brain and our emotions. So there's nothing wrong with that. It doesn't make you a bad person. It doesn't make me—or even Jack—a bad person if we see the man and the woman standing at the lectern crying and the only thing we're able to muster is faux concern.

It's not that we're bad people, it's just that we're people.

"Too many guns," I say.

"Yes," Jack replies. "So many guns. What are they all about? Why do we have them? Why are we always trying to shoot people who haven't done anything to us? Is there really any point to it? And don't even get me started on the lack of mental-health care in this country. It's criminal."

"Yes," I say. "Did you hear about the other shooting?" I don't know what shooting I mean, but there's always another shooting so it's always a safe bet to just ask if the person heard about the other one. It makes you sound informed, and sympathetic, and all of those other things that good people are.

Jack nods again in affirmation. "I did hear about it," he says. "Terrible. Just terrible. It's the kind of thing that makes you wonder about the nature of people. Why do they do it? Why do they do anything like that? What drives them? Who are these people?"

Jack and I continue to go back and forth about the people, and about the tragedy, and about how we're both fed up with the process and the shootings and we hope that we're giving Sharon everything she needs in order to feel good about things and in order to think that neither of us are bad people. After all, we're not bad people. We're just people caught up in the cycle of humanity and trying to get by.

The thin droplets of water at the corners of Sharon's eyes have transformed into full-blown tears. They streak down her face—but do not mar her makeup—and she wipes them away and sniffles. "He was just a kid," she says. "To do that to a kid. I just don't understand it."

Jack and I both know better than to say anything. This is the type of moment in which you don't offer words but you simply let the silence do the work of expressing grief. So he and I both purse our lips and nod solemnly and we both remain that way until Sharon says, "I need to go out for a moment."

Jack and I remain silent as she leaves. We try to leave room for her grieving.

"You know," I say, "I think I might take a moment myself."

"Yes, yes," Jack says. "You do that. We all need time to figure out these impossible-to-understand things. All of these dead people . . . what do we do with them?"

It feels like a rhetorical question so I take my chance and head to the bathroom. And there, The Kid is waiting for me.

"SO WHAT DO YOU THINK OF ALL THIS?" I ASK THE KID.

(He was already there back then. How did I forget *that*? But, then again, I can only be so surprised. It's like I told you before: I can't trust my mind. I never know what's then, what's now, and what never really happened at all.)

He shrugs his shoulders, stoic as Marcus Aurelius on Xanax.

"Well, I think it's a tragedy," I begin, full of righteous indignation. "It's an outright tragedy. I just get tired of seeing it. Get tired of turning on the news and finding out about another dead person."

"But people have always died, right?" The Kid asks.

"True," I reply. "And it's not like the news makes the deaths. I mean, CNN and Fox News aren't out there killing people in the streets. But they do add to the overall air of dread that we all feel. It's the soundtrack of America right now. The jam we all bump and grind to. People being shot is the way we mark the passage of time now. Like, where were you when Sandy Hook happened? And do you remember who you were dating around the time when those people shot up that office building? But it happens so much that you then have to ask: 'What office building?'" I try to flash a smile at the kid as my way of consoling him for the world that he finds himself in. "But it's just the way it is. There's no harm in it. Every generation had their share of tragedies. It's just that we all happen to hear about them more. Fact of the matter is, the murder rate is the lowest it's been since the 1980s. And I know you're too young to understand, but believe me when I say that the 1980s were the heyday of bad things, and crime, and killings, and drugs, and everything else."

The Kid doesn't look particularly convinced.

"But what about the people?" The Kid asks.

"What do you mean?"

"There are people that these things happen to, right?"

I scratch my chin and think about his question. "Technically, I suppose."

"And aren't we supposed to care about people? My mama said that we're all supposed to care about people because . . . well . . . because it's what you're supposed to do. It's how we all take care of each other. So you can't just see somebody being hurt and not care about them."

I shake my head, confirming that everything the boy is saying is true and real. "Everything you're saying is true and real, but that doesn't change the fact that it's impossible to care about everyone. So you pick your battles. You limit how much you invest into the world and into people. It's a type of emotional triage."

"What's 'triage'?"

"It's what they do in hospitals. It's how they tell who to help first. It's basically people prioritizing other people into more or less important."

The Kid thinks about this for a while. He sniffles as though he's suddenly come down with a cold. He balls his small black hand into a small black fist and places it under his chin like an inky rendition of Rodin's *Thinker.* "It just doesn't sound right," The Kid says, somber as an elegy.

"I hate to tell you this, but nothing ever sounds right after a certain age, Kid. The older you get, the more you find out it's all just falling apart and, even worse than that, it's always been falling apart. The past, the present, the future. They're interchangeable when it comes to bad news. Tragedy and trauma are the threads that weave generations together. Hell, being Black, we should know that better than anyone."

WHEN I COME BACK, SHARON IS STILL GONE AND JACK IS STARING AT his watch. We're getting close to being over on time and I can't tell if he's happy about the extra money or frustrated that we're keeping him from something else. Either way, he seems eager to see me. "Now, tell me about your book."

"Well, I mean, you read it. What would you like to know?"

"Tell me what it's about," Jack says. "Pretend I'm a stranger and I haven't read your book. Now tell me what it's about."

I think for a moment. "Well," I begin, "my book's about this character named—"

"I'm going to stop you right there because you're wrong," Jack the Media Trainer says. "But don't feel bad. That's a common mistake among first-time authors. They think their book is about the characters or the story or, if it's nonfiction, the subject matter. But that's all wrong. That's like saying the *Mona Lisa* is about a woman with a wry smile."

I hate to admit it, but Jack the Media Trainer has just managed a pretty profound notion.

"Thank you," he says, as if he can hear my thoughts. "I've been working with authors for well over a decade now. I've media trained people for countless novels, memoirs, short-story collections. The list goes on. And here's one thing that they've all had in common: their books are never about what the authors think they're about. No, sir. Their books are about whatever the hell we want them to be about." He points to the lectern, and the microphones, and the camera at the far end of the room. "When the time comes, when you're sitting up there on Oprah's couch. Lots of good things come out of that couch. Let me tell you!"

"I thought she stopped doing that," I interrupt. "You know, after that whole *Million Little Whatevers* controversy back in—"

"Carrie?!" Jack shouts. "Did Oprah's couch stop running?"

"May 25, 2011," Carrie calls back, somberly. "In the industry it's known as 'The Day the Milk Ran Out.' We hold a moment of silence on that day each year."

"But she's back now, right?" Jack asks. "She didn't turn off the faucet again, did she? Dear God, I hope not!"

"No," Carrie says slowly. "She hasn't gone away again." Her voice is so heavy, I imagine her staring off into the distance for a moment, like watching the credits roll on some favorite movie that she'll never see again. Then she manages: "She's still back . . . but it's never been the same."

"Sorry for your loss," I say. And, without being prompted, we all have a moment of silence for the way things used to be.

AFTER MOURNING THE IMPERIAL SPLENDOR THAT OPRAH'S COUCH used to be, we get back to business. Sharon joins us, looking much more composed, and we spend the next hour and a half talking solely about my wardrobe for the book tour and for interviews. "Right now," Jack says, "with the jeans and button-down shirt combination you're wearing, you've got a bit of an 'Aww shucks' country guy thing going on. That's all well and good, people like that. It's relatable. But it doesn't exactly sizzle. We've got to get you into a sport coat."

"I told you," Sharon adds.

"It's a subtle difference," Jack says, "but a vital one. It's the difference between an author whose wardrobe says 'You should read my book' and an author whose wardrobe says 'You have to read my book.'"

"Which is a seventeen percent difference in sales," Sharon says.

"Exactly," says Jack. "So, first off, sport coat. Then, when you're not in a sport coat, you should be in a suit. Have you ever seen an author on the *Today* show not wearing a suit?"

"Well . . ."

"You haven't," Jack says. "The suit—or sport coat—is the backbone of a good interview. Speaking of interviews, has Sharon given you her interview primer?"

"I have," Sharon says.

"Good," Jack says. "Now get up there and show me what you've got." He turns and nods toward the lectern at the far end of the room.

I get up and walk toward the lectern, because what other choice do I have? Jack's a professional media trainer. This is his business. And me, I'm a guy who's spent his whole life in customer service and who just happened to write a book someone wanted to publish. When I stop to think about it, I can't remember ever seeing an author on the *Today* show who wasn't wearing a full suit. So Jack and Sharon must know what they're talking about. Which only makes me all the more nervous.

My legs feel like concrete as I take my place at the lectern. I count nine microphones in front of me, all of them placed there to make me feel uneasy, I guess. To push me out of my comfort zone.

"Excellent," Jack says. "One more quick thing." He walks over to the camera standing in front of the lectern and switches it on. "There," he says. "Are you ready?"

"Not really."

"Good," he says. "Because life never waits until you're ready. First question: What's the title of your book?"

"*Hell of a Book,*" I say.

"Let me stop you right there," Jack says. "You didn't thank me for asking you that question. You should always thank your host for their first question about your book. Let's try that again: So, what's the title of your book."

"Um . . ."

"No 'ums' or 'uhs.' Try again."

"Thank you for asking," I say, my voice shaking like the precursor to an earthquake. "My book is called *Hell of a Book.*"

"Wow!" Jack says, far more excited than he should be. "That was great! Ready for your next question? Here goes: What's your book about?"

"It's about . . ."

"Title," Sharon says, sending yet another email from her phone.

"What?" I say.

"Repeat the title as often as you can," Jack the Media Trainer says. "Go again: What's your book about?"

"Thank you for asking," I say tentatively, like sticking a toe into deep and unknown water, "*Hell of a Book* is about—"

"So here are the key points that you need to make about *Hell of a Book,*" Jack interrupts. He leans forward on the table, ready to whisper the great secrets that I later found out my publisher was paying $350 an hour for me to hear.

"Okay," I say.

"Who are you?"

"I don't think I understand." I know for a fact that I don't understand.

"Who are you?" Jack repeats. "It's the only point that you need to make about your book. It's the only point anyone ever really needs to make about anything. Who you are defines the world in which you exist." Jack smiles. "Who you are defines your book more than any plot point, more than any character arc. Every time someone asks you about your book, what they're really asking is 'Who are you?'"

"And don't forget plot," Sharon says.

"'Who are you in plot form?'" Jack corrects. And then he leans back in his chair, more than a little pride stretched across his face.

"Wonderful," Sharon says. She's looked up from her phone this time. She looks mesmerized. Awestruck, even. She turns to me after a moment. "Didn't I tell you this would be wonderful?" she says.

"Jack?" I say.

"Yeah?"

"I don't understand."

"That's okay," Jack says. "You don't have to understand. Not right now, at least. It'll come to you later." He points to Sharon. "She gets it already because it's not about her. It's about you. It's always easier to see the truth about other people than it is to see the truth about ourselves."

"Is this because of that labyrinth inside of me?"

"My work here is done," Jack says. "You're on your way to becoming an author. You're on your way to becoming a professional author. One last thing, though."

"What's that?"

"This probably goes without saying, but I'm going to say it anyway: Don't write about race. Specifically, don't write about being Black. You can write about Black characters, but just don't write about being Black. No."

"Why not?"

"Trust me on this. I've crunched the numbers. I've seen a dozen writers like you come and go. You've got that crossover talent, my man. You live in both worlds. That's the smartest thing about *Hell of a Book.* You need to hang on to that. The last thing people really want to hear about is being Black. Being Black's a curse—no offense—and nobody wants to feel cursed when they read something they just finished paying $24.95 for. Know what I mean? Here's one thing I've learned: when someone treats you terribly, the last thing they want is for you to behave as if they've treated you terribly. If I punch you in the neck, I don't want you bringing up that time I punched you in the neck. It's your job, as the punchee, to grin and bear it and treat me like I never did it. Make me feel good. Help me forget the whole neck-punching adventure. It's common courtesy, really. And that's just the same for the person who said they loved you and then showed it not to be true as it is for the country that kidnapped you and chopped off your left foot. Nobody wants their monstrosities brought up. And if you should happen to do it, they'll hate you for it. Just ask Frankenstein's monster."

"Say what?"

"So here's what I want you to do: I want you to make sure that you keep things as light as possible—as a person, as an author, and as a book."

"But I'm not a book."

"Of course you are. And, as such, don't plant flags anywhere. Ever. Don't commit to anything. Just exist. Just like that maze inside of you, the future of this country is all about patriotic, unity-inducing language. Post-Racial. Trans–Jim Crow. Epi-Traumatic. Alt-Reparational. Omni-Restitutional. Jingoistic Body-Positive. Sociocultural-Transcendental. Indigenous-Ripostic. Treaty of Fort Laramie–Perpendicular. Meta-Exculpatory. Pan-Political. Uber-Intermutual. MLK-Adjacent. Demi-Arcadian Bucolic. That is the vernacular of the inclusive, hyphenated, beau-American destiny we're manifesting here! You and me! Book by book we're making it happen! But it doesn't happen by planting flags and picking at the scabbed-over wounds of a certain Dispossessed Neo-Global Cultural demographic committed at the hands of a onetime *possibly* improprietous proto-nation."

It's such a beautiful word soup he's feeding me. Simply beautiful. But not without its lumps.

"Wait . . . just wait," I say, scratching my head. "Am I the . . . the, uh, the Dispossessed Neo-Global Cultural demographic?"

"Listen. The key takeaway here is that if you're going to write, write about something universal that fits into that fervid, sublime nationalistic archetype I just mentioned . . . Write something like love." Jack leans back in his chair and rubs his chin, pleased with himself. "Yeah," he says. "Write about love. Love and Disney endings. Not suffering. Not oppression. Not fear. Not the slights of the past—imagined or documented. Not disappointment. Not death. Never death. Only love. Tell a love story. Always tell a love story. Love is a form of absolution—if not expressed, then implied."

. . . Like I said: this is a love story.

It was the belly of summer and the cicadas trilled their familiar song as Soot's father, William, jogged through the night. The air still smelled of fireworks. Now and again, he ran past clusters of people in their backyards. Al Green, Marvin Gaye, Wu-Tang, Donna Summer, J. Cole, they all rolled out over the muggy night air as Black bodies danced and laughed in the dim glare of porch lights.

He ran past the Browns' house and caught the smell of a barbecue. His stomach growled and a voice called out about coming in to get a plate and William yelled back that there were miles to cover yet but maybe he'd come by tomorrow and get whatever was left over. And then the person yelled something back and disappeared into the night behind William as his run unfolded.

Soon, he entered the stretch between the houses. The lights all fell away, leaving only the dim light cast by a sliver of moon and a swath of stars. The only sound he heard was his breathing and his feet flapping against the pavement.

His run took him out through the long arms of the countryside. He crossed over a small bridge and heard the splash of something leaping into the water. He wanted to stop and find out what had made the sound, but it didn't quite feel right so he kept going. But the feeling came back to him, again and again, as he ran. He throbbed with the need to stop and linger, the urge to wait, to stretch out the moments and mysteries that were given to him, in case they were suddenly taken away from him.

More than anything, it felt good to be out here, lost in the darkness of the world, away from everyone. He felt at home within himself, at home in his skin. He could believe, just then, that the whole world was gone away and all of the eyes that had been watching him were finally gone. He wasn't being watched anymore. He didn't stand out. Every moment of his life, he felt that he stood out. Too tall. Too skinny. Too Black. All of it swallowed him up some days. There were eyes everywhere, watching him, staring at him.

He saw that same worry in Soot and hated the world for it. But, more than that, he hated himself for not being able to fix it. He'd wanted so much for his son to learn to disappear. To be able to go away, become unseen and safe. It was the only thing he wanted to give his son, and he was failing at it day after day.

But even that sadness and guilt went away when he ran. Out here, beneath the black sky, surrounded by the black earth, he was just himself.

He was no one.

He was unwatched.

He was unseen.

He was safe.

THE WAY BACK HOME WAS MORE OF THE SAME SPLENDOR. HE PASSED the dwindling moments of other parties. By now, people were too tired, or drunk, or just having too much fun to see him jogging past them in the night. It was when he was reaching his home that he saw the glimmer of the blue lights behind him.

The siren chirped and William moved to the side of the road and looked back over his shoulder. Blue lights hovered. Headlights blinded him. He turned back and saw his home—the little square of wood and nails and memories destined to come to an end. He could throw a stone and hit it if he wanted. Or he could run to it and be there inside seconds.

The police car came to a stop behind him. He heard a door open. "Hold on right there," a heavy voice called out.

William took a deep breath and turned. All he saw was the glare of headlights and the flash of blue. A silhouette climbed out of the car and said, "Just wait right there."

A flashlight shined in his eyes and, reflexively, he lifted a hand to shield his eyes from the light.

"Don't do that," the silhouette said. William felt a shiver run down his spine. He lowered his hand slowly. "What are you doing out here?" the silhouette said.

"Running home."

"Why you running in the dark?"

"Gets too hot in the daytime. That's all." William turned and pointed at his home. "That's my house right there."

"Mmm-hmm," the silhouette said. "You got some ID on you?"

"No. Like I said, I was just out running. My house is right there. I left my ID at home."

"You should have your ID with you. Turn around."

"What? Why?"

"Turn around."

"I—"

And then the world exploded.

William fell to the ground. His legs failed him. His lungs trembled in his chest and he felt as though he were drowning. His arms still worked, but they did not know what to do with themselves. "Calm down," he said to himself. "Calm down. You're going to be okay. You're going to be okay." Those were the words he wanted to say, but all that came out was a pain-filled moan.

The shape behind him shouted something, but William couldn't hear the words. He needed to get home. If he could get home, everything would be okay. His wife would be there and his son would be there and, together, they would all be okay. They would be safe.

If only he could make it home.

He rolled onto his stomach as the blue lights flashed in the grass around him. He tried to crawl, but his body could not comply.

He looked up and saw, there in the doorway of his home, his wife and his son, watching it all. Her face contorted in terror and the boy's . . . the boy gave no reaction.

Then it happened. The boy began, slowly, fading away. It was not darkness that clouded William's eyes—that would come soon—but something else. The boy was disappearing. Effervescing like steam. Melting away into nothing.

Drifting off . . . into The Unseen.

Finally.

Finally, he would be invisible.

Finally, he would be unseen.

Finally, he would be safe.

The disappearance of his son was the last thing William saw. He smiled in death.

Because my life isn't enough of a traveling sack of chaos, I make the mistake of telling The Kid that there's a love story coming down the pipe as well. I know it's a mistake even as I'm doing it. Ever since Renny smacked me around and told me I'm Black and I need to talk about it, The Kid's been stalking me a lot more. And while I've done my best to keep him at a distance, I can feel him starting to get to me. Every time I try to just get back to the way things used to be, he shows up again, smiling that smile of his.

We're sitting together outside the airport watching all of humanity pass us by and he's still a bit sore about the notion I buy into that you can't treat people as real beings, no matter how much your local PBS station and *Sesame Street* tell you otherwise. I try to explain to him that adulthood just isn't built for believing in the existence of other people. If we all believe in everyone—really believe they existed—then we have to care about them. We have to change our lives. We have to admit that maybe some of us actually have it better than others and, in having it better, we have to admit that maybe we could get by with a little less so that others can have a little more and that means giving up some of the things that we have.

"What's so wrong with that?" The Kid asks, glowing with naivety.

"The Fear, Kid."

"The Fear?"

"That's right. The Fear. Fear's the oldest state of being in the human hustle. Comes in all shapes and sizes. But there are two versions of it that'll affect you the most, being who you are."

"What do you mean?" The Kid asks. I can hear the hesitation in his throat. Every word digs its heels into his tongue, doing what it can to stay in his head. But The Kid shoves them out anyways, knowing full well that they'll come back to bite him. He's onto the fact that he's opening up a grease gun of knowledge that he doesn't really want. But he does it anyway.

Yeah, safe to say this kid's got moxie. And, in this world, moxie'll either take you far or get you killed. Or maybe it'll take you just far enough to get you killed.

Either way, if he's willing to ask me for it, the least I can do is give it to him. So I do, with both barrels, straight down the line: "Live long enough," I say, "and you'll eventually see all sorts of things taken away from you, Kid. Toys, sandwiches, money, people, and eventually time. And the longer you go in life, the more you worry about something being taken away and you worry about going back to not having enough. We're all afraid of being at the bottom of life's shit stack. We're all afraid of being poor, being injured, helpless, handicapped, all of the things that make us look at other people and say, 'How bad. Somebody should do something to help them.' The thing we're most afraid of is being the 'them' in that equation." I shake my head to push home the horror of what I'm saying to The Kid. I can't tell if he's understanding me or not. I can't tell if any of this is really getting through or if I just sound like another cynical heel. But this is the truth I know.

The Kid mulls it over in silence, and that impossibly ebony skin of his swallows the sunlight in the most beautiful way.

"What's the other one?" he finally asks.

"The other what?"

"You said there were two big versions that would affect me. What's the other one?"

I sit there for a second, thinking about whether or not I should go into that one. I don't have the heart to tell him that the second one is even worse than the first. I don't have the heart to tell him about how I came to learn it on the day my old man died and how it's haunted me every step of the way ever since. I can't tell him how much it's taken away from me.

So I just don't tell him. Decide to save that horror for myself. For now, at least.

"I'm sorry, Kid," I say.

"What for?"

"For telling you all of this. For breaking the illusion."

The Kid shakes his head. "Nah," he says. "It's okay. I decide if I really believe what you're saying or not. My mama taught me that. She said I can always pick what is true about the world. I can't pick the facts, but I can pick what's true. But she apologized too."

"What did she apologize for?"

"She wouldn't say. She just got sad all of a sudden. Did your mama tell you that too? That you could pick what is true about stuff?"

I flinch at the mention of my mother. Doesn't this kid know it's impolite to ask about someone's family? Doesn't he know that such things just aren't done? I mean, I know I asked about his mother but that was only after he brought her up. That's how you do things. That's how you interact with people. You let people keep their secrets. You let them be whoever it is they want to show you. You let their ambassadors live. The thing you don't do is go prying into people's lives and asking about parents, and loss, and pain, and all the things that keep them awake in the late hours of the night after they've had nightmares for a week.

"Let's not talk about my mother," I say.

"Why not?"

"Because I'm going to show you the key to getting through this life, Kid. I'm going to show you the trick to really being happy and really being able to take in reality and make it something you can stand up to day after day after day for all the years of the rest of your long and happy life."

The Kid and I sit together on this bench watching the airport crowd and eating the last of a lunch that I managed to steal off of an interviewer who was nice enough to meet me here and ask me all those types of questions that interviewers ask.

I look over the travelers shuffling to and fro as I finish off my sandwich and wipe my hands on my suit pants. "Now," I begin, "What's your favorite animal?"

"A peacock!" The Kid says, eyes dancing.

"Peacock?"

"Yeah! My uncle used to raise them. They're awesome. At night, they would fly up in the trees and sleep up there. Sometimes, in the middle of the night, you would hear them screaming." The Kid throws his head back in laughter. "Sometimes, my cousin from

New York would come down during the summer. Every time the peacocks made that sound in the middle of the night, he would jump out of his skin!" The Kid buckles over. He grips his stomach with his dark hands and laughs. His mouth is all teeth, and tongue, and unsung glory. "It was the only time he was ever afraid and I wasn't," The Kid says. "The only time ever."

"Okay," I say. "Look over there." I raise a finger, pointing to a large azalea bush growing at the edge of an artificial pond.

The Kid looks. "The flowers?"

"No," I say. "The peacock. The black one."

I point again, aiming my finger directly at the beautiful bird that stands no more than twenty feet away from us.

It's an onyx peacock. Black as anything. A dark star with plumage. From the bottom of its thin, delicately clawed feet, to the top of its thinly crowned head, to the final reaches of its train that is spread as wide as the horizon, ebony like a wall of night that has been bottled, and molded, and shaped into a sculpture worthy of song and wonder.

I can tell from the boy's eyes that he can't see it.

"It's okay," I say.

"What is?"

"We've got time. I've got time to teach you to see those types of things."

The Kid thinks for a moment. He looks at me and then back at the place where he can't see the peacock. "Do you really see a bird there?"

"Just as sure as I see you," I say.

"But I'm real," he says.

"I know."

"I'm just invisible to people that I want to be invisible to. I told you. My mama taught me. It's my gift." For the first time, he doesn't sound certain. Neither of me nor of himself. I know what he's feeling. Been there. It's that feeling of the sand slipping out from beneath your feet and not knowing that you're about to be pulled along with it.

"I know," I say. "And it's a glorious gift. Your mother sounds like a wonderful person."

"She is," The Kid says.

"But did she ever tell you why she taught you this gift?"

"To stay safe."

"Yeah, but from what? From who?"

A cloud settled over his face and he was sad all of a sudden.

"Want to talk about it?" I ask.

"No," The Kid says.

I don't have the heart to tell him that I know perfectly well what his mama was trying to protect him from. My mother tried to protect me from the same thing. My dad too. They both failed. And my guess was, The Kid's mama had failed too. He just doesn't know it yet.

We sit for a while and I watch as the onyx peacock walks back and forth beside the pond. Its inky plumage scintillates in the afternoon sun, refracting the light through the lens of darkness and shooting out something more beautiful than I've ever seen before. It looks the way jazz might if it had a form that you could see that wasn't that Miles Davis.

I stand and walk toward the bird. As expected, it spooks and takes flight. It sails off into the distance of the unknown city and disappears among the clamor and clap of humanity. I pick a feather that it's left behind.

"Here," I say, handing it to The Kid.

"What?"

"One of the feathers."

The Kid stares down at my hand and, for a moment, I can't tell if he can see the feather or not. My gut says he can, but The Kid's hard to read. Especially with that dark skin of his. It hides so much of him that, even if he isn't able to turn invisible, I'm not sure he has much trouble disappearing in this world. It's when his hand reaches out for the feather that I'm able to see just how much alike he and the peacock are. They're cut from the same cloth, the same impossible shade of darkness. The same blackness. The same splendor.

Just before his fingers touch the feather, he pulls his hand back.

"I don't see anything," he says.

"It's okay," I say. "It doesn't matter anyway." I toss the feather away. "Say, Kid, you think about love very much?"

I LOVED MY MOTHER, AND I LOVED MY FATHER AND DADDY HENRY. And as I got older, I loved people in different ways. You met the receptionist. But I've never been much of a dater. The main problem I've found with dating is that, at some point in the process, you have to include other people. You have to actually interact with another human being. And when it comes to people . . . well . . . I've never really been a fan.

But, like anybody else spinning through the void of space on this watery rock of ours, I've had days where I thought it might be good to not be alone. To feel someone else's hand on my flesh. To tell a joke and hear laughter other than my own.

The only flaw I've ever found with writing is that you can call out to it, but the page never answers you back. Writing is an act of obsession, after all. And obsession is, by nature, a one-way street.

Only love can ever answer back.

And for that you have to have another person. And in order to have another person, you have to leap into the maelstrom that is dating. To dip your toes.

Exhibit A: Kelli

It's the middle of summer and I meet this lovely woman with hair down to the center of her back and a peculiar sense of humor and it's enough to gain my interest. She tells me that her name is Kelli and I tell her that's a great name—which it is—and eventually we agree to have dinner together. She invites me over to her house and promises to cook me dinner even though I tell her that she doesn't have to.

"I've never actually made Buffalo wings before," Kelli says. We're standing in her small kitchen that smells of sandalwood and spices. "I'm not much into fried foods," she continues. "My aunt swears by this recipe, though." She lives in a loft on the hipster side of town. Her home is filled with books and family photographs. She has a slight midwestern accent.

"You don't have to do this," I say, politely as I can. "I can eat anything, really." Truthfully, I'm allergic to bananas, but there's no sense in telling her that just yet. First dates are matters of ambassadorship, not diplomacy.

"No," she says, equally polite, "I want to. I love learning new things."

Then we both smile our best first-date smiles. She reaches over and turns on the knob on the stove. The cap beneath the pot of oil leaps to life with a soft *fwoosh* sound.

"Do you know what I like about you?" Kelli asks.

"Charm? Dashing good looks? Modesty? Take your pick."

She laughs a little. Then: "No," she says. "It's that you don't try to tell me what to do. I swear, I keep meeting these guys who just, I don't know, they're just always trying to tell me what to do. You're not like that."

"Not at all," I say.

The cap beneath the pot of oil continues billowing out heat. I stare at it, unable to look away now that I've noticed she's got it turned on high. "I know exactly what you meant about those types of guys," I say. Then: "Hey, I think that cap might be turned up a lit—"

"I just don't think you understand just how good it feels to spend time with someone who isn't trying to be my father. You know?"

"I totally get you," I say.

Wisps of smoke rise from the pot. The oil inside shimmers. There's a gentle crackle like miniaturized lightning as the oil continues to heat.

"You . . . uh . . . you said you don't do much frying, right?"

"Yeah," Kelli answers. "Cholesterol, and fats, and all that."

She grabs a fistful of breaded chicken and holds it over the pot of sizzling hot oil that is, already, on the edge of throwing a tantrum.

"Listen, Kelli," I say, "I'd never tell you what to do. But—"

"But what?!"

Her mouth is a tight line. There's a fire in her eyes that says, "I dare you to finish that sentence." Both of our very lives could be on the line, but I'll be damned if I'm going to say anything. I don't want to be another one of those men who is always trying to tell her what to do. I don't want her to reject me. I don't want to be sent home to an empty house where there's only a computer and a half-done manuscript filled with memories of my dead parents waiting for me.

So I say nothing.

The chicken wings get dropped.

Then we're standing in front of a burning building with smut on our faces and smoke in our lungs. Firefighters jostle us, racing toward the inferno. Water erupts from fire hoses. The burning apartment is a small, luminous sun.

"So you'll call me?" she asks.

"Probably not."

"I totally get that."

"I'm going to leave now."

"Drive safe."

"Yeah."

And that was one of the better dates I've had.

Exhibit B: Kellie

It's springtime. Warm in the sun, chilly in the shade. Birds in the trees. I'm in a car with a very attractive woman named Kellie.

This isn't the same Kellie as before, by the way. It's a totally different spelling.

For whatever reason, the universe chooses to send me lots of Kellys. Kelly, after Kelli, after Kellie, after Keli. I have no idea why. My mother's name wasn't Kelly. My first love wasn't named Kelly. Freud would be pretty disappointed, I imagine. I never wanted to kill my father and marry my mother. Fact of the matter is, my father was a good fella. I liked him.

SPEAKING OF MY FATHER, LET ME TELL YOU A LITTLE BIT ABOUT THE old man:

Picture me at age nine. I'm tall for my age. Thin, but not really skinny. I look smart enough, but not so smart-looking that you might think me the kind of kid who might grow up to be a pain in the ass or anything.

I live in a small, old, gray house. The outside paint was chosen decades before I was born. It's hard to say whether or not gray was the original color. Maybe it was a soft shade of blue once. But then the sun came around, and time passed, and nobody cared for it the way they're supposed to because the money was never there and so the paint leached away and all that's left is a home that seems sad and forlorn.

But this isn't a place of sadness.

Inside the house, the flooring is wood. Old and slightly faded, just like the outside of the house, but with an air of warmth about it. It seems like the type of floor you could put kids on and forget about them and everything would be okay. It's the type of floor children remember sleeping on and feeling the heat rise up through the floorboards in summer and feeling the chill of winter creep through at Christmas while they waited for jolly old Saint Nick.

It's the type of floor a life is built on.

The house has two bedrooms. Small, narrow rooms that fit all the other small, narrow outlooks of the house. There's seventies-era wood paneling on the walls. It's that tacky, deep-hued flavor of brown that everybody who couldn't afford any better were into at one time. Makes it look like you covered your walls in mahogany, only you've never actually seen real mahogany before so you got sold a bad approximation and you don't even know it. It's tacky as all get-out, but eventually they get taken down and the wall painted a soft blue color called Last Summer Sky Before You Die. So, depending on your imagination—whether you want to imagine the paneling or the paint—the walls are either forest or sky. Whichever you prefer. Whatever you choose probably says something about you.

There's a living room here. The biggest room in the house. When I'm nine years old, there's a big, square, wood-burning heater in the corner of the room. The kind you don't see anymore because of all the houses they burned down. Pig iron arsonists, that's what they were. A soot-black plume of aluminum reaches out like a burnt arm from the top of the heater. It punches straight through a hole in the wall to the concrete block chimney wearing a mildew-green patina and running up the outside of the house. That old heater was a beast. Had more tricks than a carful of monkeys. I still got a scar on my leg from one of the embers that broke out of the belly of that thing one time when my father was shoving pine into it.

Nostalgia's a funny thing, though. Even back then, when it happened, I knew it wasn't a particularly terrible experience. Even though I wound up scarred for life I wasn't scarred for life, you know? That's what I call "Now-stalgia." When you know a time in your life is gonna last forever, even before the moment is over.

In the opposite corner of the room is the most important piece of equipment: the television. My father works a lot of hours. Swing shift in a sawmill. Mornings one week, afternoons the next, overnights the following, and on, and on, and on. Later, after my father's dead, there'll be articles published on just how bad swing shift is on a person. The body clock being always unable to adapt. No consistency. The brain, and heart, and liver always chasing something that will never come: normality. It's brutal. And the father in this story knew it long before the eggheads in lab coats did their study and figured it out. But only certain tax brackets get the luxury of knowing something'll kill you and being able to choose not to do it.

Swing shift isn't the cause of the old man's death—cancer won that particular gold watch—but it contributes to the state of his life. The same way a grain of sand contributes to the existence of a beach.

My old man is as tall as they come. Six-foot-six. Skinny as a bank account after Christmas. He's got a wiry mustache and a small goatee with sprigs of gray cropping up around the edges. He wears work clothes every day of his life. Day in and day out, the same uniform of scraping by: dark blue button-down Dickies or tan-colored button-down Dickies. More pockets than he ever had money to put in them. Always one size too big so that they hung loose on him, like the Scarecrow and Cowardly Lion decided to swap rags one day. Not long before the cancer got him—on one of those last lucid days—he told me that it was because of how he got picked on back in the day. They made fun of his gangly silhouette so he thought he'd mitigate it by dressing big. Didn't work, by the way. You can't hide who you are. Not really. But he still tried.

My old man was just as broken as the rest of us and he knew it.

I tell you, those baggy duds were like skin grafts on my old man. I swear. Only time I ever saw him in anything other than that was when somebody turned up dead or married, and when those days came around even he didn't seem to recognize himself. He'd walk and sit as rigid as Christ on the cross. Like nobody gave him the instruction manual on how to operate the stranger he saw in the mirror.

At age nine, I'm sitting on my father's knee as that old black heater growls in the far corner of the room. The TV's on, throwing that soft mist of blue light and sibilant voices over the both of us. The old man loved those old black-and-white tough guy pictures.

You know the ones: fast-talking private dicks dressed in double-breasted danger, getting steered between bullets by some hardcase dame that can't be trusted half as much as she can be loved. All the fistfights are one punch and the murders bloodless. Just a lot of stiff-spined pantomiming and falling down slow. I figure blood would have screwed up the wardrobes in those pictures. I think that's what my old man liked most: the suits. The suits and the certainty about their world. The lack of fear.

The characters in those noir pictures were never afraid of anybody. Not really. Even when the lead started flying, they'd just duck down behind some '48 gangster tank, tighten gray mouths into sideways exclamations, and fire back a few shots of their own. Fear never came into it.

Maybe that's what the old man wanted. To live that kind of life. I'm older now. Seen a few things. And, looking back on it, I think my pops was afraid. Always afraid. Every second of every day. His whole life was one long, sustained terror that he tried with all of his might to keep to himself. Not just to keep it secret, but to keep ownership of it. He wanted to be selfish with it.

I think it was always running, my old man's fear. Perpetual and widespread.

Fear of being a bad father. Fear of being a bad husband. Fear of being arrested. Fear of being called skinny like when he was a kid. Fear of being poorer tomorrow than he was today. Fear of giving too much of his life to swing shift and not enough to his son. Fear of cops. Fear of lawyers. Fear of getting injured. Fear of dying. Fear of living. Fear of a past that he couldn't change. Fear of a present that was always out to get him. Fear of a future that might turn out to be nothing more than the present with more gray hair. Same failures. Same struggles. All of it with fewer chances to get it right.

Every day he wore his fears just like he wore those Dickies of his.

But the people in those movies, they didn't go in on wearing that particular suit. Like I said: they weren't afraid of anything. I'm pretty sure that's what my old man wanted. That's why he loved those movies. That's why he passed them on to me.

Thanks to my father, by the time I was nine I'd all but memorized Fred MacMurray's voice-overs from *Double Indemnity.* Hands down, that one was the old man's favorite. "A perfect story," he'd say. "True as can be, even if it ain't real."

And when we weren't watching grayscale racketeers, my old man told me stories. Even though he wasn't particularly good at telling them, he made it clear that a good story was the only way to tell the truth. He didn't go in on those long-toothed yarns about one-eyed giants with clunky names and boozehound gods that couldn't keep it in their pants. No. My old man told me about real people. People with Social Security numbers. He told me stories about my great-grandfather, a man so strong that one time he punched a mule and knocked it cold. Then there was the story of my great-grandmother, a woman so tall that people came from three counties over just to try and look up her dress. He told me hunting stories about the ones he got and the ones that got away. He told me stories about men down at the sawmill who lost their favorite body parts to the saw blade but who still came back to work and acted as if nothing had happened.

He seemed to feel there was a heavy lesson in that.

My old man told me once that he wanted me to grow up to be a writer. "Stories are the best things," he said.

"Writing chooses us," I once told a fan at a book signing. "All we can do is heed the call."

But if I'm honest with myself, I have to admit that the old man led me to this world. By watching movies, by talking about forerunners I would never know, by showing up in my life day after day, right up until he had used up all of his days.

He was a swell Joe, my old man. Safe to say, I loved him.

He died slow. But that was a good thing. And by that, I mean that there was enough time to bear up to it.

Picture that living room with me and my father. The wood-burning heater. The old television. The black-and-white movie swirling on it. Picture a large rotary phone sitting within reach. The phone rings—a loud, old bell sound, the kind of phone that rings so loud you could hear it from the backyard. My father answers.

On the other end of the line a doctor says: "You've got cancer, buddy."

The old man, without missing a beat, says back to the doctor: "Happens to the best of 'em." Then he hangs up the receiver and we finish watching the movie.

His last moments came and went a year later under slanted sunlight that came in through the windows of a hospice center and cast hard shadows over the day. The cancer had already won. By now, it was just doing victory laps, so they kept him run up on morphine, which meant he slept more than he did anything else. Practicing up for the future. I guess.

I was ten years old then. My mother and I camped out at the edges of his hospital bed. She kept telling me that everything was going to be okay. I told her I believed her.

Together, she and I did what we could to keep a cycle of those old movies of his dancing on a loop on the TV on the far wall. The hospice people said that even though he was sleeping, he could still hear what was going on. My mother believed that story. I didn't, but I went along. Maybe for her sake. Or maybe just in case.

The plan neither of us said out loud was that we hoped to have him drift off on a soundtrack he'd known all through his life. Dames telling brutes: "Get your mitts offa me!"

Hardheads barking back: "No dice, toots."

It was a good play, but at the very end it came up short. A swing and a miss. Nobody's fault, really. Just how things go sometimes.

Here's how it fell apart:

The old lady had just stepped out to find food. Can't remember how long it had been since either of us had eaten, but it was long enough for my stomach to turn on itself. So there I was, decade-old me, dressed in jeans and my best t-shirt and my only pair of sneakers. Credits had just finished rolling on *The Maltese Falcon* and while I was swapping out one movie for the next on the TV, the news broke in like it always does. The story of the hour, running on every single channel—the only show in town, you might say—was about some dark-skinned man gunned down by a cop in his own front yard. There was a lot of the usual side-picking: excessive force versus resisting arrest. The details were still up in the air, but the one thing that showed through in the muck was the fact that, no matter how you cut it, the man had died in front of his wife and son. They'd watched the whole thing from the comfort of their very own front porch, awash in the flickering glow of blue lights and a deafening crescendo of eight gunshots.

The dead man on TV was barely past thirty, but hell if he wasn't the spitting image of my old man. It was downright uncanny. Just as skinny. Just as dark. Even had on a pair of dark blue Dickies, if you can believe it. And the icing on the cake? In one of the photos of the dead man's life that flashes up on the screen, it's a family shot. Him, his wife, and a little troublemaker that wasn't too far down the handsome scale from yours truly. Aged ten years, just like me. I mean, the kid was damn near my doppelganger. The only difference was his skin: impossibly dark, impossibly beautiful.

That's when it started.

The picture of the dead guy, it sent a bolt through me. The longer I watched the news story, the more I saw my father stretched out in the morning grass, a tarp draped over his body and bullet holes in his back yawning at the sky—same color blue as those walls I told you about. Before long, it wasn't some stranger on the TV but it was my old man, one hundred percent. Even as I turned and looked at him there in the bed, dying by centimeters, he was there on the screen, already dead. Somehow, he was dying and dead all at the same time.

Schrödinger's father.

I got tight in the chest and sweaty in the palms. "It's not real," I told my young self. I said a prayer to God and Batman at the same time. After all, if there was anybody who knew what it was to lose their parents and lose their mind both, it was the Caped Crusader. But that didn't do any good. My eyes still saw my old man on the TV, dead as a target at the shooting range. So I slammed them shut. I knew it had to be my overactive imagination yanking my crank, so I focused on doing what I could to curb the insanity, curb the fear.

The Fear. That's the thing that was really dangerous. It had a fist in my stomach and wasn't about to let go. My whole body felt like it wasn't mine anymore. Like maybe it had never been mine. Like it might suddenly be taken away from me at any moment and there was nothing I could do about it. What's worse, there was nothing I would ever be able to do about it.

That's what the Fear really came down to. That's what all of the other fears were derived from for people of a certain skin color living in a certain place. But it wasn't just a fear, it was a truth. A truth proven time and time again for generations. A truth passed down through both myth and mandate, from lip-to-lip to legislation. Certain bodies don't belong to their inhabitants. Never have, never will again. A persistent, inescapable, and horrific truth known by millions of unsettled bodies. The Fear.

It had always been there, but I could see it now. Could really recognize it. And once that happens, once you see it, you can't look away. Can't ever quiet it. Can't ever forget that you don't belong to yourself anymore, but to the hands, fists, cuffs, and bullets of a stranger.

You can never come back from that knowledge. Not ever. At least, not without a mild, prolonged psychotic break. Not without going more than a little mad. And we don't know anybody like that, do we?

"No . . ." a ghostly voice whispered. It was my father, of course. The first time in thirty hours and he chose now, of all times, to wake up. His eyes—milky, red, and wide as saucers—stared in terror at the TV. It was a shattering type of fright that I saw in him just then. Greater than any of the fear I'd seen him wear throughout his whole life. Like the TV had finally, here at the end, held good on some gruesome promise made before he was even born. But it wasn't just terror, it was something else. Like he knew the face on the screen hanging before us both.

". . . God . . . no . . ." he rasped, lungs sounding like rusted bellows.

He tried to raise his hand, but all he got was a half-showing of weak, ebon fingers stretching in the direction of the face on the television. His whole body trembled from the effort, but still he tried, like he was reaching out to grab the dead man and pull him back into this world. His brow, doing what his dying body couldn't, rose up, mournful and aghast. It was an expression like nothing I'd ever seen before. Sadness and regret. Horror and recognition. It was like finally, here at the end, he saw not just a truth but *the* Truth.

He cried then. Small, shining tears slid over the dark, quivering earth of his woeful face and, still, he reached for whoever it was he saw on the television and his dry, dark lips contorted, building a word. The silent, breathless cave of his mouth looked the way it looked whenever he called my name.

For maybe the first time in my life, I knew my father's fear. I knew what haunted him. What stalked him. What hung over his whole goddamn life. I knew it because I felt it now too. I don't know if he passed it on or if I just, finally, saw what he had been seeing for his whole life. Either way, his fear was mine now.

Sometimes, I think that's what really killed him.

Cancer just took the credit.

His fingers fell limp. His brow relaxed and he just melted back down into the bed. His eyelids came down—one last sunset. Then the lights switched off and the clockwork stopped spinning. My name went unsaid.

ANYHOW, KELLIE AND I ARE DRIVING ALONG ON THIS BEAUTIFUL spring day and we're smiling and talking to one another, because that's what people do. "God," I say, "can you believe this weather? It's just absolutely beautiful!" One of the federal requirements for a first date is that you talk about the weather at least once.

"I know," Kellie says. "It's just terrific." Then: "Are we still on for the museum tonight? I hear that Rembrandt exhibit is supposed to be amazing."

"Definitely still on," I say, as chipper as you please.

Then, as we're driving along on this spring day and making our way through the quaint downtown of a smallish city you may or may not have visited, she spots someone standing on the corner. I see her see this gentleman. He's average height. Clean-cut. Wearing a half-decent suit. Not the kind you buy on 5th Avenue, but maybe the one you'd find at a really good Dillard's in a really good area if your luck is really good. The guy is staring down at his phone, texting.

"Hey, can you do me a quick favor?" Kellie asks.

"Sure. What's up?"

"Pull over for me? I'm going to step out here for a second. Meet me down there at the corner, okay?"

It's an odd request. But who among us hasn't made the odd request in his or her lifetime? So I pull over and let her out in the middle of the block. The cars behind me in traffic don't honk their horns because this isn't the type of town where people do that type of thing. This is a good place filled with good people who know that they'll get wherever they're going when the time is right. It's a philosophical city.

She steps out and shuts the door.

"Just be ready for me down at the corner," she says.

"Definitely," I say, confused but willing to play along.

I cruise slowly along the street and I watch Kellie as she moves through the crowd. She's like some jungle cat stalking its prey. She slips between people, almost unseen. And all the while, she doesn't take her eyes off of the guy on the far end of the block.

He's still staring down at his cell phone. Lost in his own little world.

Kellie begins to move a little faster. Not quite running, but not a leisurely stroll either. If she were a horse, I would say that she was cantering very nicely. Well, the canter soon becomes a slow jog. Then a full jog. And then, like some flower blossoming, the jog becomes a full-on sprint.

It all happens so fast I can hardly keep up with it. She's sprinting along the block, barreling her way through the crowd, slipping and dodging people as if they were linebackers. And the poor bastard on the corner—who still hasn't taken his eyes off of his phone—still has no clue what's coming.

Just as she reaches this guy Kellie leaps into the most perfectly executed flying punch I've ever seen. It's a thing of beauty. The moment freeze frames. She's got her fist squarely on this guy's jaw. He's bowled over. One shoe is flying. The poor cell phone is airborne.

And all of it hangs there in suspended animation for just a moment as my brain tries to process what it's seeing.

And then, just as suddenly as the moment began, it's over.

Time resumes. The poor schmuck on the corner tumbles to the ground. Kellie, having never broken her stride or rhythm, is dashing toward the car. She looks back over her shoulder and I hear her shout: "I warned you, Vince! I fucking warned you!"

Then she dives into the car shouting, "Go! Go!"

I pull out with my little car's tires squealing.

"So," Kellie says half a block later. "What time are you picking me up tonight?"

And I know what you're thinking. But, in my defense, would you have told her no just then? To this day, I get paranoid when I look down at my phone for too long. Who knows when the flying punch will toll for me?

Soot awoke to blue lights flashing around the walls of his bedroom. They danced in and out of existence like fairies. He heard his mother's voice screaming his father's name. There was horror in her wails—the sound of things falling apart, the sound of dreams breaking. Soot scrambled out of bed and raced to his mother. She heard his footfalls on the old hardwood floor and, without taking her eyes off of whatever it was she was watching outside, shouted, "Go back to bed! Please!"

She wiped her face and stepped out of the front door onto the first step of the stairs. She moved slowly, like walking along the edge of the world. She carried her hands before her, both of them aimed at the sky.

"Please don't do this," she spoke to the blue lights shimmering in the front yard.

Soot wanted to follow her, but he didn't have the courage to disobey her. So he climbed up on the old couch and squinted out of the window with his heart beating in his ears.

Outside, caught in the blue and white lights, Soot saw two shadows. One tall and lean, one square and hard. One stood with his hands in the air, the other with one hand on his hip. He knew from the lankiness of the shadows which one was his father.

"Mama?" Soot called, but his mother did not hear him. She was out on the stairs with her hands in the air, calling her husband's name.

"William?" she called.

Then the world exploded.

His father's shadow fell to the ground.

Soot ran out onto the porch and grabbed his mother by the waist. She was screaming, screaming with her fists clenched and her body a taut cable of pain.

In the glare of the headlights, with the blue flashes blinding him, Soot saw his father turn to him. He saw the man's eyes—full of pleading and fear—and the only thing Soot wanted was to disappear. And, somehow, he felt himself growing light. He felt as though he were moving, but the world only stood still.

Unseen, he felt warm and calm, safe and unafraid.

It's the end of the evening in San Francisco. Seems like folks had a good time. I've been a good distraction for everyone. A good way to make them ignore the river of youth still flowing past outside the bookstore. But every tide must recede eventually. And soon, the Black bodies and voices—even my own—are gone and all that is left are my readers. All of them basking in the performance I have just given.

I managed to talk about *Hell of a Book* for over an hour and not remember any of it. It's like I wasn't even here. And I'm thankful for it. But out in the crowd, people are sobbing. Women wipe the corners of their eyes and grown men turn away, maybe even wiping a few tears of their own.

Whatever *Hell of a Book* is about, it must be something powerful.

I wish I knew what it was.

"Hell of a show," the woman with the platinum blonde hair says when it's finally her turn to step forward and get her book signed.

Her voice is full of confidence and energy, like Richard Simmons has come and taken over her life and made her a better person and now she's ready to share that with the rest of the world. But all I can think about is the fact that she's the last thing I have to do in San Francisco. Once I'm past her, the night is mine.

"Thanks," I say. "It was a barrel of kicks for me too. Hope you had a few laughs."

"I guess so," she says, her face tightening into a query.

"Something the matter?" I ask.

"How long can you keep it up?"

"What do you mean?" I say, narrowly resisting the urge to respond with "That's what she said."

"All of this," the woman says, making a gesture with her hand to indicate my novel, the bookstore, the people, my whole entire existence from the day I was born until this very second. "How long can you keep it up?"

I flinch like I've been bitten by something.

"I'm sorry," I say, remembering that it's easier to talk to someone when you speak in someone else's voice. I bring out the Bogart that's served me so well in strange cities with strange women before. "But have we met someplace before? Some hotel somewhere in the late hours of the night when the scent of jasmine comes wafting in and—"

"No," she interrupts, holding up her hand. "We haven't met before. But just because we've never met doesn't mean we don't know one another." She smiles the most perfect and disarming smile I've ever seen in my entire life.

"My name's Kelly," she says.

Of course it is.

"Of course it is," I say. Then I bring the defense system online. "You know, that's a nice set of pillars you're standing on."

"Wow," she says. "That's your opener?"

"You'd be surprised how often—"

"Stop. Just stop." She looks me in the eyes and there's something in the softness of her eyes that threatens me with something wonderful if I'm willing to let down the defenses. But, dear God, how long has it been since that's happened?

"Just try introducing yourself and asking me out to dinner," she says.

"Excuse me?"

"We both know you want to," she says.

What the hell?

"Hi," I say, reluctant as frost on a spring morning. "My name's ———. Do you want to get some dinner?"

"Much better," she says. "Let's go."

She's immediately interesting. And that's never good. I've got to be careful with interesting women.

SO THERE WE ARE, MYSELF AND THIS LATEST KELLY, SITTING IN A San Francisco restaurant. All the while I'm sitting there, all I can think about is her hair, her smile, her confidence, and the fact that I shouldn't be here. I should be back at my hotel, and achieving the Kama Sutra's most difficult maneuver with some woman I barely know and will never see again in this or any other lifetime. But, for better or worse, here I am.

Just then, my phone rings. It's Sharon, so, as rude as it is, I have to take the call. So I give a penitent nod and step away from the table.

"Hello?" I answer.

"This is a mistake," Sharon says.

"What do you mean?"

"This woman."

"What woman?"

"This platinum blonde woman with the smile and confidence."

"How do you know about her?"

I look around, certain that I'm about to find Sharon sitting at a nearby table, watching. Sharon knows everything.

"I know everything," Sharon says. "And this woman is no good for you. You should be promoting *Hell of a Book*, not going out on dates. It's one of your commandments."

"What about the other women I've met?"

"Those weren't dates. That was sex." Sharon sighs. "Look, you've got a second book to be working on right now."

"But I'm still promoting the first book," I say, feeling my stomach drop to the soles of my feet. I knew it was just a matter of time before she brought up the second book again. *Hell of a Book* was part of a two-book deal. Sharon said it showed "confidence and excitement" from the publisher. But what all that confidence and excitement really boiled down to was three months of me telling them what kind of book I wanted to write and three months of my editor telling me why the books I wanted to write were "not quite the type of book we publish." Whenever I told them I thought the whole point of publishing was simply "to publish good books," both Sharon and my editor laughed.

The child had told a joke.

"Even though you're just two weeks into your tour, *Hell of a Book* has come and gone," Sharon says. "That's the nature of the business. Nobody cares about what you wrote last, only what you're writing next. You're only as good as your next project. That's why publishers give out advances: to lock in that next project. And, speaking of which, you haven't—"

"No! I haven't spent the advance money," I shout.

There's a long pause. I think Sharon's using her agent and publicist powers to peer into my soul. Finally, she speaks: "You have, haven't you?"

She knows. Dear God, she knows.

"I haven't spent the money," I say. I speak the words slowly, brick by brick, trying to build a levee behind which I can hide. "Sharon, look, it's all sitting in my account, untouched, just like you told me."

"First you're on a date with this woman and now this," Sharon says, her disappointment as thick as motor oil. "You're digging a career grave. You know that, don't you?"

"Listen, I need to go. I'm in the middle of dinner." My date with Kelly is my only way out. Better to admit to being on a date than to admit to having spent all of the advance money.

Ask me what I spent the money on and I couldn't say. All I know is that it was there one moment and gone the next. All of it. Tens of thousands of dollars. Nothing but a memory. I'm not even sure how I'm going to pay my rent once this tour is over. "I'm going to hang up now, Sharon. My dinner is getting cold."

"You haven't even ordered yet," she says.

"Stop doing that!"

"Fine," she says. "But when this all comes crashing down around your ears, don't say I didn't warn you." Just before she hangs up, she says, "She likes your sport coat, by the way. I told you people like authors who wear sport coats."

"You did," I say.

"One last thing," Sharon says. "I'm trying to set up a big interview for you in Denver. Papers, TV, libraries, sizzle reel, the whole deal."

"Denver? Why Denver? Why not New York or LA?"

"Because I know where all the bodies are buried. That work for you?"

"What does that even mean?" I say.

"In means don't ask questions, and trust in your agent like you trust in God."

"I'm an atheist."

"Only rich people are atheists. And who made you rich enough to be an atheist?" Sharon asks, reaching the big bang of one hell of a verbal artillery shelling.

"You did," I say.

"Exactly," she says. Then she's gone.

I make my way back to the table, a little confused, maybe even a little woozy. I'd love a drink. I'd love to get drunk. To slide away into that numb, familiar area where I'm not worried about Sharon, or *Hell of a Book*, or the next book that I haven't even started writing, or what my publisher is going to do when I haven't turned in a manuscript and don't have their money. Or the fact that I think I just saw my dead mother sitting at the bar, looking at me as if there's something I'm supposed to do for her. The Kid is here too, watching me the way he does. Waiting for me to do something or say something that he has yet to tell me. He reminds me of Poe's Raven. Lingering at my imagination. Waiting to shout "Nevermore!" when I demand peace of mind and a glimpse of the way things used to be.

"Nevermore," The Kid whispers.

"Fuck you, Kid," I say.

"What's that?" Kelly asks.

"Nothing."

"That really is a great sport coat," Kelly says when I get back to the table.

"Thanks," I say.

"Is everything okay? That call sounded pretty serious."

"Not at all, I say. Let's just forget about it and focus on the two of us. I don't usually do this sort of thing, you know."

"The hell you don't," she replies. "You've got 'man-whore' written all over you."

"Are you sure we haven't met before?"

"I'm sure."

"Okay," I say. "I suppose now you'll want to talk about my book."

"Not really," Kelly says just as the waiter comes walking up to our table. And, in spite of myself, I believe her. She doesn't want to hear about my book.

When you're an author on tour, all anyone wants to talk about is your book. They want to hear the pitch. They want the plot points. They want to hear where you got the idea from so that they can go to wherever that place is and pick up one of their own. They want to hear what stores your book is in because that's how most people judge the success of someone who says they're an author. The more stores you're in, the more likely they are to believe in you.

Sometimes, you tell people you're an author and they'll pull out their phone and Google you, right there in front of your face. They'll type in your name and, depending on the search results, decide for themselves whether or not you're truly what you say you are. The modern author is only as important as their search results.

And after they've found out that your book is actually in actual stores, they'll want to know how you got your agent, how you got your editor, what software you use to write, how long it took you to write it, how much money you got paid, how many copies you sold, whether or not they're going to make your book into a movie. "Hollywood always knows how to find the worthwhile books," a reader once told me.

There's almost no end to the things people want to know when they meet an author, an actual author. But they rarely want to know anything about you. Your book becomes your identity, your identity becomes your book. Maybe Jack the Media Trainer was wrong when he said, "Every time someone asks you about your book, what they're really asking is 'Who are you?'"

"Red wine, please," Kelly says to the waiter.

"Wait a second," I say, blinking like a hazard light. "So you don't want me to talk about my book?"

"Nope."

"Not at all?"

"Nope."

"But you know I'm an author, right?"

"Yep. I was at the reading."

"Don't you want to ask me how I got an agent? How I got published? All that?"

"Not really," she says. And, once again, I believe her, this latest and most perplexing Kelly.

"Then what *do* you want?"

"Just a date with a man I thought was attractive," she says, and I can't detect any irony or insincerity in her voice. "In fact, I haven't even read your book. And I can't honestly say that I will."

"But it's a hell of a book. Of course you've read it. Everyone's read it. It's a bestseller!"

"I actually didn't know anything about it before tonight," she replies. "Didn't even know it existed. I just swung by the bookstore because there's a very old and hard-to-find book I've been looking for and I thought I'd check. Then, when I got there, it turns out there was an author coming for an event. I've got the night off from work so I figured: Why not?"

"Wine for you as well, sir?" It's the waiter speaking. I've totally forgotten that he existed. Right now, there is only this anomaly of a woman. This Kelly. This first person in months who doesn't want me to pitch my book, who doesn't want to talk about sales or interviews, who isn't going to ask me, "So what's your next book about?" Right now, in this moment, I'm myself again. For the first time since I found my agent, I am not the thing that I do. I am not my book. I simply am.

The waiter is patiently waiting for my order. The instinct is still to order wine. To get the alcohol into the veins and drift away. To give in to the fear. But then I might miss something. The lady, this latest Kelly, she's interesting. And interesting things deserve our full attention in life.

"Just water for me," I say.

"That's good," The Kid says. He knows that since he's invisible, I can't answer him back without looking like I belong on certain psychotropic medications. So I only smile at Kelly and pretend The Kid isn't there. "It's okay," he says. "I'll leave you alone for now. I just wanted to say that it's good that you're not drinking. You drink too much. I don't think it's good for you."

I want to tell The Kid to fuck off. I want to tell him that my coping mechanisms are my own and shan't be interfered with. But when I turn, he's already gone. Little bastard got the last word in. And when invisible kids want to get the last word in, they get it.

Being The Unseen felt like the beginning of "I Got 5 On It." Like the opening before the bass drops. Like the first thump of the bass. Like the first whisper of the first verse. Like the hook that bobs you up and down in your car. Like that.

Like you got the glow. Like you're Bruce Leroy, and Turbo, and Ozone all at the same time. Like you're out there with that broom dancing back and forth while din-daa-daa echoes all around the world and that breathy sound that drives the rhythm is the sound of your own breath and you're in control of it all. Like Freaknik back in '96. Like you just woke up in a sea of blackness and there ain't a white face in sight and you didn't know that feeling existed until that very moment and it's so foreign, and yet so beautiful, that you don't know what to do with it and while a part of you loves it, another part of you wants to know where the White people at just in case these niggas get out of line because that's what you've been taught that niggas do when left to their own devices.

Like a cold winter's morning and the only place you can find warmth is under your favorite blanket and you fall asleep there and wake up there all at the same time and it feels like your entire body and soul are caught up in the perfect warmth of that moment and all you know is that you don't want to ever leave this place because it feels the way life is supposed to feel.

But then the problem is that Soot began to understand just how much of a gift he had been given and he didn't know what to do with it. He wanted his father to have the gift so that his father could feel the same way but his father was dead . . . wasn't he?

The idea of his father's death flashed into Soot's mind and he winced like he'd been hit, but no sooner did he feel the sting of pain than it receded, and he could believe it had never come at all. That his father was not at work, or elsewhere. What mattered still was here—his gift.

It was too much of a dream, The Unseen. It was too smooth. Too perfect. Too Miles Davis. Too Prince. Too *Soul Train.* Too *Martin.* Too *Def Comedy Jam.* It was too much of a perfect and pristine thing to sit back and keep it to himself.

The thing that he loved the most about being unseen was not seeing his own skin anymore. He had escaped his dark flesh. He had escaped Soot and, because of that, when he closed his eyes and thought about himself, he finally got a chance to see the boy who had been living behind his eyes for the very first time.

The boy was small and vibrant-looking. He smiled. He laughed. He seemed happy with himself and the world. He was not a boy who was afraid. He was not a boy who got picked on while riding to school each morning. He was not a boy who watched the news with his father and heard reports of "Black-on-Black" crime and tried to understand what that meant, and tried to understand why there was no such thing as White-on-White crime, or tried to understand what it meant when his teachers told him that one in every three Black men would end up in prison.

The boy, that Soot, was free of all of that. And he looked at Soot and smiled at him and didn't pity him because the boy in The Unseen didn't even know what pity was. He only knew what happiness was, and what compassion was, and what meaningfulness was, and what excitement was, and what swimming without being self-conscious was, and he knew that thump of the bass that came through and he knew that it meant that everything was going to be okay.

But then he came out of it and his father was dead, killed right there on his front lawn under the light of the July moon, with his wife and son watching.

Later that night, Kelly and I walk through a small park somewhere in San Francisco. It's picturesque in that way things only ever are in romantic comedies. You know the type:

Boy meets girl.

Boy loses girl.

Boy gets girl back.

Credits roll.

On the drive home, you realize the girl was something, the boy was a chicken, and nothing was ever at risk for anyone.

Chinese lanterns dangle from a small footbridge as we make our way through the park. The lanterns become small suns burning in the distance and I can believe, just for a moment, that all of us people are wandering the universe together as one. One of the truths we often overlook is that we are, all of us, always wandering the universe. We are perpetually hurtling on a rocky raft through the void, taking the tour of the cosmos at 67,000 miles per hour, every second of every day, and yet we still find time to stop and talk over bridges in the late hours of the night and maybe reach out and touch someone else's hand.

Renny has chosen this spot as the second part of our date. And as the two of us walk through the park together, Renny drives along nearby in the town car, watching like a concerned parent.

"Never had a limo driver as a chaperone on a date before," Kelly says.

"Renny's a good guy," I reply. "Purely on the up-and-up."

"You've got an odd way about you. Why do you talk that way? Like you just stepped out of a mobster movie."

"I guess we've all got to be somebody in this life. So why not be somebody that does it differently? That's my policy. And I get a feeling that you're somebody that does it differently too, Dollface. Just look at that platinum hair of yours. That's not exactly out of the Martha Stewart playbook."

"I guess," she says, and she pulls a hair away from her face and I want to be the hand that touches that hair that touches that face. "But don't ever call me Dollface again."

"Okay." I can't help but smile and I don't know why.

"So when do we get to the part where you ask me what I do for a living?"

"You spend all day breaking rocks, does that make you a hammer?" I reply. "I don't think so. I think the better question to ask someone is this: Do you like what you do?"

"A lot," she says.

"Then that's enough for me."

"And what about you?"

"What about me?"

"You write books. It's what you do. But is it who you are?"

I want to answer, her question sends me into fits. My throat goes all tight and a cold chill runs over me. Too many memories. Too much death and pain in my brain that's suddenly trying to claw its way to the top, all triggered by a simple question about who I am as a writer. I've found that the best way to beat back moments like this is with a fistful of liquid courage. As we pass an outdoor bar I eyeball the liquor lining the counter and all I want to do is have a good drink because when I look over at the tables placed around the restaurant I see *her*: the reason I write, the reason *Hell of a Book* handed me all my dreams and wrapped them in pain at the same time.

She's in her mid-fifties, and she's wearing a hospital gown, and her eyes are slightly sunken, and her skin is a little saggy from sudden weight loss, and she looks clammy, and tired, and sad all at once. She looks over at me and she tries to smile but it's too much for her to manage so she manages only a thin grin and even that is gone almost as quickly as it began. There's an IV stand next to her and it drops clear chemicals down into the IV bag, which funnels them down the plastic tubing and into the back of her hand, and I can almost hear it making that drip, drip, drip sound and it hurts my ears and my throat tightens even more and my mouth goes dry and my lips feel like they've got glue on them and all I want is alcohol.

Nobody else sees the woman in the hospital gown. She's just for me.

"I'm never really sure what I am," I manage to say to Kelly. "It's hard to tell what's real some days."

I'm able to make it over to the bar, where I order a shot of whiskey and I down it almost before the bartender can finish pouring it. When I look back over my shoulder, the woman in the hospital gown is gone.

"Hit me again," I tell the bartender.

He does.

Kelly looks at the newly emptied shot glass.

"You know what they say about writers and alcohol, baby," I tell her.

"That it's cliché?"

"You ain't just whistlin' 'Dixie.' But clichés gotta start somewhere."

Just then, her phone rings. She steps away and answers it. A little rude, but she'd mentioned earlier in the evening that she was on call for whatever her job was and that the call could come at any time. So I don't stress too much. Besides, I'm busy making sure that woman in the hospital gown doesn't show up again. A man's got to have limits when it comes to the world of the imagination. Sometimes you've got to put your foot down and say, "Sorry, you haunting vision of something that doesn't exist anymore. I'm afraid you'll have to come back and play later."

So that's what I did.

I've just ordered a third shot of whiskey by the time Kelly makes it back over.

"Hey," she says, "I'm sorry, but that was work. I've got to go take care of something."

"Ah," I say. "I get ya."

"What?"

"Nothing," I say, feeling my teeth tighten. "Don't sweat it, Dollface. You think I'm all wet and you want out. It's okay. You're not hurting my feelings."

"No," she says. "That really was work. And I told you not to call me Dollface."

"Sure it was," I say, fully able to see through her ruse. "What are you, a pilot or something? No, that's not possible."

"Why can't I be a pilot?"

"Because pilots always let you know early on that they're a pilot. Never met a more arrogant and insecure group of bastards in my whole life." I wave my hands dismissively—at least, I think I do; by now the whiskey is doing a little dance inside my head; I should have eaten more at dinner. "It's okay," I say. "You're not hurting my feelings."

"No," she insists, "that really was work."

"Whatever," I say. "It doesn't matter. It's better this way anyhow. You're interesting."

"What's wrong with interesting?"

"I've got a condition."

She stares at me for a moment as I order yet another drink. As I lift the drink to my lips, she snatches it from me and pours it out. Then she takes my hand and says: "Let's go."

RENNY'S BLACK TOWN CAR. PARKED OUTSIDE A FUNERAL HOME. THE sign out front reads WORMFUD FUNERAL HOME.

I've never understood the need to call them funeral homes. They're neither funerals nor are they homes. And since the funerals themselves do not reside within the location, they cannot accurately be called funeral homes.

Yet we do anyhow.

"I don't want to go in there," The Kid says, suddenly sitting in the back of the car with me. He was polite enough to wait until Kelly stepped out before appearing and deciding to let me know about what he likes and doesn't like about the current situation.

"You don't have to go in," I say.

"Yes, I do," Kelly says.

Of course she thinks I'm talking to her.

"Give me just a second," I say. "I need to make a phone call." I close the door of Renny's car and claim the privacy.

"Listen, Kid," I begin. "I appreciate that you've got a thing about funeral homes—most people do—but the fact of the matter is that I'm going in there. You don't have to go if you don't want to. You can leave whenever you want and crawl your way back into the wacky confines of my imagination."

"I'm not imaginary," The Kid says.

"Of course you are," I say. "That's why nobody else can see you. You're a figment of a fragile mind—*my* mind—and I know it. Therefore, I have some power and authority over what you say and do."

"I'm not imaginary," The Kid repeats. He adds an edge to his voice. A little roar that I imagine is scary to kids his age.

"Then why can't anyone see you?"

"Because I don't want them to. Because my mom taught me how to be invisible. How to be safe."

"No such thing as invisibility or safety in this world, Kid. Just reality." I stare him down like he owes me money. Like more than anything else I just want him to pay what he owes and go away.

The Kid's jaw clenches. He looks in the direction of Wormfud Funeral Home. "Okay," The Kid says. "You don't want me around. That's fine. I'll let you go in there by yourself."

I can't help but laugh. "That's your threat? I've been asking you to leave me alone all night and now you're threatening to give me what I want?" I toss the kid another laugh and step out into the night.

"Everything okay?" Kelly asks.

"Yeah," I reply. "Just a phone call with an unbelievable person."

Then I take her hand and smile as she leads me into the funeral home.

INSIDE THE FUNERAL HOME, MY SKIN IS CRAWLING. EVERYTHING IS painted in neutral colors and there are paintings and placards placed around the room designed to calm me and to remind me that death isn't a bad thing. Meant to convey the message that death is just an event that happens and, while it certainly needs to be taken with a dose of somberness, it doesn't have to be sad.

The greatest lie ever told.

KELLY AND I ARE STANDING IN FRONT OF A LARGE PAIR OF WOODEN double doors. There's a sign above the doors that reads PREPARATION ROOM.

"So you're an undertaker," I say.

"Funeral director."

"That's an undertaker."

"I suppose so."

PREPARATION ROOM.

"But I thought you said you liked what you do for a living."

"I love it."

"But you're an undertaker."

"Funeral director."

PREPARATION ROOM.

"I'm guessing that's not where the Keebler Elves make such delicious cookies," I say.

"Nope," she replies.

"That's swell, Dollface."

PREPARATION ROOM.

"That's just swe—"

I fold in half and dry heave myself into oblivion.

WE'RE INSIDE THE PREPARATION ROOM AND KELLY IS DRESSED FOR preparation. She's wearing a blue smock and a surgical mask over her face. On the table in front of her is a dead body. It's the body of a middle-aged man. I can't tell what killed him. No gunshot wounds, or stab wounds, or strangulation wounds, or anything along those lines. It just looks like someone pulled his batteries out.

As for me, I'm standing on the far side of the room with my back against the wall and my arms pressed flat against it and I feel like I'm on the top ledge of the Empire State Building. At any moment I could go falling and maybe I'll never stop.

It's irrational, I know. But I've never been one to claim to be rational.

"I was right about you," I say as she picks up a large scalpel. "You really do it differently, don't you?" She takes the knife and begins carving on the dead body. "You're just going to jump right in there, huh?"

"Assholes and elbows. That's what my dad used to say."

"That expression feels a little strange right now."

She has the nerve to smile. As if she were just working behind the counter at Starbucks and I'd come in to order a cup of joe.

As she works, there's this wet, squishing sound. She's changed tools from the scalpel to things I can't identify and fluids are draining through the table drain and I don't want to think about what those fluids are and I don't want to hear the sound of them running down the drain. All I want right now is to be anywhere else on this planet but here.

It's when she picks up the cadaver's hand and snaps one of the bones in the fingers that was curled into a fist that all thought of her as a viable love interest goes flying out the window.

"I never felt the need to know how sausage was made," I say. "And now I realize I never wanted to know how funerals are made either."

More bone snapping.

I turn my head.

"So how's a pretty girl like you wind up in a place like this?"

"Well," she says between snaps and cuts and draining sounds, "when I was a kid, my aunt gave me a book about ancient Egypt. Mostly, the book was about the ancient Egyptians and their connection with their dead. Embalming, reverence for the deceased, the afterlife, all of that. And, well, for whatever reason, I became fascinated with it. Then I stayed fascinated with it."

"So what you're saying is that ever since you were a little girl you've always wanted to be an undertaker?"

"Yep."

"That may be the scariest thing I've ever heard."

She laughs. And her laugh is light and vibrant. It's a bluebird singing the aria of an entire universe trapped inside its small, delicate chest.

"I've never seen anyone react quite like you to the embalming process before," Kelly says.

"I have no idea what you're talking about," I say as I run my hand over the wall behind me, lovingly. Because, at this particular moment, this wall is the only thing in the world holding me up. How can I not love it the way I do?

Another bone snaps.

I close my eyes. I try to will myself away. There are images coming up inside my mind that I don't particularly care to be a part of and they won't go away—a woman in a hospital dying, my father's chair sitting empty in front of a television that goes unwatched but still plays his favorite movie.

My legs tremble. They want to run but they're too weak. They want to collapse but they're frozen stiff. Everything inside of me is pushing and pulling at every other part of me. It's all on the verge of exploding and imploding.

I want to call out for The Kid. I don't know why, but if he were here now, I think I could get through all of this. It's now that I understand his threat. Imaginary or not, there's something about The Kid. There's something about the fact that I'm the only one who can see him. There's something about the things that he makes me think about. He's a part of me and if he's not here I can't really connect with myself.

"Recite a poem for me," Kelly says.

"What?"

It's enough of an odd request that it gets me to open my eyes.

"Tonight, during the reading, you said that you used to be into poetry," Kelly continues. "Recite something for me. People still do that type of thing, don't they? Maybe it'll help distract you."

She doesn't stop working as she makes the suggestion. Nope. She's still in that cadaver literally up to her elbow. But she is also waiting for me. Patiently. Maybe even caringly. This woman, whom I only just met, whose last name I still don't know, seems to care about me. When I'm not even sure I care about myself.

How very amazing.

I search for a poem and find none.

"I seem to be drawing a blank," I say just as Kelly snaps another finger. I expect her to let me off the hook, but she doesn't. She only flashes me a smile and then continues working, continues waiting, continues believing in me and my ability to think up something that will distract me from the terror I feel inside. She believes I can save myself if I try hard enough. She believes I can be me, here, now.

I'm not sure anyone else has ever really believed that about me before.

And then I hear the sound of a heart monitor beeping. It's very soft, very far away. But I hear it. That digital pulse singing like some fairy-tale bird that has fallen in love with a metronome.

. . . beep . . . beep . . . beep . . .

The sound gets under my skin. All I can do to calm it is pace back and forth. But even that's not helping. The sound wells up inside of me.

. . . beep . . . beep . . . beep . . .

I look over at the cadaver again. It's not the middle-aged man. It's someone else. A woman. A beautiful, delicate woman that I don't want to recognize. Her from the outdoor restaurant earlier. My mother, perhaps.

All of a sudden, the poem is there:

"That we were frightened by your death—no . . . it is that your harsh death darkly interrupted us, divided what-had-been from what-would-be: that was our concern; coming to terms with it will accompany everything we do: Today; tomorrow. Again and again. You have gone on. . . . But you were frightened too."

I didn't write that poem. But, then again, none of us ever do.

I look over at Kelly. She's staring at me. I can't tell what her expression is. And since I can't tell what her expression is, I can't bear to look at her, so I look away. And that's when I see it.

On one of the gurneys behind her, dangling out from beneath a large, white sheet, is a small, black hand. It's the darkness of the hand that catches my attention. It's impossibly black. As if it has captured the pigment of an entire nation.

"Who's that?" I ask.

Kelly's eyes follow mine. "Nobody," she says. She walks over and adjusts the sheet to cover the hand.

But I know what I saw. I walk up to the gurney and reach for the sheet.

"Stop," Kelly says.

"Why?"

"The rules," she says. Then: "Plus . . . you don't want to see that."

I make sure to move before she can stop me. I pull the sheet off.

There, lying on the gurney, is The Kid.

He looks smaller. Blacker, if that's possible. But his skin is tinged with some other hue. But I can look at the skin only for a moment before the horror of it all catches me.

Bullet holes. Eight of them, blooming through The Kid like some macabre flowers. Chest, legs, arms, head. He is covered by this terrible wreath.

"Kid?" I whisper.

Kelly covers the body of The Kid. "I'm sorry you saw that," she says.

"What happened to him?"

"You haven't heard?" Kelly asks. "It's all over the news. The shooting. This is the kid from the shooting."

And now I remember the talk of the shooting. The talk of some kid somewhere who caught the wrong end of a bullet. The talk of the police. The talk of excessive force. The talk of Black lives mattering, and Blue Lives mattering, and All Lives mattering. Now I remember the pundits and politicians. The talk show hosts and celebrities. The presence of this always. Now I remember all the screaming, and crying, and rallying, and arguing, and the memes and the thoughts and prayers, and the talks of regulation and investigation, and the bumper stickers, and gun rights laws. Now I remember it all.

I can remember all of that, but I can't remember actually seeing The Kid in any of the noise. I can't even remember his name. Isn't that strange? I'm sure someone must have said his name at some point in all of those reports. I'm sure he must have been a hashtag. A t-shirt. A rallying cry. I'm sure the Black bodies from before must have called out his name but I can't say exactly which belongs to The Kid.

In his death, he's just The Kid.

"Are you okay?" Kelly asks.

All I can do is leave. So I do. I run out of the room without looking back.

I race out of the funeral home and into Renny's car.

"Hotel," I say.

"What about your lady friend?" Renny asks.

"Take me to the hotel. Please, Renny."

"Okay," he says reluctantly.

The car clunks into gear. We're off into the city, away from interesting women and remembrances of the dead.

THE NEXT THING I KNOW, I'M SITTING ON THE FLOOR OF MY HOTEL room wearing a complimentary leopard-print bathrobe and taking swigs from a large bottle of whiskey. I can't even remember when I bought it. That heart monitor sound is still there, at the edges of my reality.

. . . beep . . . beep . . . beep . . .

Casablanca is playing on the television. There's Bogart, looking forlorn and gutted. And there's Bergman, looking beautiful and unattainable. But the longer I stare at the screen—and the more whiskey I take in—the less it looks like Bogart and Bergman. The more I realize it's actually my Kelly and me.

We're at the runway scene at the end of the movie. The plane is waiting. The Germans are on the way. A dialogue balloon appears next to my head: "Had to go."

"Sorry." Kelly replies in a dialogue balloon of her own.

"Not your fault."

"Now what?"

"I go home tomorrow."

"Need a ride to the airport?"

I look from the television to my phone and realize the whole conversation is just a string of text messages.

"I'm getting too old for this shit," Renny says, suddenly appearing out of nowhere. He's standing by me, holding up my wet and slightly vomit-stained shirt. "Not sure that'll ever come out," he said. "You're going to be wearing San Francisco for the rest of your life."

Then Renny looks down at me and, just from his expression, I know I'm a sad sight. He sighs. "Damn writers," Renny says. Then: "Okay. Let's go."

Renny squats down and places an arm beneath my shoulders and helps me up to my feet. He's as gentle as a hospital orderly. God only knows how many other sad-sack writers he's had to help up over the years.

"What's going on?" I ask, my words slurring.

"Just come with me, State College."

"Okay," I say. "But just so you know: I never put out on the first date."

"Bullshit," Renny says.

After the death of his father, the small house in which Soot and his mother lived grew larger than it had ever been. And it was the empty expanses that had never been there before that filled Soot's mother with the greatest sadness. Every inch of the house was a place where her husband had once existed. Every chair longed for his shadow. Every room yearned to be filled with his laughter. The eaves of the house howled in the late hours of the night when the wind blew in from the south, moaning and asking where he had gone. And through it all, Soot's mother made sure that her arms were constantly filled with her son. She hugged him with a compulsive frequency and a singular desperation. It was as though she had never held him before and she might never hold him again. At night, she slept in his bedroom on account of the emptiness that had now come to take up residence in her own bedroom.

Soot watched her and wished that he could do something to take away her sadness. There were so many tears to be shed now. The sound of her sobbing woke him in the middle of the night as she lay in the bed next to him, asleep, not knowing that she was crying. He lay there, sometimes, and watched her mourn in her sleep.

Soot wanted to absolve his mother's sadness. But, more than that, he wanted to hide from his own. He felt it at the edges of his world, the persistent sorrow, stalking him like some raw-boned animal. But it was not sorrow over the death of his father, as he expected. In fact, he didn't think about his dead father very much.

It wasn't that he had not loved his father. Soot knew that he loved his father and, sometimes, he missed him. But, hour by hour it seemed, Soot's memory gave up just a little bit of what it held of his father. It was as if the death of his father was too much for his mind to hold on to, and so it gave it up, little by little, in the hopes of saving itself.

And the memory of his father, and his father's death, was never farther away than when Soot was lost in The Unseen. He could do it on command now: disappear and become The Unseen Kid. And each time he did it, the pain of his loss drifted away a bit more. He came back, each time, remembering a little less of his father. He came back hurting not quite so badly. Being Unseen was saving his life by taking parts of it away.

There were other distractions as well. People. So many people.

Every day since his father's death, Soot's house was filled with people. Women from the church brought food and condolences. They held prayer circles in which black hands gripped one another and called out for Jesus to become the deliverer that He had promised He would be. There was singing of sad songs and there were promises of justice—both earthly and divine—and, more than anything, there was the promise that God had a plan for everyone and everything and that the last thing Soot's mother should be was sad.

"He's gone on to God," they made it a point to say.

To which Soot's mother offered a nod and a weak, placating smile.

And while there were those who came and talked of Jesus and peace, there were those who came and talked with angry tongues of earthly justice by any means. Lead among these was Uncle Paul. Paul was Soot's uncle on his mother's side. A large man, with large hands and dark skin and a beard like coiled wire, he was the type of man under which the floor seemed to move each time he stepped.

"This is exactly the kind of shit I've always been talking about," Paul said as he entered the small country home. People gave him a wide, respectful berth because there was no other choice for a man of his proportions and temperament.

"Hey, Paul," Soot's mother said.

Paul wrapped her in a hug. "I'm so sorry," he said. "I just can't believe this shit. Right there in the front yard. His fucking blood is right there in the goddamn mud of the front yard!"

When the hug was over he marched over to Soot, the entire frame of the house shaking underfoot. "And what about you, little man?" he said, aiming his focus at Soot.

He reached down with his large, black hands and lifted the boy up into his arms. He hugged him gently—in spite of his large, strong stature—and Soot could feel his uncle's wiry beard rubbing against the side of his cheek.

"I'm so sorry," Paul said. "But don't you worry none, we're going to fix this. It ain't going to just get by. He ain't going to get away with it. I swear to God."

"Don't say that," one of the older women interrupted. "Don't be swearing to God like that."

"I'll swear to whoever the fuck I want to," Paul bellowed. "And if He don't like it, tell Him to come down here and do something about it. And maybe while He's here spanking me on my ass for taking His name in vain, the rest of you can ask Him where He was when Will got shot in his front yard by that damn cop."

The room was cowed in silence.

"You hungry," Soot's mother asked.

Paul offered a belly laugh. "Look at me. A nigga my size always hungry."

Paul, Soot, and his mother all went into the kitchen and Paul helped himself to the food dishes that the women had brought along with their condolences. "One good thing those old biddies in there are good for is their food."

"They're just trying to help," Soot's mother said.

Paul bit into a chicken leg and grunted an affirmation.

"This ain't gonna stand," Paul managed between bites. "I just want you to know that. That cop what did the shooting, he lives up near Lumberton."

"How do you know that?" Soot's mother asked.

Paul laughed. "C'mon, now. Ain't nobody around here that can hide from nobody. County ain't but so big. They're supposed to be sending out some investigators to look into all this. But you already know how it's going to go," Paul spat. "Ain't nothing going to happen to him."

"You don't know that," she said. She sounded tired all of a sudden. As if a great weight had just been placed on her back. It was the weight of knowing that no one will seek justice for people who look like you.

"I know it as well as you know it," Paul rebutted. Then he looked at Soot. "This is one of those things you need to learn," Paul began. "Ain't nothing going to happen to the man that killed your daddy because that's how the world works for people like us."

"Paul!"

"What?" Paul asked. He was halfway through loading food onto his plate. Now and again he looked back over his shoulder at Soot and his mother. "Don't tell me you ain't talked with him about it yet."

"Just . . ." Soot's mother looked at her son. She opened her arms and he went over and let her take him into her arms.

"If you ever thought you could keep him from it, that decision's already been taken from you," Paul said. "Got taken away right here on your front lawn."

"No," she said. She leaned down and whispered into her son's ear: "Go. I don't want you here for this."

"But Mama," Soot began.

"Please," his mother said. "I need to know that you're safe. I need to know that you're happy. I need to know that you're invisible and hidden and in such a good place that none of this can reach you. I want you to go and come back and tell me what it feels like. Tell me what it feels like so that I can feel something other than the thing I'm feeling right now, the thing I'm going to feel for the rest of my life."

Her eyes were slick with tears. Her voice was a plea offered up not only to Soot but to the universe itself. How could he defy her?

He nodded and, when his uncle wasn't looking, slipped away into invisibility, into The Unseen, where he would feel safe and happy and forget just a little bit more of his father and his father's death.

The last thing he saw as The Unseen enveloped him was his mother's smile, tinged with sadness, but almost thankful.

I'm in the back of Renny's car, half-asleep and staring blankly out of the window, and everywhere that I look I see The Kid. He rides in the passenger seat of a nearby Honda, dead and filled with bullet holes, staring at me. I look away and I find him standing on a corner, he's holding up a sign that asks for money, and he is dead and full of bullet holes. When we stop at the corner, he comes up to the car and knocks on the window, asking me to roll it down. He is dead and full of holes. What else could I do but look away and pretend not to see him? That, I am starting to see, is what I do.

We roll on into the shimmering night.

Renny's car pulls up in front of the most beautiful home I've ever seen. It's a house so large and sprawling, it looks like it ate another house. I'm still pretty miserable just now, so, as he parks, I'm just laying with my head pressed against the window and my extremities feeling far away and it's easy for me to think that this is all just a figment of my imagination. There's nothing I wouldn't put past myself right now.

But it turns out, I'm not dreaming.

The Roman columns, the vaulted foyer, the massive windows, the sprawling front lawn in a city that has almost zero front lawns, it's all real. And it all belongs to Renny.

I finally lift my head from the window—my mouth hanging slightly ajar in surprise—and look over at Renny. He smiles one of the largest smiles I've ever seen and says proudly, "I told you, State College. I went to Harvard. Now you've got the meet my Martha. In spite of what you might have heard about her, I love her."

"I haven't heard anything."

"You've heard of evil, haven't you?"

He snorts a laugh and so do I.

The interior of Renny's home is just as stunning as the exterior. Vaulted ceilings. Marble tiles. A large kitchen counter that looks as though it was sculpted—not cut, but sculpted—from a single slab of marble. I feel like I've died and gone to capitalist heaven. And maybe I have. The way my head is throbbing just now I wouldn't put anything past me. But the scent of jasmine wafting through the air makes me believe that maybe I haven't died just yet.

A short, vibrant, sixty-something woman who smells of jasmine emerges from the kitchen and greets Renny and me at the door and she doesn't seem to mind the fact that I'm still wearing only my robe and slippers from the hotel. "Honey," she says sweetly, kissing Renny on the cheek.

"This is—"

"The book man?!" she asks, not even waiting to hear my name.

"Yes, honey. The book man."

Martha claps her hands together in excitement. "That's

wonderful," she says, offering a handshake. "It's so wonderful to have someone as respectable as an author in my house."

I thank her by accidentally vomiting all over her marble floor.

WE'RE IN RENNY'S IMMACULATE KITCHEN A LITTLE LATER. HIS WIFE, Martha, is making us a late supper. I think she's forgiven me for earlier, which is damned nice of her and I tell her so. "This is damned nice of you, Martha," I say, holding my head between my hands because there's a really obese man inside my skull right now and he's doing a little dance around the inside of my brain.

"No problem at all," Martha says. "I can't sleep most nights anyhow. So at least this way, while I'm awake, I get to actually do something."

"Why can't you sleep?" I ask Martha.

"Dreams," she says.

"Bad dreams?"

"No," she replies, "just dreams. Never really cared for them."

It's a profound statement and I tell her so. "That's a profound statement, Martha. Damned profound."

"Your mother will still be dead tomorrow," Martha says.

"Pardon me?"

"Pardon you what?" Martha says, looking more than a little surprised.

"What did you just say?" I ask.

"Nothing," she says, and her face tightens into a large question mark and I'm left to face the fact that, very likely, I only imagined her saying that line about my mom. I've been known to imagine things. I've got a condition: I'm a writer.

"So," I begin, trying to recover, "how long have you two been hitched?"

"Too damned long," Renny says immediately. "Martha fought in the Peloponnesian Wars. Isn't that right, honey?"

"Your mother," Martha says.

I reach across the kitchen counter and grab a bottle of scotch that Renny and Martha must have paid a fortune for. I open it without asking and pour myself a glass before either of them can say a word. The two of them watch. Maybe there's pity in their eyes.

"You got any family, State College?" Renny asks.

"Nope," I say.

"Friends?"

"One."

"Good friend?"

"Good as any other."

"Then you got family," Renny says. He walks over and pours out my glass of scotch and takes the bottle out of my hand and replaces it with a bottle of water. "What I'm trying to say here, State College, is that I look at you and I see a man adrift."

"Untethered," Martha corrects.

"That's what I said," Renny replies.

"You went to Harvard and the best you can come up with is 'adrift'?"

Renny points an accusatory finger at me. "This man went to a state college!"

LATER, WE'RE STANDING OUTSIDE OF RENNY'S HOUSE. IT FEELS LIKE we can see all of San Francisco from here. Even with the mass quantity of alcohol in my veins, I can appreciate how beautiful this city is. It's a marvel. And the longer I stare, the more beautiful it becomes. The lights glow. The colors grow more saturated. I feel like I'm on a vision quest. I feel like I've had too many of those special brownies the woman in Colorado put in my welcome bag. I feel like Betty White is on her way over once again.

The lights of the city become fireflies, dancing over the surface of an ocean. I can't tell where the city ends and the sky begins. I think that, if I really tried, I could get lost in either of them. I could disappear in both of them. I like the idea of disappearing.

I think I hear the sound of that heart monitor again.

But then I close my eyes tight and take a deep breath and when I finally let it go, the sound is gone and San Francisco is just a city again.

As if he's reading my mind, Renny says, about driving, "Keeps me busy," shrugging his shoulders. "You slow down in life and, well, that's when it all comes to a stop. I've always liked driving. So now that I'm retired, I get to drive as much as I want. I get to meet people I probably wouldn't otherwise meet—people like you. Plus, it gets me out of the house and away from that madwoman."

Immediately Martha sticks her head out of the back door and shouts, "Oh yeah? Well, did you tell him you were impotent at forty?!"

"That's not what your sister said," Renny barks back immediately.

Martha only waves her hand dismissively and drifts back into the kitchen.

"I really do love that woman," Renny says warmly. Then: "We'll put you up in one of the spare rooms."

"Thanks, Renny. You're a swell fella."

"Can I tell you something, State College?"

"Can I stop you?"

"No."

"Then yes."

"I don't know much about you," Renny says, "but one thing I do know is that if you keep this up, you're going to hit a wall pretty hard. At some point, you're going to have to face whatever's chasing you . . . whether you want to or not."

"You're probably right, Renny," I say.

"Of course I'm right," Renny says. "I went to Harvard."

A LITTLE WHILE LATER, RENNY AND MARTHA HAVE BOTH GONE TO bed and they've pointed me in the direction of my room. I almost get lost in the halls of their mansion, but it always feels good to wander the corridors of someone else's home. It's a good way to remember that lives are lived every day in a way that's different from your own. It makes you feel like you're a part of something.

In one of the hallways, I spot a group of wedding photos. Renny and Martha have kids. From the looks of it, Renny and Martha have a lot of kids. In the photo, one of their daughters is getting married. In another photo, Renny and a different daughter are dancing together. Renny's smile is all pride. Martha, in the background, is all tears of joy.

I stand and look from photo to photo, and a life is built. It's a life of love and caring. It's a life of family. The longer I stare, the more the photos become real. Renny and his daughter begin to move over the dance floor. I hear the music playing—a slow waltz. Since Renny's a Harvard man, his waltz is perfect. He and his daughter flow like mercury over the surface of the dance floor.

I can smell the chicken that was served with dinner. I can taste the wedding cake in the back of my throat.

As I keep looking at the photographs, I can see myself in them. I'm standing in the back corner, smiling. I'm happy. I applaud Renny and Martha and their daughter. I walk over and hug them. I'm a part of the family. Behind them, in the back of the photograph, blended in with the crowd, I see a couple dancing. The man is tall and thin as a flower's shadow. The woman: short, rotund, with long hair pulled into a ponytail. My mama and dad. They stare into each other's eyes, smiling and twirling around in a small circle, swaying in time with the music. My dad belts out a laugh, my mother manages a smile. He is not dead. She is not sad. I can walk over and hug them both if I want.

But, in defiance of myself, I do not.

Then the dancing stops. The photographs become just photographs again and I'm a thirty-eight-year-old writer standing in the hallway of a stranger's home trying to build myself into his life. I'm just drunk and lonely all of a sudden.

So be it.

I make my way to my bedroom and flop down on the bed. I'm still wearing the robe and slippers from the hotel. I close my eyes and begin to drift off to sleep.

"Hi," a voice calls out. It's The Kid.

I sit up. "Hi," I say.

The Kid is sitting in the corner of the room with his knees pulled to his chest and his arms wrapped around his legs. "Are you okay?"

"I was going to ask you the same thing."

"I don't want to talk about me."

The Kid's fingers fidget with the material of his blue jeans. There are a few specks of mud around the hem of his pants, like he's spent the afternoon playing in the front yard the way I used to do once upon a time. The Kid reminds me so much of myself that it makes it hard for me to remember that he isn't me. He's a dead kid.

"I'm sorry," I say.

"For what?"

"For what happened?"

"You mean in the car?" The Kid asks. He looks genuinely surprised. "It's okay," he says. "You were just afraid. I should have gone in there with you, though. You shouldn't leave people alone when they're afraid, even if they're being jerks." He grins for the first time tonight.

"No," I say. "I mean I'm sorry about what happened to you."

"What happened to me?"

His dark brow furrows and he stops fidgeting. He stares at me with wide, brown eyes and waits for me to tell him that he's been shot and killed and that he's not real. He waits for me to tell him that whatever gift he thinks he has didn't save him from the barrage of bullets and there's no way to take that back. He waits for me to tell him that he's not real. That he's a ghost. No, that he's a figment of my imagination.

So I give him what he wants. Even with figments of your imagination, it's best to be as honest and forthcoming as possible.

"You're dead," I say.

After a beat, The Kid laughs. "No, I'm not."

"Yes, you are," I say. "Dead as a doorknob, as my dear, departed daddy used to say. And, more than that, I'm a little offended that you wouldn't tell me that you were dead this whole time. Here I was thinking you were just a part of my condition and it turns out you're something much more than that. Turns out you're a real boy who got shot and killed a few days ago. I saw you. I saw your body."

Again The Kid laughs.

"No," he says. "That's all wrong. Are you high?"

"Drunk," I say. "Not high."

"Well," The Kid says, "either way, you're wrong. I'm not dead. That would be stupid. I'm real. I'm as real as you are. I don't know what you saw tonight or who that was, but it wasn't me."

As much as I don't want to believe anything The Kid is saying, I can't deny the fact that I'm starting to believe him. After all, that's the catch-22 of imaginative conditions like mine: you can't trust things or people in regard to their reality. If a thing spends all of its time telling you that it's real, eventually you've got to believe it simply because of the fact that most of the people you meet in the world are real and it would be terrible to treat real people as imaginary.

"But if that wasn't you, then who was that kid I saw at the funeral home?"

"Don't know," The Kid says. "But it wasn't me." He lifts up his shirt to reveal his impossibly black chest that is free from bullet holes or any other sign of trauma. "See?" he says. "I'm fine. Nothing bad has happened to me and nothing bad ever will. I'm safe and I'll always be safe because my mom and dad gave me this gift."

"Yes," I reply, my head thumping like an 808. Maybe from the liquor. Or maybe from trying to understand what my life and mental state have become. I take a seat on the floor beside The Kid. I pull my knees to my chest and cross my arms around my legs as though I could become small enough to be safe from the reality that exists beyond this moment. "I'm tired," I say.

"Me too," The Kid says. "I miss my mom."

"Where is she?"

"I don't know," The Kid says.

"Do you want us to find her?"

"No," The Kid says. He pulls his legs tighter to his chest.

I want to ask him why not, but something in me tells me that it's the wrong question to ask. So he and I just sit together and hold whatever this is that we're both caught up in. I don't have it in me to bring up again the fact that I saw his corpse tonight. And I don't have it in me to bring up the fact that I saw my dead mother tonight. I don't have it in me to bring up a lot of things, so the two of us just sit in the room surrounded by the unsaid things.

"What about that girl?" The Kid asks. "She seemed nice."

"Don't think it's in the cards, kiddo."

"You should try it," The Kid says. "You're lonely. I can tell."

"How can you tell?"

"Most people like us are lonely," The Kid says. "Anyone who imagines things is lonely. I've always been lonely. Since as far back as I can remember. The kids at school pick on me for being so dark. So does my cousin Tyrone. I like him a lot. He's the coolest kid I know. But he's mean too." The Kid shrugs his shoulders. "But he's still my favorite cousin. So I take his jokes and I don't say anything and I forgive him even when he doesn't ask for forgiveness because we're cousins, because we're family. And that's what family does: they forgive each other. We're in this together."

"Did Tyrone tell you that?"

"How'd you know?" The Kid asks.

"Just a hunch," I say.

We sit together for what seems like a longer time than is possible. I keep waiting for the sun to rise but time is moving slowly, and still The Kid and I sit together, both of us holding our knees, both of us languishing in loneliness. I worry about if The Kid is really imaginary, dead, or something else. The Kid worries about me being alone. We're a pair, he and I. Both of us worrying too much about the other person.

"Do you want me to teach you?" The Kid asks.

"Teach me what?"

"To be invisible."

"No," I say. "I've already got my preferred means of dealing with the world."

And then there is nothing to do but sit alone in the quiet and wait for sunrise.

Somewhere along the way, I fall asleep.

When I awake, the boy is gone and my phone is lying on the floor next to me. I remember something and after a few swipes I dig through my messages to find the message from Kelly: "Need a ride to the airport?"

THE NEXT MORNING, RENNY AND I ARE STANDING OUTSIDE MY HOTEL. I'm wearing my traveling suit. Renny's wearing his limo driver's outfit. We're both looking down the street.

Renny looks left. I look right.

Renny looks right. I look left.

No Kelly.

"Well," Renny says, "there's always my car."

No sooner do the words leave his mouth than a small Honda Civic comes screeching up beside the curb in front of me. Kelly waves from the driver's seat.

Renny smiles.

He helps me load my luggage into Kelly's trunk. "Don't forget me, State College."

"Never happen," I say.

Renny gives me a hug that reminds me of my father.

Then I get into Kelly's car and we start off for the airport.

AS WE MAKE OUR WAY THROUGH TRAFFIC, I FEEL COMPELLED TO speak. After all, I ran out on her in the middle of the funeral home. A pretty ungentlemanly thing to do. "Listen . . . about last night . . ."

"Shut up," Kelly says.

She hits the radio. "Crazy" by Gnarls Barkley plays. An honest-to-God theme song.

WE REACH THE AIRPORT WITH SORE LUNGS AND TIRED MUSCLES. We've been singing the same song all the way here. The outside of the airport is bustling with people. Everyone's headed somewhere.

I step out of the car and unload my luggage. Kelly closes the trunk. Then, once I'm all squared away, she comes over to me and says, "Take your shirt off."

I hesitate for only a moment, but do as I'm told.

Kelly reaches into the glove compartment of her car and retrieves a large Magic Marker. She writes something on my undershirt. The letters tickle. The people swirl around us, seemingly oblivious to what she's doing. Which makes me wonder if she's really doing it or if I've slid off into my imagination again.

I've got a condition.

When she's done writing, Kelly says, "Read it when you get home."

I go to speak but before I can, Kelly leans in and kisses me.

Fireworks. Music. Sunlight. Ginger and cinnamon. The moment our lips touch, these things are the only things that matter. The bustling crowd of airport travelers around us suddenly drops their luggage and erupts into dance. It's a joyous, vibrant jazz number. Heavy on the drums. The trumpets, they're giving it the business. Count Basie's fingers are doing the Charleston and The Running Man on the ivories, sounding like how I imagine stars would sound if you could point your fingers to the sky and birth them from nothing. All the drab, comfort clothes are gone. Everybody's dressed for a night out in high society or for a night in the smokiest juke joint this side of Harpo's.

All around Kelly and me the world is light and sound, bodies and bass lines. My heart is in my throat. My hands are on her cheeks, siphoning the electricity and maybe giving back a little of my own.

And then the kiss is over. The music stops. The costumes fade away and everyone's back in jeans and sweats and mild depression. Life is life again. Only the memory of imagination remains as reality sinks its teeth in. "I live three thousand miles away," I say.

"The sun is 93 million miles away," she replies. "But you can still feel it on your face, can't you?"

I WALK THROUGH THE AIRPORT IN A DAZE. TSA, WHOM I USUALLY love, notices my distraction. Or maybe they don't. All I know for sure is that the pat-down felt awkward for the both of us.

"Did you ever make that switch to boxers?" the TSA agent asks.

"Huh?"

"No one ever listens to me," he says. Then: "Next!"

I'M SEATED ON THE AIRPLANE, STILL DAZED, STILL FAR AWAY FROM everything. How I got here I can hardly say. While the rest of the plane is still boarding, I make my way to the bathroom, lift up my shirt to read Kelly's message: FORGIVE YOURSELF.

I'M BACK IN MY SEAT. A LARGE HAWAIIAN MAN SITS DOWN NEXT TO me. His bulk spills over onto me, but it feels comforting. Makes me feel like I'm a part of something other than myself.

As the plane continues to board, I watch the baggage handlers toss luggage onto the conveyer. One of the baggage handlers looks up at me. It's Kelly. A dialogue balloon appears next to her head: "See ya 'round!"

I smile. The baggage handler looks confused. It's not Kelly anymore. My phone vibrates in my hand. A message from Kelly shows up. Guess what it says?

AS WE'RE TAXIING ON THE RUNWAY, THE LARGE HAWAIIAN MAN NEXT to me begins to sing Whitney Houston's rendition of "I Will Always Love You." He's a better singer than he should be. Before I know it, we're both singing. Both belting it out. Both leaving something behind in San Francisco, maybe.

The whole town turned out to solve the tragedy of William's death. While the man's body lay on a slab in the coroner's office over in Whiteville, an old church in a small town groaned under the weight of people too angry, sad, and afraid to put their own thoughts into words. And so they sought God and a man of God to speak for them.

"And I know," Reverend Brown said, "we're not the first ones to grapple with this particular type of beast but just like Jonah, we know that God is here and we know that God will not turn His back on us."

"What about Will?" somebody in the congregation asked. There was anger in their voice that the reverend and everyone else could hear.

"God never let him go," Reverend Brown said. "God just called him home."

Then he reminded everyone of Daniel in the lion's den. He spoke on Daniel's fear. He asked his congregation how many of them could have walked before the mouths of lions and not been afraid. "How many of you have that faith?"

It was an amazing thing to Soot, watching Reverend Brown. The old, bald man stood in the middle of the church recounting stories of God and His miracles and the congregation hung on his every word. The stories grew larger and longer as things went on and, still, the people listened and nodded in agreement and called out "Amen!" now and again and, sometimes, they even seemed a little bit healed by the stories they heard. There was no shortage of weeping faces in the church when Reverend Brown first started, but the longer he went on, the more stories he told, the fewer salty tears the old church pews had to catch.

Soot didn't know it then, but he was becoming a believer. Not in God, as Reverend Brown and the rest of the church-bound southern community might have wanted, but he was becoming a believer in stories. He saw, there in the wake of his father's death, that a story could take away pain. He saw smiles, however brief, where there had been tears. He saw fellowship where there had been loneliness. He saw hope where there had been despair.

And he began to wonder if stories were something that he might be good at one day.

As Soot wondered, Reverend Brown continued to salve those he could. Among the crowd, there were those who nodded their heads in agreement and allegiance to God Almighty and the reverend kept his focus on them and tried not to pay attention to those who were shaking their heads and looking around the church for others like themselves who were fed up with the way that things were going and who would not continue to wait for God.

Soot sat by his mother and watched it all while his uncle Paul stood huddled together in the back of the church with a group of other men. They talked to one another and shook their heads instead of nodding with the stories of God.

But the sermon went on.

By the end of it, the pastor seemed to have won the day on account of the fact that the men at the back of the church all excused themselves and went out into the parking lot. They paced back and forth in the glow of their old pickup trucks' headlights. They grumbled to one another about how something needed to be done. They made promises that they wouldn't stand for what had happened to William, what had happened to men and boys like him all across the country. They swore that they would find a way to mend what the law had failed. They reminded one another that the law was always going to fail them. That was the one thing that they knew and understood clearly.

The law was always going to fail them, just as it had failed their parents, and their grandparents, and their great-grandparents, and on and on. "The laws were never made for Black folks," Paul said, and the chorus of men grumbled and chirped in agreement. The other men all took their turns in explaining all the ways in which they had been failed by the law. They told stories of their own, different from Reverend Brown's, but with all the same weight. Instead of God, there were dead Black bodies. Instead of whales and lions, there were police and judges, prisons and loan officers, politicians and legislatures. In the vacuum left behind by God, their black skin and all that came with it filled the void.

The men all took turns trading what-if scenarios about all of the things that could happen to their children and how that loss would gut them if it ever came and took root in their lives. They all agreed that something would have to change. They cited Sam Cooke and Martin Luther King. Then somebody called Cooke a liar and they called MLK a failure. They said, "Ain't shit changed and maybe it's time that we do." Then somebody went to their truck and came back with a cooler full of beer left over from a long day of fishing on the river and the stories rolled on.

It was all anger, and fear, and sadness, because that was what their lives had become. Perhaps that was all they had ever been.

Outside the church, the men grew tired of talking and the men grew tired of drinking. And now that it was all over, Paul came back into the church and picked up Soot and carried him to the truck in his arms.

The next day, Soot woke up early and found his uncle sitting sleeplessly on the couch.

"Come with me," he said in his dark, booming voice. Paul led Soot out into the driveway beneath the dim glow of the rising sun. They went over to his truck and Paul reached into the glove compartment and took out a small pistol.

"This world ain't gonna take care of you, so you need to know how to use this. It's the only thing they respect, the only thing that will ever get you heard."

Here's an experiment that everyone should do:

Go to any bustling public place—make sure it's one with a nice, flat floor and lots of foot traffic—then toss a good, high-quality marble onto the floor. Now, you might think that you know what's about to happen, and maybe you do. And maybe you even think that it's not really possible. You might think that dropping a marble onto the floor won't actually cause people to take a good tumble. After all, this isn't an episode of the Three Stooges, it's real life.

But, again, just trust me on this one.

Take that marble and drop it into the crowd and wait. Eventually, it will happen. Someone will step on it and, if you're lucky, they'll actually take a fall. But the thing about it is, if you've chosen your time and location properly, it won't be just them that takes a fall. It'll start a chain reaction as the first person falls and tries to grab someone in order to break their fall. And then the second person goes down. Maybe a third. Fourth. And so on.

Before long you'll have laid waste to a whole team of individuals.

But then the interesting part happens. After everyone has taken their spill, after they've checked to be sure that they're okay and gotten over that sense of embarrassment that we all feel after such a thing . . . they'll go right back to their lives. They'll re-enter whatever conversation they were having. They'll continue on to the bathroom, game room, out the front door, wherever they were going before it all happened.

You see, the thing about people is that we're all creatures of habit. We like order, routine. We struggle to make a pattern out of our lives in order to mitigate the deep-down belief that there is no order to anything, that we're all just marbles banging off of one another in a cold, infinite expanse.

So when something comes along and upsets the norm, the first thing we human beings do is reestablish our routine and get back to our lives. And ain't I a human being?

So that's what I did after Kelly. I went back to what I knew.

I got back out there on the road. I got back to beating the metaphorical and literal concrete. I sold some books. I did some interviews. I drank some exotic alcohols. That's what a Joe like me does. He digs routine. Makes a schmuck feel like they're in control of something. And there's nothing better than feeling like you've got Life by the horns rather than being the used sucker glued to its bootheel. I been there. And there's no way I'm going to let something like a little psycho-emotional instability send me back there. Know what I mean?

But the problem with a vivid imagination is that it doesn't know when to go kick rocks. So next time I'm on an airplane I have what you might call a strange encounter.

It started with Magdalene. She was a flight attendant from Tulsa and she had a smile that could break a man in half if he wasn't ready to stand up against it. We met somewhere above the West Texas stratocumulus and, from the moment I saw her, I had visions of her and me bodysurfing the bedsheets until dawn. But she's not the story here.

This was just after the snack cart had come and gone by for the last time and everyone else was down for the night, dreaming at thirty thousand feet. I was sitting there, minding my own inconsolable business, when I got a soft tap on the shoulder. "You look familiar," Magdalene said, rolling out that million-dollar smile of hers.

"We all have to look like someone," I said, smiling like I have in every other interview. "And it's very possible that I've been this way before. I lose track of things pretty easily. I'm an author."

"I knew it!" Magdalene said, her eyes lighting up like Roman candles. She turned on her heel and ran down the aisle and when she came back, she had a copy of *Hell of a Book* in her trembling, non-wedding-ring-wearing hands. How could I refuse her when she asked me to sign?

I haven't talked about it much, but signing books is trickier than you might think. When you get right down to it, signing a book is akin to etching a piece of yourself into the soft stone of another person's memory. When you sign something, people remember it. The item in question becomes a totem, a symbol of a moment in time that meant something but that will never come again. The person on the other side of the equation wants you to give them physical proof that their chaotic lifepath crossed yours. They want something to be able to show their friends. They want something to hold over their heads when Life shits on them from a great height—figuratively speaking. They want to be able to pop open that dusty tome and find wisdom, inspiration, a timeless monolith full of stars—again, figuratively speaking.

And all of it hangs on you inscribing something meaningful.

It's a lot to hang a hat on.

So a while back I just decided on one thing to write in every book I signed.

I was halfway through this signature of mine when I got politely interrupted. "Do you mind if I get one of those too?" a deep voice asked from across the first-class aisle. It was a voice I knew, but didn't believe. Know what I mean? One of those voices that fires up synapses in parts of your brain that you'd forgotten were there. "Eerily familiar" is the easiest term for it.

"You betcha," I said, finishing up Magdalene's book.

I couldn't yet see who was talking to me on account of Magdalene still standing between us, reading the inscription I'd just left her. When she was done reading, she was all red-eyed and sniffly. She wiped a tear, took a breath, fixed her mouth for words, but all that came out was a sorta half-sob sigh.

Sister, I been there.

She ran off down the aisle, barking off that choky sob sound.

Once she was gone another copy of *Hell of a Book* got shoved in my face. "I really appreciate this," the voice from across the aisle said. "It really is a hell of a book."

"So I've heard," I said, and I finally pulled these brown eyes of mine up out of the mud to take a look at who I was talking to. Eye contact goes a long way in this business. One of the many things I learned in media training is that you need to connect with your readers at every opportunity. You need to look them in their eyes and make them feel like they're the center of the world, you know?

Like they're your old friend that's been lost among the many savage existences of the world for decades and now, at long last, they've slogged their way back home to your waiting arms. Makes people feel good to believe they've been seen.

So I looked up, planning to give this Joe all of those good feelings, and that's when I saw that the man on the other side of the aisle wasn't just some anonymous book buyer destined to be forgotten even as I locked these pretty browns lasers with his. No. This fellow traveler was special. It was, and you gotta believe me when I say this, none other than the one and only Nicolas Kim Coppola.

Better known to the layperson as Mr. Nic Cage.

That's right.

Nic Cage.

Mr. *Leaving Las Vegas.* Mr. *Raising Arizona.* Mr. *Windtalkers.* Mr. *Mandy.* Mr. *Face/Off.* Mr. *The Rock.* Mr. *Joe.* Mr. *Color Out of Space.* Mr. *Ghost Rider.* Mr. *Vampire's Kiss.* Mr. *Bad Lieutenant.* Mr. *Snake Eyes.*

You might not know it to look at me, but I've always thought that Mr. *Ghost Rider: Spirit of Vengeance* was the greatest thing since somebody got the idea to put corn sweat in a barrel and call it bourbon. Hell, if I could have a spirit animal, it would be Mr. *National Treasure.* Maybe he didn't do everything my father and Fred MacMurray did for my life, but he damn sure filled in the gaps. Just something about the man. You never know what he's up to now or what he's going to be up to in a week's time. It's like he rebuilds the world in every movie, rebuilds his reputation, rebuilds his outlook on sunshine. And if that don't speak to someone like me, I don't know what the hell does.

"You can just write anything," he said. "You've already written so much, ya know?" He flashed that smile that you and I have seen for 109 feature-length movies—and counting—and all I could do was sit there for a moment, Cagestruck, trying to find words that wouldn't come to me. All tapped out. At the end of my brain's bank account, reaching for syllables and coming up with not even verbal pocket lint. Little more than a slack jaw and a slow drool.

Mr. *Con Air* wore tattered designer jeans and a pair of old leather boots, an Al Green t-shirt, and a jacket covered in zippers and buckles. He looked exactly the way I always imagined he would.

"It's okay," Mr. *Bangkok Dangerous* said. "I know what you're thinking right now. But, for the record, I'm not who you think I am."

It was a mystery that snapped me out of my stupor. "You're not?"

Of course he was. Mr. *Bad Lieutenant: Port of Call New Orleans* couldn't put himself across the aisle from me, look me in the eyes, and tell me he wasn't who he was.

"You're not understanding me," he said, leaning in a little. A classic move that sends across the message of intimacy. "Don't get caught up in this," Mr. *Gone in 60 Seconds* said, making a motion with his hands. "Any of it. None of it's real." I couldn't tell if his motion was pointing to his duds, the man beneath them, or maybe even yours truly.

Needless to say, this was the kind of talk that made the wool on the back of my sport coat stand up and salute. Did he know about my condition? Or was he a part of it? I hoped for the former. I mean, I wanted to be able to say that I actually met Mr. *City of Angels.*

"You know what's *really* crazy?" Mr. *Wicker Man* asked.

"What's that?" I asked, certain that my thoughts were being shot out into the belly of deep space and—by mystical, tele-Cagic means—funneled into this SAG Award winner.

"Expectations," he began. "That's what's crazy. The notion that we, every single day, expect things. We expect things from the universe. We expect it to behave a certain way, you know? Bibles and scrolls and laws, all dancing the same dance, arguing they know how it all goes down. We expect things from ourselves—and we're almost always wrong about those things, by the way." He clucked another quick laugh, as if maybe someone else's memory had just burst into the orbit of his mind, which I could pretty sure believe.

"But even more than all of that," he continued, "we expect things from other people. Take, for instance, this particular moment. Right now, you're sitting across from me, right? And we both know who I am—or, rather, we both think we do. You know me from a fistful of big, forty-foot-tall poly-cotton screens in a chain of dark rooms with sticky floors spread out across decades of your life. Or maybe you know me from that little rectangular box that sits in your living room telling you what to expect from this whole spinning world. And you believe it because you have no other point of reference."

I was being pulled into quicksand and I knew it. I could feel my mind being deconstructed, swallowed up by the gaping maw of some creature reaching out from time immemorial. I wanted to call for Magdalene, just to help me find my bearings, but I couldn't break eye contact with Mr. *Fire Birds.* He had me in a death grip. I was stuck in this Cage.

"You can't get to know a person until you've, well, gotten to know them," he said, his voice gentle all of a sudden, like he knew I was about to drown and wanted to have a little mercy on me. "Your book talks about that a little so I know you know what I'm talking about. But you know what your book doesn't talk about? It doesn't talk about how you can't get to know someone by believing what you see on television. Or by driving past where they live and drawing ignorant conclusions. Or by dancing to cherry-picked pieces of their music because you want to feel counterculture. You ever noticed how the people who do that make sure to leave out the songs that point fingers? The songs that secretly imply that, maybe, the very people you don't know might know you better than you know yourself. Like, the people you judge remember all your secrets and you resent them for it. That's horrifying for somebody to face. It's a mirror nobody wants to gaze into. It's easier not to. So you know what you do about it? Not you, in particular, but national socio-political identity, I mean."

I shook my head.

He reached across the aisle and poked a finger in my chest. "*Americae excommunicatus*," he said. "You know that term. You know what I'm talking about. You and the Sioux."

"I . . . I do. But I've never heard anybody el—"

"Don't interrupt me," he said, sounding like an apology. Then he brushed my shirt where he had poked me with his finger. "You want to know what else?"

"I severely want to know what else," I said, spellbound.

"You're terrified right now. Scared all the way down to your socks. Because at some point you saw yourself on that little box in your living room—the same one that brought me into your world—and you started to believe the things you were told by people who truly didn't know you and were terrified of you. You saw pictures of yourself in prison, in riots, shooting other people who look like you, sacrificing yourself to the bloodthirsty monster just to save the hero—who looks nothing like you, by the way. And when you saw it all it built up a story in your brain, a story so convincing that it eventually swallowed up reality itself. And you started to think:

'Shit. Maybe that really is who I am. Maybe I really am the socio-narrative villain.' And that's when it happened."

"What happened?" I asked, breathless.

"You became terrified of yourself. You became afraid of your own voice. And I think you still are."

"Holy shit," I managed.

"Damn right," he said. "See. That right there. That's the thing. That's the moment! You just realized that maybe what you heard about me isn't true, which means I'm an unknown. And you also realized that maybe what you've heard about yourself isn't true, and maybe you're an unknown, even to yourself." He shook his head. "That's some terrifying shit."

"So what do I do about it?" I asked.

In my gut, I was on my knees. It had finally happened. The universe had given me a guide. My very own Virgil, willing to lead me out from the underworld of my existence.

And then Mr. *Drive Angry* did the worst thing ever. He just sat there and said nothing. With that tall, smooth forehead, with those slightly sunken eyes that know how to go crazy like nobody else's. He sat there and waited for me to unravel whatever in the hell he'd just told me all on my own.

If I'm square with you, I hated him a little bit right then. He had one job: be who I expected him to be. Let me feel good about myself. But, shit, that doesn't seem to be the theme of my life when I get right down to it. He had single-handedly spoiled my meeting of him. Had put the full kibosh on my entire Cage-view. It would have been easier if he'd just let me sign his book and let me have what I thought I knew of him.

Because he was, apparently, still picking up my thoughts from deep space, Mr. Cage motioned toward the book in my hand. "Go ahead," he said. "Write anything you want. I got to catch a little catnap before we land. Filming a new movie."

"Can I ask you—"

"No," Mr. Cage said. "Don't do that. Don't waste this experience by asking questions I can't give you answers to. You're better than that. Life's too short for that sort of thing. We could die right now. Hell, we might already be dead, you know? In fact, if you want to get philosophical, we are already dead, somewhere down the timeline. Everyone is. We're all just chasing after the moment when the timeline catches up to us and we blink out. So don't waste any of this, for God's sake!"

Mr. *Family Man* punctuated his rant with another poke in the chest. Then he fixed his jacket and sat back in his first-class seat and exhaled a satiated breath. "I think I was a dragon in another life," he said to himself—at least, I think he was talking to himself. Then he closed his eyes, his sights set firmly on copping a fistful of winks before Texas came and grabbed both of us by the ankles.

There I was, at thirty thousand feet with my very own Golden Globe–winning Oracle of Delphi . . . and I did not know what to say. Something sharp and glib to cut through the cigarette smoke of confusion buzzing around my head. But I knew that he was already onto whatever I was thinking. One doesn't have to speak when the universe already knows your thoughts.

"It's scary," he said, half-asleep. "But you'll find your own way. In the meantime, take care of yourself and I'll see you on the next one."

"The next what?"

"You think this is over?" he asked, opening his eyes again. He looked around his seat as he spoke, searching for something. "This is just book one. Just an introduction."

"An introduction to who?"

"To whom," he corrected, finally finding what he was looking for: a blanket. Then he leaned back in his chair again and shut his eyes and before I could even ask another question, he was already asleep. Deep and instant slumber, like somebody had just closed the lid on the universe's laptop.

I'm not sure when I'd stopped breathing or how long I hung there, confused and breathless like a fish that woke up on top of the Empire State Building, I just know that all of a sudden my lungs sucked in a bellyful and whatever trance I was in had finally taken a hike.

I wanted to wake him. I wanted to continue our conversation. I wanted to have someone—anyone—solve the riddle I understood the least: the riddle of my existence, the riddle of my skin and my mind. But I knew it wouldn't do any good. So there I was, across from a sleeping prophecy, holding a book that he would carry with him, a book I was supposed to sign, a book that in the front of which I was supposed to say something profound.

So I did the best I could. I signed what I always sign when I autograph a copy of *Hell of a Book*. It's the only thing that makes sense, so I write it, again and again and again, I burn it into every copy of my book that I touch. I just change the name at the beginning:

Dear Mr. Lord of War:

The whole world of my life spins under a radiant marquee of fear. Day in and day out it kills me, over and over and over again. Kills me dead, just to restart it all tomorrow. And all I can do about it is tell people that I'm fine.

"Thanks for reading."

Followed by a smiley face.

Then I thumped the book closed just like I've done a thousand times before and placed it gently in his lap and, at some point after that, those little sleep elves got the better of me and put me down for the night.

When the plane landed the man of the hour stayed asleep. Even when time came to deplane, he slept, and the flight attendants and everyone else let him sleep. I looked back as I walked off the plane, caught one last glimpse of fact or fiction.

THAT SHOULD HAVE BEEN THE HIGH POINT OF MY TRIP. SERENDIPITY, some might call it. But, no. Joes like me don't have no such luck. It still felt to me that very little was going along fine at all. I was still on book tour and so I never knew what city I was in and everyone was still asking me, "So, tell me what your book is about," and every time I told them, it was becoming more and more difficult to not hear the words that I was saying.

That's been my secret to getting through the book tour: I'm able to talk about my book without actually hearing what I'm saying. It's like watching television with the sound turned off. My lips move and words come out but all I hear are my thoughts about how much I don't want to be there, and how tired I am of being asked the same questions, and wondering what city I'm in and whether or not the bookstore will have a good turnout when the time comes, and what Sharon is going to say the next time she calls and asks about my book and tells me more about this big Denver interview she can't seem to stop talking about, and maybe I might actually tell her the truth: that I haven't actually started the second book.

All I have is a first sentence: "It was a dark and stormy night . . ."

And I stole that from someone else.

But the bigger problem is that now I've been on tour for so long that I'm beginning to hear my own voice in interviews. I can hear someone that sounds exactly like me saying that my book is about death. I can hear someone that sounds exactly like me saying that my book is "an attempt to cope."

Those two things both sound like a pretty serious rap, so I tune myself out when I can. That's what the dames were for. I'm no bounder, you see, but sex is a great way to distract yourself from whatever it is that starts breathing down the back of your spine when the 2 a.m. shadows show up and the rest of the world goes quiet and there's just you and a brain that won't shut up about all the broken parts of your life as it turns them around, right there in front of you, over and over again like some kind of goddamn insecurity zoetrope.

In my experience, the only poultice for that particular malady is a heavy dose of sex and alcohol.

You might not believe me when I tell you this, but I never really had a taste for alcohol until I started this death march of a tour. It's the truth. I'd drunk maybe five drinks in my whole life before I became a success, before I became a bestseller. Now I'm making up for lost time.

But I'll tell you what: one thing that's making life more bearable is The Kid. He's around all the time now, like a shadow after Hiroshima. Maybe it's my seeing his corpse at Kelly's place or maybe it's just the night of he and I sitting together and holding our knees and not saying anything to each other. But, whatever the reason, we're getting along like gangbusters. I've learned to not worry about the fact that I'm the only person who can see him. And, most important of all, I stopped seeing the bullet holes in his soot-colored body. It's like he's never been shot at all. All of it has passed away.

People have even stopped talking about the shooting. News travels fast in this world and the dead kid—this particular dead kid, at least—is three news cycles old now, so there's no one to remind me of how he died, or why he died, or of the outrage I'm supposed to feel about his death.

Dead kids don't linger on the brain like they used to.

Now he's just The Kid again. So I take him on. I accept him. I see him as he is and I really put in the sweat to see him for who he is. And, folks, let me tell you: he's a riot.

The Kid has one hell of an imagination. And I don't mean that in the way that most folks say it when they talk about kids. Most folks, when they talk about the imagination of kids, what they're really saying is that kids can imagine monsters or whatever. But that's not true imagination in my mind. The Kid . . . The Kid's onto something different.

When The Kid imagines, he sees people being different than they are. He gets his biggest kick out of looking at people and saying something like "What if she really understood how smart she was?" Or maybe he sees something dire on the news—because everything is dire on the news—and when he sees it, he says something like "Wow! What if we just went there and helped."

Revolutionary ideas like that seem small on the surface but, if you ask me, are a hell of a lot more imaginative than any talk of dragons or monsters or any of those usual tropes of what we think kids are supposed to sign up for.

The Kid loves telling jokes. And not just any jokes, but those bad kind of jokes that only the very young and only the very Dad are able to laugh about. Those jokes where the punch line is the thing that makes you grimace more than it's the thing that makes you laugh but the bottom line is that you came here to grimace or laugh to begin with. And I've always found that those types of jokes aren't really about the joke itself but about the willingness to embarrass yourself for the sake of the other person. You know the joke is bad. They know the joke is bad. And somehow, you both agree that the telling matters and the listening matters and so you both laugh together at the end because it's funny in its own particular way.

When we go into airports The Kid's always at my side. Sometimes he holds my hand as we go through the chaos of the TSA. Every time we hit the sky he acts like it's his first time flying even though he's been with me in every city since Missouri. The trip seems a little more sane now that I see him on my flights. He's always sitting a few seats in front of me or behind me or maybe across the aisle. And I've learned to pretend that I'm dictating into my phone whenever I talk to him so that the people around me don't start to think that I'm losing my grip on reality, because that's not what's happening here at all.

THE KID IS A BAD INFLUENCE ON MY ALREADY RUINED DIET WHEN we land in a particular city in Pennsylvania. It's not far from the city where they make Hershey's chocolate and The Kid can't talk about anything else. It's like this is the one event he's been waiting for ever since the beginning. It's like he planned it all.

We go to a small college, a stone's throw away from the factory, and I sell my books, and I shake hands, and I make jokes, and I come across as a mostly sober and relatively competent human being, but all the while, The Kid is in my ear whispering about chocolate, and Twizzlers, and everything else in the Hershey portfolio.

I keep trying to focus on the job at hand but The Kid won't be left alone. So, finally, I tell everyone that I'm sick and I catch a cab over to Chocolate World on the outskirts of the Hershey factory and no sooner are we in the door than the kid makes a hard and fast run for the nearest chocolate. He rips it out of the package and shoves it into his mouth and I can't help but run over and grab him by the hand and hiss, "Stop! We gotta pay for that!"

"They can't see me."

"That's not the point, you little bandit. We still got to pay for things."

The Kid thinks about this for a moment and nods. The rest of the time, he waits as patiently as he can as we go around filling up a small basket with all of the things we both wanted to eat but never should have decided to eat.

A little while later, we're sitting out on a hard concrete bench watching people file into the Heart of Chocolate and stuffing our faces with all of our treats. The sun's bright and hard; an angry gold eyeball staring down to see what comes next. Because it knows what's coming next.

Now and again, people sitting on small concrete benches in this little park area I find myself in stare over at me as though they haven't seen an author in a three-piece suit shoving his fists into a sack full of candy and, occasionally, talking to someone that only he can see.

"I still can't believe you did that."

"I said I'm sorry."

"No. You didn't."

The Kid bites through another candy bar. "What difference does it make? Nobody can see me."

"What does that have to do with anything?"

Everything around us smells like cocoa. The sun, the sky, the grass, the squirrels dry humping in the bushes with no sense of decency or decorum. Never can trust a horny squirrel.

"If nobody can see me," The Kid starts, trying to ignore what's going on in the bushes, "then what difference does it make what I do? Especially when I'm only hurting myself. That's what people say about candy, right? They say that it's bad for you and that when you eat a lot of it you're only hurting yourself. That's what my mom said, anyway."

I think about this for a moment. I've always been a little bit of an anarchist and I can't deny that there's more than a little sound logic in what he's saying. But I also can't deny that I know it wasn't right.

"Just because somebody can't see you doesn't mean you're allowed to do something like that."

"Why not?"

"Because you have to believe you matter, whether someone else sees you or not. Especially for a kid like you. Even Nic Cage knew that."

"Nic Cage?"

"Never mind."

A stiff, cocoa-scented breeze blows over the world. Cooling me down for a second as the sugar I've been scarfing down starts to hit my bloodstream.

"What do you mean a kid like me?"

"I mean that you're different. You know what I mean."

"No, I don't. What do you mean?"

The Kid stops eating his chocolate now and looks at me with sugar-stained lips and a furrowed brow.

I can't help but sigh. I mean, is it possible that this kid's mama and daddy didn't have The Talk with him?

"Didn't your parents ever tell you the truth about who you are?"

The Kid clucks a laugh. "You sound like you're about to tell me that I'm a superhero or something."

"No," I say. "Nothing like that. Just trying to say you've got to know that you're different. That the world is different with you in it and that you might not always be treated the exact same way that everybody else has been treated. That's just something that you've got to know."

"Why would I be treated differently? Because of my gift?"

It's just enough of an unexpected answer to make me wonder why I haven't thought that it's the only answer he could have ever mustered. Of course, a kid who's able to turn invisible might think that the world was going to treat him differently than it treats other kids like him. It's a beautiful idea and a beautiful thing. And now it's my time to shatter it.

"No, Kid. They're going to treat you differently because of that skin of yours. You can't tell me that you don't already know something like that. A kid of your years? You've got to come into this game knowing what the rules are and knowing that you can't ever win it. All you can ever do is try to break even and survive for a little longer than the next person who looks like you. That's all you can expect. But the thing to know and remember is that you can never be something other than what you are, no matter how much you might want to. You can't be them. You can only be you. And they're going to always treat you differently than they treat themselves. They won't ever know about it—at least, most of them won't. Most of them will think that everything is okay and that you're being treated well enough and that everything is beautiful. Because, I guess for them, all they can imagine is a world in which things are fair and beautiful because, after all, they've always been treated fairly and beautifully. History has always been kind to them."

I'm getting on a roll now and it feels good. It's rare that I really know where I'm going with anything but right now I know and I like where this train ride is going. I still can't believe this kid's mother and old man never took the time to lay out the road map of the world for him. Or maybe they did and it just never went across properly. I've seen that happen before. I've seen those times when people try to let their kids know what's happening in the real world but the kids are so blinded by Walt Disney and DreamWorks and a thousand other storytellers that can't relate to their reality. You see, the thing those fablers don't get is that certain kids don't get a fair chance to chase the dream. The world murders them first. Murders them, but fails to kill them. So these kids, they die young and grow a little more mad every day from then on out.

"But the thing that you need to know," I tell this soon-to-be Mad Kid, "is that history has given you a specific role in this world. A specific burden to bear. And it's not the prettiest one. And the sooner you learn that the rules are different for you, the better off you'll be. But I can also understand why your folks never sat you down and had this heart-to-heart with you. The fact of the matter is that if I had a bambino of my own, I might hesitate to strip down illusion and build up the reality that's bleak, and painful, and full of woe and sadness. A parent sees a child come into the world and all they want is for that child to have everything the world has to offer. But for kids like you—and for the kid I used to be—all that the world has is a collection of traps and walls. If the traps don't get you the walls will keep you away from all of the things that you've been taught you're owed. And that's a hard thing to lay on a kid. It's hard to stand there and tell your children that they're always going to have to be afraid of the police. It's hard to say to them: if a policeman stops you, you should trust them, but you should also keep your hands where they can see them and you should never ever talk back to them and you should never do anything that could be seen as a sudden move and even if you do all of that, there's still no guarantee that you'll come out of it alive. The cop could shoot you right then and there and you'll die without ever knowing what you did wrong."

I take a second to look up at the sun. I stare straight into it, just like you're not supposed to do. It hurts, but I keep doing it, like hurting myself will somehow fix something. It's the exact thing I told The Kid not to do and here I am doing it.

Sounds about right.

"It's hard to tell a child that being who they are, being born with a certain skin, is an act of counterculture in and of itself," I tell The Kid without ever taking my eyes away from the sun. I wallow in the pain and continue paying my pain forward. "It's hard," I say, "to tell a child, 'You're the mirror that nobody wants to see. And, because of it, you and everyone like you is born excommunicated. A whole nation, unwanted and unsought, born into exile in the belly of another nation. *Americae excommunicatus*! Always have been.'

"What kind of thing is that to tell a kid? What kind of moment does it create? What does it take away? What does it leave them with?"

Finally, I blink.

But the sun is still there.

The pain is still there, even though nobody else can see it or feel it but me.

I can hardly process it all. I can still remember when my folks had this talk—*The Talk*—with me. The old man was on the edge of breaking into tears and my mother was on the edge of rage. They both, in their own way, felt like they'd failed me. Maybe they thought that they could do something about the world before I got old enough to be affected by it. But they had lied to themselves. They had ignored the fact that from the moment I came out with all of this black skin, the world was already turning its blades against me. The traps had already been set. The walls had already been built. The schools. The prisons. The self-hatred. It had all been done before I ever showed up and my parents had the audacity to think that they stood a chance against any of it. They dared to believe that they could change anything.

Pipe dream of a pair of Mad Kids if I ever seen one. World proved them wrong. And they went on living in madness, eventually becoming mysteries unto themselves. Trying to figure out why the world wouldn't let them be who they were. Trying to figure out why the world wouldn't listen to them, wouldn't see them. Trying to figure out whatever happened to the soul they used to be before the world drove them mad.

And, now, here I am face-to-face with another kid about to turn mad.

It gives my stomach knots. The whole of an indigestible lifetime bubbles up inside of me like some sort of Vesuvian existential crisis. It's amazing how much you can get used to the intolerable, right up until the moment when you realize you have to pass it on to some pair of bright eyes that have no choice but to be dimmed by it. And now, here I am, breaking this kid's world just like mine got broken.

The irony is enough to fill me to the gills and beyond. So my stomach does all it can: it vomits up all of the chocolate, all the Twizzlers, all the lynched dreams, the redlined hopes, the color-blind promises that got Stopped-and-Frisked, the brutal, melanin-driven epigenetically inherited Americana that nobody—not even me—wants to talk about . . . it all comes erupting out of me faster than the red glare of those famous rockets bursting in air.

And all the while, the poor Kid watches, powerless to do anything about it. It's all he can do not to get covered in my bile.

NOT LONG AFTER THE VOMITING, AFTER THE KID HAS GONE—IN THE wake of what I just told him before the heaving started, I can't blame him for wandering off—but before I've had a chance to brush my teeth and settle my stomach, I get a phone call from Sharon.

"How's the next book coming?"

"Fine," I say. The easiest lie I've told today.

"Good," she says. "The publisher is going to need it soon."

"I'm sure."

"So do you know why I'm calling you?"

"I have no idea."

"Are you kidding?"

"Why would I be kidding about not knowing why you're calling me?"

"I'm calling you about the dead boy."

"Somehow, I'm not surprised. That kid has been clouding up my world more and more lately. You'd think that I could get away from him, but he's tenacious and so is his death. Which is rather rude, if you ask me."

"What?"

"Never mind. Okay, so you're calling about the dead boy. The one who got shot so many times the wind can whistle through him."

"That's horrible."

"The world's horrible."

"The point is, I'm sending you to the town."

"To what town?"

"To the town where it happened. Where the kid was shot."

My stomach falls to the floor. "Jesus Christ! Why the hell would you do that?" My hands are shaking all of a sudden. I'm sweating. My tongue feels like a flounder stuck in my mouth.

"Because you need to be there. You need to be a part of this." From the sound of her voice, Sharon is standing in her office and yelling at her phone. I can't be sure of it, but I know that's how I would picture it in my head. Her voice is strong and hard, slamming into the receiver and smacking the satellite, breaking through the cell tower and crashing into my ear. "We can't just keep pretending that this shit isn't happening."

"Who's 'we'?" I manage to find a little credulity. I'm always suspicious of group pronouns.

"You. Me. All of us."

"But that shooting was a race topic. I distinctly remember you and Media Trainer Jack telling me to stay away from being Black. I mean, that's a real thing that happened, right?" I want to be right, but I can never be sure of my memory. But, in this case, I'm mostly sure, which is the best I can ever hope for.

"To hell with that," Sharon says. "Did you see the photos of that boy's body?"

"No," I say, and The Kid's bullet-ridden body flashes before my eyes like lightning striking a dove: all awe and horror. "I don't need to see the photos."

"Then you understand. And, plus, there's that thing with the mother. Why haven't you said anything about that yet?"

"What thing with the mother? Whose mother?"

"The boy's mother!" Sharon barks. "My God! She's been going on TV saying that she wants to contact you."

"Contact who? Me?"

"Yes!" Sharon sighs. I feel like I've disappointed God Herself. "She did an interview the other day saying that she wanted to talk with the man who wrote *Hell of a Book.* I've been trying to contact you since then but you don't answer your phone anymore."

"Well, how was I supposed to know?"

"Answer your phone!"

". . . Touché."

"So I'm setting it up to have you meet with her in Denver. That'll make the Denver interview even bigger than it's already going to be. So first you're going to go to a couple of events and, if everything goes to plan, meet with the mother of the boy who was killed."

I'm sweating like a pig being led to market. "But why? I mean, why me? I don't do well with mothers."

"I don't know exactly what she wants. But she definitely wants to see you. I thought you might know her or something."

"How the hell would I know her?"

"Because she's from your hometown. The Kid too," Sharon adds. "The shooting, all of it happened there. It happened in your damn hometown. How the hell do you not know this?"

"Wait. She's from my hometown but we're going to meet in Denver?"

"That's right," Sharon says.

"Why?"

"Dramatic tension."

"Excuse me?"

"Never go small when you can go climactic," Sharon continues. "Why have two big events when you can fold them together into one? You, her, your little hometown, they're famous right now. And we're going to swing through there to drum up a bit more interest in your book and then take the whole damned thing to Denver and really make history! When you get up on that stage in Denver you'll talk about your book first, and before people can even finish impulse buying it from Amazon you'll be there taking questions from the mother of this poor kid. And by that time anybody that didn't impulse buy in the first wave will be clicking like blue jays fighting over acorns."

I'm about ready to fall over at this point. Too much going on too fast. All this talk of Denver and dead kids and mothers and my hometown and birds that click.

My phone falls to the ground. I can't believe any of this anymore. Or I won't believe it. It's clear that I'm having another break. Too much daydreaming. This conversation can't be real. I can't be real. I don't want to go back to that town. I left there for a reason all those years ago. Bolton was never good for my mental condition. My therapist said that whatever trauma I might have suffered must have happened there. I don't believe that, but I know, for a fact, that I don't want to go home. And that's the only thing that matters. That's the only thing I really need to know.

I won't go back there. I won't. I don't care if The Kid's from from there. I don't care. I won't care.

I just know that I can't go home again. Too many thoughts

there. Too many memories. Too much reality. Too much fiction. Too many blurred lines and not enough alcohol in this whole world to set them straight.

No.

Like I said: I can't go home again.

"There are things you are going to have to learn," the mother said, "and sometimes I will have to be the one to teach you. I'm sorry."

She stood in the doorway holding the old leather belt in her hand like a limp snake. She sighed.

Soot was not afraid of his mother, but he feared his mother's discipline. He feared the snap of the leather belt and the sting of the switch. He feared the gentle "whip-whip-whip" sound they made as they cut through the air and connected with his flesh.

But he never feared his mother.

Just now, Soot couldn't remember exactly why he had been compelled to steal the other boy's comic book. It was a simple thing that he thought the other boy wouldn't notice. He'd had a whole stack of them: Captain America, Iron Man, The Hulk. But it was the Silver Surfer issue that caught Soot's attention. The Silver Surfer was always his favorite superhero on account of the fact that his skin was neither black nor white but something other. A raw, beautiful silver.

He existed outside of all of the things that Soot hated about himself. His skin shined while Soot's only seemed to consume light. The Silver Surfer could also fly away whenever he wanted to. He spent most of his time away from people, out among the stars, in a place not unlike The Unseen that Soot knew and loved.

How could he not love the character?

And when he saw the comic book mixed in with the rest that Shane carried, impulse got the better of him.

He almost got away with it. Almost.

When the whipping was over, Soot sat on the edge of his bed in tears and his mother sat beside him, and she reached into her pocket and took out a cigarette and lit it between shaking fingers and took a drag and exhaled and said, "God, I'm tired."

Then the two of them sat in silence for a long time.

"Thank you for not doing it," Soot's mother said eventually.

"Doing what?"

"Hiding from me. You could have done it. But you didn't. So thank you."

"Yes, ma'am," Soot replied.

"This will get worse as you get older," Soot's mother said. "Or maybe it won't," she added. "I hope to God it doesn't. My father, he beat me and my brother too. But he did it differently. Harder. Belts and switches were just the beginning. He'd swing at me with anything he could get his hands on when he got mad at Paul." She sighed. "We were both terrified of him from the time we were born until the day we moved out. And, honestly, even then I was scared of him. I'd be out somewhere and I'd be worried that I'd come around a corner and find him there, waiting for me, and I'd have done something wrong. I'm not sure what I would have done wrong, but I know it would have been something and he would have been all over me for it just like he did when I was a kid."

"Why did he beat you like that?" Soot asked.

"Because he loved us," his mother replied.

And then she looked down at him.

"We don't beat the people we love," she said. "But this world isn't safe for us. That's why your daddy and I taught you to be unseen. That's why we worked so hard to give it to you. He didn't have that when he was a kid. Neither did I. I think that terrified my father."

"Why did it scare him?"

"Well, it wasn't exactly that he was scared. It was everything that not being able to disappear like you can leave you open to. And I think he felt guilty about the fact that he could never give it to me and Paul. I saw that in a lot of parents back then and I still see it in them. Our parents beat us and now we beat our kids, all because we're terrified. All you really want is for the people around you to be safe. And there's nobody in this world that you want safety for more than your children. So when you can't give that to them, it swells up around your life. It swallows you up. You get afraid to let them leave the house because the monster of the world might come along and swallow them up. And the thing is that, eventually, that's exactly what happens. Every child like you in this country has been swallowed up by the monster since before they were even born. And every Black parent in the history of this country has tried to stop that monster from swallowing them up and has failed at it. And every day they live with that."

"How does that make them beat their children?"

"Because even though you're going to lose them and you know

you're going to lose them, a part of you would rather be the one to give them that pain because then you can control it. You can put a limit on it. You can build a wall around how much hurt they're going to feel and if you build that wall high enough—with whippings, and spankings, and beatings—maybe you can keep them safe for just a little bit longer. Maybe you even go so far as to believe that you can actually keep them completely safe. That's a lie, of course, but when the truth is bad enough, you'll buy into any lie that you can. You'll even go so far as to make the lie your own."

Soot's mother finished her cigarette by letting it burn down to her fingers. "But that won't happen to you," she said. "Your daddy and I saw to that. You'll always have this gift. You'll always be able to be safe. We succeeded where everybody else failed. We did it. We saved our boy."

"Then why do I still get beatings?" Soot asked.

His mother thought for a moment. She reached for another cigarette and found none. "I guess just because it's always been done that way. And because I love you. And because you still need to know that . . ."

"Need to know what?" Soot asked.

His mother hung there, on the edge of telling him all the things she did not want to tell him. She teetered on the edge of changing who her son was, how he saw the world, all by telling him the truth about how the world saw him. It was a leap she always knew she would have to take. And now, with the moment finally before her, she didn't have the heart for it. She didn't have the heart to break her son.

"Nothing," she said. "Just . . . just ignore me. Just be a child. Just be who you are, son, for a little while longer."

Too much alcohol finally makes me sleep on a plane. I wake up in terror as the airplane's tires slam into the runway tarmac and again I feel like the whole world is crashing. But, this time, I know where I am. Maybe that's why I can feel everything falling apart.

The humidity hits me in the face as I step out onto the jet bridge and I know for sure that I'm back in North Carolina. I know all the smells: humidity, pine trees, thinly veiled racism. It's what home feels like for me.

Down in this part of the world, we got it all: fifty-foot Confederate flags planted along the interstate, statues put up by the Daughters of the Confederacy, plantations where you can have wedding pictures taken of the way things used to be; we got lynchings, riots, bombings, shrimp and grits, and even muscadine grapes.

Yeah, the South is America's longest-running crime scene. Don't let anybody tell you otherwise. But the thing is, if you're born into a meat grinder, you grow up around the gears, so eventually you don't even see them anymore. You just see the beauty of the sausage. Maybe that's why, in spite of everything I know about it, I've always loved the South. Was born and raised in a small southern town called Bolton. Chances are you've never heard of it, and if that's the case, don't you go worrying about that or feeling bad. The fact of the matter is that there's no reason for anybody to have ever heard of Bolton. Which is to say, it's a hick town in the middle of a hick county in the lower leg of a hick state, so not knowing about it is probably a sign that you're not a hick and that you've been raised a little bit better than myself.

When I come down the small airport escalator I look around for either The Kid or whoever has been picked to be my Renny in this little piece of the South. I'm back home so I already know what airport this is but I keep hoping I'm wrong.

When I come down the escalator, I'm greeted neither by The Kid nor by any typical Renny but by my agent, Sharon, instead.

In case you were wondering, Sharon is a tall, lean woman who dresses in New York couture and nothing else. She's the type of woman who judges a person based on where they bought their newest piece of clothing and her judgment is as cruel and sharp as any Khan of the Old World.

"You're late," she says as I come down to meet her. As she talks, she never looks up from her phone.

"I was on the plane," I say. "If I'm late, it's just because the plane is late."

"We don't have time for excuses," Sharon says. "Just because the plane was late doesn't make it okay. Do you have any idea how many book sales we lose when an author is late landing in a new city?"

"Well, I . . ."

"Seven sales per minute," Sharon says.

"That can't be a true statistic," I say.

"And that's if you're lucky," she continues. "That's if you're selling well. Which you, by the way, are barely doing. Have you looked at your sales numbers lately?"

"No," I say. "But everyone I've talked to has told me that things are going pretty well."

"Things aren't going badly yet, I'll give you that. But things never go badly right up until they do. And when they do, there's nothing that you can do to fix them. And when you stop selling books, you lose the publisher's faith, and when you lose the publisher's faith, they don't want to read anything more from you and then, before you know it, nobody wants to work with you. And do you know what that means?"

I'm terrified to answer.

"I can guess what it means," I say.

"I'm sure you can. Now let's go."

We walk out of the airport and into the sweaty open mouth of summer in the South. The humidity is thick enough to push the air from your lungs if you're not careful. I'm sweating in places I probably shouldn't be sweating in the time it takes us to walk from the concourse to the limousine that Sharon has waiting. Sharon, by the way, hasn't the slightest bit of sweat on her person. It's like she's invulnerable to the wiles and ways of the southern sun.

"Where to?" I ask.

"You tell me," Sharon says. "It's your town."

LONG BEFORE WE REACH THE THIN CITY LIMITS OF BOLTON, WE MEET the protesters. Thousands of them stand along the highway leading into the small strip of pavement that is Bolton. They wave signs and shout about justice and, just like the way it was back in San Francisco, they are all youths. All of them between the ages of two and twenty. It's amazing how my hard-luck imagination travels so well with me. I could swear that when I look at those youthful faces standing outside the walls of my beloved hometown, I can see the exact same faces that I saw on the other coast. One of the small children wears a shirt that says I CAN'T BREATHE and I find it poignant and ironic that someone who isn't potty trained is socially conscious enough to hop a flight from the West Coast to the East Coast and stand out here in the middle of this Carolina heat and humidity and protest.

Even with all the signs, I can't quite make out the name of the person that they want justice for. But even though I can't read the name of whoever needs justice, I feel like I know.

One thing that's common on the protest signs and t-shirts, one thing that comes through loud and clear in the chants, whoever it was that got shot by whoever else it was, well, he was a young Black youth. And there's only one Black youth that I know who's been shot.

The Kid.

It's been a day or two since I've seen him and I wonder where he is as we turn off of the main highway and onto the small two-lane blacktop that leads through the heart of town.

Nestled in the sweaty armpit of Carolina swampland, surrounded by gum trees, and pines, and cedars, and oak, and wild grapevines, the town of Bolton is the land that time forgot. Go back far enough into the town history, and there used to be a railroad stop and a sawmill here. And that was at its pinnacle, somewhere around sixty years ago or so. Back then, the town had a population of maybe around three thousand people.

The main exports of Bolton are lumber and Black manual labor. The wood comes from the forests and swampland—all of which are owned by the local paper mill—and the labor comes from the town's seven-hundred-odd residents. I wish that I could tell you that something more than those two chief exports comes out of Bolton, but there's nothing else. Bolton isn't a town that gives, but neither is it a town that takes. It's the type of place that keeps to itself. It's self-sustaining, the way the past always is. And though it changes a little now and again, the way an old piece of metal seems to change colors over the years as some thin patina comes along and begins to grow over it, at its core the town is the same that it has always been. And that's how the people like it.

But, apparently, now the town of Bolton has two new exports: tragedy and a famous author.

AS WE TURN DOWN THE MAIN STREET LEADING INTO TOWN, THE young protesters begin to find themselves being supplanted by locals holding up signs that read WELCOME HOME! And those that aren't holding up WELCOME HOME! signs are holding up copies of *Hell of a Book*. It's a hell of a sight to see.

"This your doing?" I ask Sharon.

"Nope," she says sadly, looking out of the window. "But I wish I'd thought of it." She scans the small town as we pass. Coming through, we cross paths with nine churches over the course of the town. "Why does a town this small have so many churches?" Sharon asks.

"Because God needs the little people more than he needs anyone," I say. There's a knot in my stomach the size of Texas all of a sudden. I haven't been back to Bolton in years, and with good reason. It's a town with tendrils. And as soon as those tendrils get into your skin, you can never get rid of them. You can never get away. The truth of the matter is that I'd managed to get out of Bolton only because I snuck away under cover of darkness and something akin to invisibility. I never really fit into this town when I was a kid. I was always too much of something for the other kids I grew up with. I was too much of a bookworm. Too nerdy. Too weird. Too clumsy. Too skinny. Too black of skin. Too white of temperament. I never liked hunting and fishing enough. I never liked fighting or chasing girls enough. I never liked God or hated the devil enough. I never grew things in the garden. I didn't eat okra and butterbeans. I couldn't stand dumplings.

My family did the best they could to not make me feel like the freak that I always was. My cousins, God bless 'em, they loved me like I was one of their own even though I'd argue that I didn't really belong to anyone. Especially after the emergence of my condition.

I can't say exactly when it began, but I can definitely say that it's linked to this small town of Bolton and my childhood. From what I remember, I've always been living in a different world. My therapist says that can't be the case, not for the type of condition I've got. She swears that what I've got comes about only after a person has gone through some sort of trauma. And, typically, when you talk about this type of trauma, it's got to be something beyond the scope of school bullying and general low self-esteem—both of which I had no shortage of in my youth.

My therapist and I have been through more than a few loops about what might have caused my imagination and persistent daydreaming to work the way it does.

"Can you think of any event that might have occurred?" she

asks, over and over again, for the past five years since I've started seeing her.

"No," I reply. "I had a pretty normal childhood. I grew up in a small town that nobody's heard of in the ass end of North Carolina. Well, now that I think of it, maybe you could count that as a trauma."

"I don't think that's funny."

"Neither do I. Have you ever been to Bolton?"

"You know I haven't."

"There's nothing there. It's just an empty hole decorated around its edges with people living in single-wide trailers and clapboard homes that look like the nearest breeze will blow them over."

"I think you're exaggerating," she says.

"Everyone does," I say.

"Tell me about your parents," she says.

"Why?"

"Because that's always the best place to start when we begin a conversation about trauma."

I cluck a laugh. "Well, that's a harrowing thing to say about parenthood."

"What kind of woman was your mother?"

My insides go tight, like always. "Did I ever tell you about how a man was shot in my town when I was a kid?"

"No," she says. She leans back in her chair and makes a note on her sheet of paper.

"Yeah," I say. "Was a terrible tragedy, or so I'm told."

"You don't know for yourself?"

"Nothing like that. I just have trouble remembering it. It happened when I was pretty young and so I have a hard time remembering it. I just remember a bunch of people being sad and angry at the same time. I remember people marching—I think I might even have marched along with them. I remember this long walk along this blacktop road surrounded by a bunch of people. I have this image of my cousin—he was a big boy, one of those kids who seemed to go straight from toddler to grown man. You know what I mean?"

"I think so. What do you remember about him?"

"I remember him walking behind me as we walked along this road. I remember getting tired and wanting to stop and I remember him nudging me from behind like I was some kind of mule that had refused to keep plowing. God, he was strong. He poked and prodded me and wouldn't let me stop walking no matter how much I might have wanted to stop."

"How old were you back then?"

"Not sure. Maybe around the age of ten or so."

"So this was after the death of your father," the therapist says.

For a moment, I'm not sure if she's asking me or telling me. I can't seem to remember exactly how old I was when my father died so I just hang there for a moment, thinking about the fact that I can't remember parts of my past that I probably should be able to remember.

"What's wrong?" she asks.

"Nothing," I say.

"No. Tell me what you're thinking about right now. Tell me what's going through your mind at this exact moment."

But the fact of the matter is that there isn't anything going through my mind right now. Nothing at all. My mind is just a blank, windswept expanse. One that I've spent almost my entire life crafting. And now it's here, and it's slowly killing me, and there doesn't seem to be anything that I can do to stop it.

SHARON'S LIMOUSINE PULLS UP IN FRONT OF A SMALL HOUSE SQUATting on the edge of a cornfield. A tire swing dangles from an oak tree limb by an old rope in the front yard. The "hotel" that Sharon has booked us at is nothing more than an old gray house perched at the end of a long driveway lined with trees and surrounded by cornfields.

At the sight of the house, I feel like I'm in a dream. I feel like I've been here before, but I can't say when. Maybe I know this place? Maybe I've been here before? I mean, I grew up around here, didn't I?

The house is gray with a slanted roof and white-framed windows. It sits up on concrete blocks and the black earth can be seen beneath. The whole thing looks tired, and yet the whole thing looks as though it could stand for another hundred years without breaking a metaphorical sweat.

Where do I know this place from? Why does it shake my guts and warm my bones at once?

"Because it's your home," Sharon says.

"What?"

"What, what?" Sharon replies. "I didn't say anything."

And I know there's a good chance she didn't. I can feel my imagination flaring up again.

As the driver opens the door and we step out into the humidity and bright sunlight of the day, I catch sight of The Kid sitting on the front porch, swinging his feet back and forth over the edge, waiting for me.

I can't deny that a certain degree of calm washes over me at the sight of The Kid.

"I wonder if there's internet out here," Sharon asks, eyeing the house suspiciously. "How in God's name do people live like this? It's barbaric."

I can't help but smirk.

"I'm going in to check on the internet and get down to work. You should do the same. You've got the town hall meeting to go to soon."

I'm not really paying any attention to whatever Sharon's talking about. Mostly, I'm just happy that she's walking into the house and leaving me to converse with The Kid without feeling self-conscious about talking to a boy who is there only for me.

"FANCY MEETING YOU HERE, KID," I SAY.

"Cool to see you again too."

I walk over and take a seat on the porch beside The Kid. "So how you been?"

"Good," The Kid says. He takes a long look down the driveway. He takes in the shimmering blue sky, the emerald cornstalks leaping up from the earth, the hum of the cicadas, the cool, wet breeze pushing the branches of the oak tree to and fro. "I like it here," The Kid says.

I sigh. "Yeah, me too. I grew up not far from here, but I'm sure you already know that."

"How would I know that? Because I'm a part of your imagination?" He smiles, his glowing white smile bursting from his impossibly black skin.

"Let's not start down that rabbit hole again if we can help it. I'd rather just sit here and enjoy this. It's peaceful."

And it *is* peaceful. I haven't felt the wind like this in years. I haven't heard the trees shimmering, dancing under the summer sun. Say what you want about life in the South and the humidity that comes with it, but I swear it makes the world sound and feel different than any other place on the planet. Maybe it's got something to do with air density or some other complex element of science. All I know is that there's nothing like the South.

"That field is pretty cool," The Kid says.

"Yeah," I say.

"There's a field like that not far from my house too. Looks almost the exact same. My daddy said that it was where they used to grow cotton a long time ago. My daddy was always talking about the way things used to be back before I was born."

"That a fact?"

"Yeah. It was like that was all he wanted to talk about. He used to have these books he would read to me on the weekend. These encyclopedias about Black people."

"No shit?"

"No shit," The Kid says. He pauses a moment, testing to see how I'll respond to his use of profanity, but once it looks like everything is going to be okay, he continues. "Every Sunday we would sit together on the couch while Mama was at church and, first, we would watch Clint Eastwood movies."

"Word?"

"Yep. All those old Westerns. That dude was always shooting up the bad guys and my daddy loved it. So we'd sit there and we'd watch a movie and then, when it was over, my daddy would open up these encyclopedias about Black people."

"The *Ebony* encyclopedias."

"Yeah! That's it! How did you know?"

"I've heard of them," I say, offering The Kid a smile. It's clear that he's excited not to be the only person to have heard of them.

"Yeah, so you know all about them, then." The Kid nods. "It was always weird, looking through them. They were full of all of these people that I didn't know about and had never heard of and my daddy would get real serious when we read them."

"Serious how?"

"Serious like he was trying to . . . I don't know . . . trying to do something big. Serious like how you get serious when you're trying to put a transmission in a car. Like he would just get all focused and tight. I could feel it. And he'd read the words slow. Real slow. Like reading word by word. I asked him why he read like that one time and he said it was because he wanted to be sure that he got the point across without getting anything confused. I'm not really sure what that meant."

"I think I know. My mama used to talk to me like that sometimes too."

The Kid nodded.

"And then what?"

The Kid shrugged his shoulders. "Nothing much. He'd read them to me. They seemed real important to him. He used to say those people were like me and I was like them. But I never really believed that. I'm not really like anybody else."

"What do you mean?"

The Kid gave me a suspicious look. Then he raised his ebony hand. "This," he said. "This right here makes me different from everybody. Always has and always will."

I want to tell The Kid that he's wrong. But I can't.

"The kids at school used to pick on me about it. Said I was a freak because of how dark I was. Used to lock me in lockers, beat me up on the bus. A lot of other stuff too. One time, this kid got on the bus one morning and poured a whole can of motor oil on me just as we were getting to school. Poured it right over my head." The Kid made a pouring motion with his hand. Then, believe it or not, he laughed. "Can you believe it?" he asked, half laughing. "It was so messy. The bus driver got so mad because he was going to have to clean it all up. We both got sent to the principal's office."

"What? Why'd *you* get sent to the office?"

"The other kid said that I started it. He said that he'd brought the oil onto the bus to take to shop class but that I started messing with him and we were fighting over it and I spilled it all over myself."

"And they believed that shit?"

The Kid shrugged his shoulders. "I'm not really sure. I don't think so because they didn't try to make me clean it up. They just called my mama to come and get me, but she was at work so they got one of the teachers to take me home so that I could clean up."

"Kids can be assholes," I said.

"I don't really worry about it," The Kid replied. I could tell by the sound of his voice that he had been broken long before they poured motor oil on him. "It's just how stuff goes sometimes. But that's why when my daddy looked through those books I never really understood why he thought I was the same as those people. You think any of them were picked on by kids on the bus? You think any of them got called 'Midnight' and everything else? No. I'm something different and those kids never let me forget it. Yeah, I was Black, but I was also something else. Something that didn't quite fit into being Black so they let me know that each and every day that they could."

The Kid looked down in the dumps. And why the hell wouldn't he after a sad-sack story like that.

"Fuck 'em, Kid," I say. "Fuck 'em all."

For three weeks, Paul came around and took Soot off into the depths of the forest and taught him how to shoot. It was an old, rusty pistol that became the tool of indoctrination into the means and ways of southern self-defense. "This belonged to my daddy," Paul said, turning the gun over in his hand. It was steel with flecks of rust and grimy black splotches here and there. "I should take better care of it. But it'll shoot the wings off a butterfly if you learn how to use it right," he continued, turning his focus from the gun back to his nephew. "It ain't never been more important for someone like you to learn how to use this thing. You ask me, you've been too long in waiting to learn this. You should have gotten a lesson in it a long time ago from your daddy." He sighed. "I'm sorry," he said. "I wasn't trying to talk about that. But I wish he'd been carrying a gun with him when it happened. I told him for years that these cops around here didn't care about us. This is the South. Always was and always will be the way it is."

"Daddy said that maybe things could be different," Soot replied.

Paul grunted a dark affirmation. "And where'd that get him?"

The sun was high and the day long and hot; all of it would be filled with the sound of gunfire. Paul had stopped by the hunting store and come out of it with an entire bag of ammo. The bag crackled as he placed it on the dusty ground and began loading the pistol.

"This is going to be all you," Paul said.

"I don't like guns," Soot replied.

"Me neither," Paul said.

"What if I don't want to do this?"

"That makes it sound like you got a choice."

Soot's jaw tightened and his uncle saw it.

"Look," Paul said, his voice firm, "I didn't make this world. But I'm damn sure going to survive in it for as long as I can. And I know you don't want to hurt anybody. But this ain't about hurting anybody. This is about staying alive. You saw what happened to your daddy. And I'm damn sorry about that. But I can't just sit by and watch it happen to you. Your mama told me how she's been trying to teach you about it. She's got her way of doing it and I've got mine. She asked me to help you, so that's what I'm doing." He looked around in frustration. "It don't matter none," he said, suddenly sounding very tired. "It's like taking medicine. Sometimes you have to do things to keep yourself from getting hurt. And the things you do feel like they're hurting you more than the thing you're trying to keep safe from. But that don't change the fact that you need to do them. So this is it for you."

For the rest of the afternoon, all the boy would remember was the gun firing over and over and over again. One shot after another.

And each time, he felt the gun recoil in his hands. Each shot made his entire body quake. By the end of the afternoon, his hands were blistered and he could barely close them but Paul seemed not only proud but thankful that it had all happened.

"Let's go," he said, loading up the pistol one last time.

The two of them settled into the truck and Paul returned the gun to the glove compartment. Then Soot was asleep.

He awoke to find that the evening had come on full and night had bloomed around him and he also awoke to the flash of blue lights again and the sound of the glove compartment opening. "Uncle Paul?" Soot called, trying to decide if he was dreaming or not.

"Just sit still," he said.

Finally, Soot was awake. The flash of the blue lights sent a chill down his spine.

Soot heard the sound of a car door closing. Before long, the policeman walked up to the truck, shining his flashlight inside. As the light fell over Soot, sweat rose up on his brow.

"License and registration," the officer said.

"I got a pistol in here," Paul said, keeping his hands on the steering wheel. "I'm just saying that so you know ahead of time. I got a permit for it."

The glare from the flashlight ran through the truck. "Where you got a gun at?"

"On the seat," Paul said. "In view. That's the law ain't it?"

"I reckon," the officer said.

The light fell on the gun, then shined in Soot's face, blinding him. "Let me see your hands!" the cop said, his voice hard as a knife.

"Calm down," Paul said softly. He turned to Soot. "Put your hands up on the dash."

Soot did as his uncle told him.

"Why don't the two of you go ahead and step out of the truck?" the officer said.

"What for?" Paul asked. "You still ain't told me what you stopped me for."

"Step on out," the officer said. His voice rumbled through the small truck and Soot felt his breath quicken.

"It's okay," Paul said. "Just go on and get out of the truck."

Soot's face was streaked with tears. "No."

"What you say, boy?" the officer asked.

"It's fine," Paul said. "He's just nervous. He'll get out."

"I know he will. The both of you are gonna get out of the truck."

The officer placed his hand on his gun.

"Okay," Paul said.

It was then that Paul looked back over inside the truck to find Soot missing. "Holy Lord," Paul said.

"What is it?" the officer said. He shined his flashlight across the seat and also found the boy missing. "Where'd he go?" The lights rose and fell in the small space where Soot had been sitting. "Where's he at?" The cop unclipped the gun in his holster. "Step out of the truck and get on the ground!" he barked.

"Yes, sir," Paul said.

No sooner had Paul opened the door than he was pulled from the truck and forced down onto the ground. "Hey!" he roared. "Ain't no need for all that."

"Shut up," the officer said. "Where's that boy? Where's the boy?"

The cop forced Paul's hands behind his back and fumbled with the handcuffs. Once the cuffs were on, the cop stood with one foot in the small of Paul's back. "Get off of me," Paul yelled.

"Shut up," the cop replied. "Stay there before I shoot you for resisting arrest." The cop's attention was focused on the inside of the truck. The door was still closed and the window rolled up, so he couldn't understand where the boy might have gotten to. He walked around to the other side of the truck and opened the door. It opened with a groan. Still, he shined the light up and down in the seat but there was nobody there.

When he heard something in the darkness beside him, he drew his gun and spun. "Who's there!" he barked, aiming the barrel of his gun at the outer dark squatting over the countryside. The sound was close by. It sounded like a foot being placed on the gravel in front of him so he dropped to his knees and aimed both his flashlight and his gun at the underside of the old pickup truck. But the only sight that greeted him was the sight of Paul on the other side of the truck, still on his belly with his hands cuffed behind him and his face on the pavement.

He stood and turned his attention back to the field of darkness beside the truck.

"Where'd he go?" the officer asked. Still, the glare of his light swung back and forth through the darkness.

The only answer he received was the gentle sound of laughter coming from Paul.

The officer came around the truck and stood over Paul. "Something funny?"

"No crime against laughing, is there?" Paul asked.

The cop squatted beside Paul. "Look at me," he said.

"What?"

"Look up here at me, boy."

Paul craned his neck, turning his face up from the pavement.

"You think I don't know who that boy is?" the officer said. "You think I don't recognize him? He ain't hard to spot." He looked at Paul's license. "You his uncle or something?"

"Something like that," Paul said. He knew what was about to happen.

"Well," the officer said, "I just wanted to let you and him and anybody else know that we don't really appreciate what happened around here. That cop that you-all are trying to get fired, he's a good man. He's got a family. And y'all are threatening his family."

Again Paul laughed.

"I'm glad you find this funny," the officer said, rubbing his hands together.

"How do you figure we're threatening his family?"

The officer placed the tip of the barrel between Paul's shoulder blades, the muzzle kissing hard against his spine. "It's about the way of life. The way of the world," the cop said. "People like y'all, you want to change the way things are. You don't know what it's like, people like you. You think this world just makes itself up the way it is. You're ungrateful. That's the biggest thing about it all that gets under my skin, I reckon," he spat. "This country is the greatest place on this whole planet. And I won't say it ain't had its troubles. But when you compare those troubles against the rest of the world, against the way things done happened in other parts of the world, even the worst person in this country has it pretty damned good." He shook his head. Paul felt the barrel of the gun pressing harder into his spine. "That man that you-all are harassing, he might lose his job." He cleared his throat. "This job ain't easy. And sometimes people fight back when they shouldn't. That's what happened to that boy what got shot. If he'd been doing what he was told to do, he wouldn't have got shot."

Paul's hands trembled in the cuffs. He strained his wrists against them, but the cuffs held. "That was my brother-in-law," Paul said.

"Hope his type of behavior doesn't run in the family." He kneeled down close to Paul's face, with his gun still in the man's back. "It don't run in the family, does it?"

The moment stretched out.

"Does it?"

Paul turned his face to the pavement.

"I need you to tell me *something*," the cop said.

"Fuck you," Paul mumbled.

"Mmm-hmm." The pistol cocked. "I reckon it's a good thing that boy ran off. Makes things easier. . . . You shouldn't resist arrest."

Paul took a breath into his lungs and waited for the shot to go off. He waited for the bullet to penetrate his spine. Maybe it would kill him, maybe it would just paralyze him. He didn't know which was better and which was worse. He saw, in his imagination, his own funeral. He saw his grave placed next to his brother-in-law's. He saw Soot, the poor, poor dark-skinned boy, standing over those graves, waiting his turn. "I'm sorry," he said.

"What's that?" the officer asked. "You say you sorry?"

The gun barrel was lifted from his spine.

"Yeah," Paul said. "I said I'm sorry. But I wasn't talking to you. You can go to hell."

The officer smirked. "Okay, then."

Again, the barrel of the gun was on his spine. The shot was coming, just as soon as the cop's finger tightened around the trigger.

"Don't!" a voice called out from the edge of the darkness.

Paul and the officer both lifted their eyes to the darkness. The cop aimed the gun at the sound of the voice. He squinted, seeing nothing but darkness. But soon there came the outline of clothes rising against the glare of his squad car headlights. Then Soot, with his impossibly black skin that seemed to blend into the night, stepped forward into the light.

"Please don't," Soot said.

"Get out of here!" Paul yelled. "Run!"

"Shut up."

Soot and the cop stared at one another. The cop squinted as though he were seeing a specter of some sort, something that came from the depths of imagination. "Damn, you're black," the officer said. "I seen you in photographs but I didn't think it was real. Saw you in the newspaper but couldn't believe that anybody could be as black as you." He laughed.

"The kids call me Soot," Soot said.

"I can't blame them. I want to ask you a question," the officer said.

"Okay," Soot replied.

"You wouldn't ever resist arrest, would you?"

"What?"

"If you were to get arrested"—he gesticulated with his pistol as he spoke—"you wouldn't fight back, would you? You wouldn't stand there shouting about rights and race? You wouldn't start talking about Stop-and-Frisk or search warrants or anything else, would you?"

"No, sir," Soot said, his voice quivering.

"You sure? You sure you wouldn't?" The barrel of his gun swung to and fro in a dark arc as he spoke. Sometimes it pointed at Paul's spine. Sometimes, for only an instant, it swung its dark eye over Soot.

"I'm sure, sir," Soot said.

And then there was only silence. A long, sprawling silence that would cast a shadow over the rest of Soot's life long after he and his uncle were allowed to leave and they drove the entire drive home with Paul not saying anything and, sometimes, he cried gently and Soot reached over and touched him and Paul pushed his hand away and stared out of the window and only shook his head, the only words he could manage being "I'm sorry you were born into this."

When I ask The Kid if he's coming with me to the town hall meeting tonight, he fires back with a surprisingly courteous "Hell nah, dude. I don't want none of what's going to be going down in that place."

"I hear you, Kid," I say. "I hear you."

IT'S A SIGHT TO SEE, REALLY. I HARDLY EVEN KNOW WHY WE'RE GOing to this meeting but if there's one person who's positive, it's Sharon. She's a sight to see here in this small town wearing nothing less than twenty grand in designer clothing. She looks like she's escaped from a Paris runway and she stands out like a lightning strike in the middle of the night as we make our way through the long line of muddy pickup trucks and 1980s domestic cars which are the staples of Bolton and all towns like it.

I wonder how Sharon feels as she walks through the parking lot surrounded by people who can't appreciate just how exclusive and expensive her clothing is. For her part, Sharon seems to be having a good enough time. In fact, I'd go so far as to say that she hardly seems interested in her clothes and how the small-town hicks react to them.

"I didn't think things like this happened in small towns like this. Chicago or New York, I can understand. But this place? It's just not supposed to happen. Some places are supposed to be immune to this type of thing."

"Nobody's immune to nothing," I say as we pass through the crowd that is growing ever more dense with each step. The people of Bolton all recognize me as I pass. I hardly recognize any of them even though I know I should. Some sort of selective memory, I guess. Just my brain's usual way of stuffing the past into the past. They nod and wave and I shake a shit ton of hands. Little old ladies congratulate me on the success of *Hell of a Book.* They tell me how proud they are to finally have someone from our small town go out and make it in the world. I nod and agree with them when they say they knew someone would make it one day. "We're a special breed," they say. "And it's high time the world knew about it." The little old ladies are all the color of mahogany. They look so much alike I can't help but wonder if they're related. There's no shortage of families in Bolton who are all connected through the various threads of marriage.

When it isn't the little old ladies telling me how proud they are, it's the middle-aged mothers and fathers shaking my hand and saying how proud they are. They tell me the same thing the old ladies told me: how proud they are to know that someone from our town finally made it out into the world and did something worthwhile. I tell them that everything they do is worthwhile and that I'm nothing special—which I consider to be true—but they silently disagree. Then they ask me if I can come over and talk to their children. "It would be great if you'd come by and say a few words," they say. "They need to know that they can do it to. They need to be able to believe that they're not trapped here. You know how it is with Black kids. They don't ever get to see any role models. Not really. Everybody they see is a rapper or a basketball player, and that's just not realistic. Those aren't real people. But writers are real people! And you, you lived here. You grew up on these dirt roads. You know what it's like and you did something. I need them to know that they can do it too."

Before I can say that I'm just as unreal as all those rappers and basketball players and dreams of changing America into a place where people like me aren't afraid to walk down the street, Sharon interrupts by saying, "He'll be there. I promise. As sure as Superman, he'll be there. Just give me your information and I'll make sure that he comes and talks to your child. In fact, maybe we'll go so far as to have him do something at the school. He could talk to the whole school and let them know about all the other options that there are for them out there in the world."

Then we make our way inside.

BOLTON TOWN HALL ALSO DOUBLES AS A CHURCH BECAUSE THERE IS no separation of church and state in southern Black towns. God is everywhere, especially in the law. At least, He's supposed to be. But I can tell by the tone and timbre of the people inside the walls of this small, ruined church that they're beginning to believe less and less in the ability of God to come along and do the right thing in their lives.

"Something's gotta be done," somebody yells at the back of the church before anyone can say anything.

"Ain't nobody gonna do nothing," somebody else yells. "Nobody ever does nothing."

The local minister raises a hand and motions for everyone to quiet down. "Please," he says in a voice so booming and firm that the choice of the crowd to listen or not is taken away. The crowd wilts into their seats and soon there is only the sound of restless people shuffling upon old, wooden church pews and, before long, that song fades away as well and everyone sits and waits for the minister to tell them what to do. Which, of course, was God's way of telling them what to do.

"First of all," the minister begins, "we've got to go ahead, right here and right now, and own up to the fact that we've been here before. We've been here too many times before so we can't behave like that ain't the case." The crowd mumbles in agreement.

"We're tired," someone shouts.

"And we should be," the minister confirms. "I'm just as tired as all of you. My mama was tired. My daddy was tired. My grand-mama and my granddaddy was both tired. And on, and on, and on. Tired, tired, and more tired. One after the other. You know it and I know it. And you and me, we're the children of all of those generations of tired people. The children of those generations of people that were so tired all they could do was hope and pray for something more. Those people that gave themselves over to God because he was the only one willing to take them in love and deliverance. That's who we are, all of us. And with every generation we grow more weary." More mumbling of agreement. "And with every generation, we grow more frustrated." Louder mumbling of agreement.

"And before long, that frustration starts to mature into something else, doesn't it?" The sounds of agreement grew from mumblings to shouts of agreement and confirmation. "And we all know what that something else is. We all know what the word for it is."

"What's the word?" somebody calls out from the church.

The minister smiles. "'Anger,'" he says. "No, 'pissed off' is more like it." A round of cheering and agreement rises up from the makeshift congregation that has come out to say their piece. "Ain't nothing wrong with anger," the minister says. It's clear that he has a specific destination in mind for where this conversation is allowed to go. And it's also clear that he's going to get it there in his own time and by his own means, but he has to make the crowd feel as though they were a part of the journey. It's not just his trip that he's on.

As a writer, I can understand that.

"I've been angry all my life," the minister continues. "Just bitter and frustrated for as far back as I can remember. Some of y'all out there might know what I'm talking about. Some of y'all might know something about that feeling. You wake up every day and you feel like the whole world is trying to grind you up. Just squeeze you and grind you up over and over and over again. You grow up poor and broke, just like all of us. This town here, Bolton, we love it. I know you love it as much as I do. But all of us here are poor. And to make it worse, we're poor and Black, and that means the deck's been stacked against us twice. But we try to get past it. We try to believe that it can change. So we go out there and we do the right things and we try to live right—we try to live the way God wants us to live. But we know that it's hard. And, even more than just being hard, it's exhausting. Because to live like that means you've got to be able to ignore a lot of things. You've got to be able to know that things are broken and beyond your control and still, somehow, you've got to be able to look that in the eyes and smile." The minister shakes his head. The congregation nods in agreement. He knows what they want better than this writer could.

I envy this minister. I envy the way he's able to give solace to these people and what they are going through, while I'm only able to come here and watch and worry about the fact that my second book is due soon and I'm still not any closer to getting it written.

Yes, there are better things in the world to be worried about. Yes, there are tragedies, and shootings, and rapes, and violence, and starvation, and human trafficking, and all those other things and I have found the way to ignore them is simply by thinking about myself.

I like to think that's what the minister is talking about when he talks about the ability to look past things and still be happy. The only problem is that I can't honestly say that I'm happy. For sure, I'm something, but I damn sure wouldn't call it happy.

Despondent, maybe. Confused, certainly. Horny, without a doubt.

But happy? No. I'm not sure Black people can be happy in this world. There's just too much of a backstory of sadness that's always clawing at their heels. And no matter how hard you try to outrun it, life always comes through with those reminders letting you know that, more than anything, you're just a part of an exploited people and a denied destiny and all you can do is hate your past and, by proxy, hate yourself.

But this minister, I feel like maybe for him the world is different. I feel like maybe he sees something very different when he looks in the mirror and I can't help but be a little bit envious. And the minister, maybe he somehow feels my envy, because he turns his eyes to me.

"We have tonight among us a special guest, as many of you

know." And then there is more mumbling and there are eyes turned in my direction and I imagine this must be how The Kid felt walking through school with everyone looking at him and casting all sorts of judgments his way.

"He's a local-grown boy who is in no way foreign to our type of pain and strife, as many of you know." He pauses then and aims an outstretched hand in my direction, indicating that I should stand. But I resist that hand. Don't want no part of it. Not my style. That's a sucker's game, public speaking. Everybody looking at you like that. Nope. I don't want no part of it. I'm just gonna sit right here and let that hand hang in the air like a fart in an elevator.

"Stand up," Sharon hisses.

"Don't want to," I hiss back. Everybody in the church can hear me, and I don't care. Nope. I shall not be moved.

"You have to."

"Why?"

"Because it's the right thing to do," Sharon says. "These people are looking for somebody to say something that they can't say. You're a writer. That's what you're supposed to do."

"You know . . . you're not the first person to tell me that. And I still don't believe it."

"Okay," Sharon says, "then how about this: they're potential book buyers. And you have yet to turn in your second novel. And I've got a feeling that you've already spent the advance money and so as soon as this tour is over you're going to be beyond broke and if you don't have a manuscript, you're going to owe the publisher a truckload of money that you don't have. So maybe you should be trying to sell every book you can. So maybe you should stand up and say something. So maybe you should be a good person." Her hissing has progressed into a dark growl with each word. A sound so deep and venomous that I wouldn't think a frame as small as hers could have ever produced it. Also: I think the best thing I can do, regardless of why I'm doing it, is stand up and say something.

But my legs still won't work. My head hurts. I'm sweating all over. I'm buried under a wall of déjà vu and I don't know why. I can't shake the feeling that I've been here before. That I've lived all of this before. But how can that be? How many times have I been to a church in the town where a dead boy was killed? Never, that's how many times.

So why does this all feel so familiar?

Somewhere in the distance, far, far outside of the church, I hear a peacock howling into the night and I remember that obsidian peacock that The Kid and I saw on the park bench that day. I remember The Kid's laughter. I remember his smile.

The memory of his smile takes away my anxiety, and so I stand up. I say something.

The first time Soot saw his dead father was the day after his and Paul's run-in with the officer. He awoke one morning to find his father standing in the doorway, watching him sleep. Soot smiled and sat up and his father smiled back, then turned on his heel and walked off into the house. By the time Soot got out of bed and made it into the kitchen, his father had disappeared. The boy stood for a moment, staring at the familiar surroundings, thinking to himself.

"Okay," he said.

He had expected to see his father eventually. In the weeks after the death of his father, Soot began to see lots of things, so he knew that, in due time, his father would come to him. He saw shadows of animals climbing the sky at sunset. As he stood on the front porch watching the sun drain below the horizon, as the sky danced in opulent hues of gold and crimson, Soot saw shadows climb up out of the horizon and take flight, sailing across the sky like living clouds. Sometimes they were the shapes of animals, sometimes people. But they were always real, real enough for him to reach out and touch.

The sunset became his favorite part of the day because he never knew what he might see. But then the things he saw broke the bonds of sunset and began to come to him at all hours of the day. And they were no longer just animals but people as well. People from books he had read and stories he'd heard. Once, while sitting in the lunchroom at school, he had seen John Henry come walking out of the lunch line carrying a plate of pizza and a big glass of chocolate milk. Soot knew who the man was because of his impossibly dark skin and the twin hammers that hung from his belt. The story of John Henry had always been one of Soot's favorites, and the sight of the man—with his mountains for shoulders and tree trunks for arms—made Soot smile with a pride he couldn't name. It was like seeing a bigger, braver version of himself. He didn't care that it probably wasn't real.

On the best days—the rarest and most beautiful—Soot looked up into the sky and saw the greatest of all these wonders. He saw another Earth. No. Not Earth. Something else. An entire planet, like this one, but different. It hung in the sky like the answer to a question his heart asked him every day of his life. This place, the entirety of it, was the color of onyx. Oceans, mountains, forests, all of them as deep and dark as the skin he hated so much. And yet, there, on that other world, he did not hate what he saw. There, he loved the color of his skin.

Because this place felt like home, he wanted to name it. If he could name it, then he could call it into being whenever he needed it. He could carry it with him, escape to it. He would never feel alone or afraid or ashamed. He could love himself at any moment. He could love himself always.

The name was the thing he needed.

He wanted to call it Africa. That was, after all, where he was descended from. But Africa was not his home. All he knew of Africa was photographs, and such a thing could never be home.

This place that he saw was not America because America knew the whole of him no better than he knew the Africa of photographs.

He was the kid that belonged nowhere. And, because of it, most of his life, he felt like nothing.

But there, on that other planet that only he alone could imagine, that place that he could not name, he was everything.

It was the place of his father and mother, of their skin and language and jokes. It was the place of his grandparents' superstitions. The place of backyard barbecues. It was the place that he carried with him, carried it on his back like a city, carried it on his back like an emblem, carried it on his back like a song, and yet he still could not name it.

It was a place where dope boys and presidents were cut from the same cloth. Where poets and Them Dumb Niggas both doled out wisdom. A place where Yo Mama So Black came out of the same mouths that, at the end of the day, declared, "Still, I rise." It was a place of slaves, singers, and Oscar winners. A place where Blerd Niggas and Hustle Man argued over 2Pac and Jack Kirby.

It was a wonderful place. It was somewhere. And for a kid from nowhere, that was everything.

But it was all a dream, and Soot knew it. He knew that none of it was real and he didn't care. The things he imagined made his reality less painful, and that was what mattered to him. So when he began to see his father in his waking dreams, he was thankful for it.

But as time unfolded, stretched out longer and leaner as the months rolled on into almost a year, Soot's ability to know what was real and what was not began to fade. One Monday morning he came in to school and made the mistake of telling his friends and teachers about the forty-pound catfish he and his father had caught down at the lock and dam over the weekend. His classmates—not even the older kids—didn't seem to have the energy to tease him the way they used to. Ever since the death of his father, not even Tyrone Greene teased him anymore. Soot was just the kid to be pitied, which was almost worse than being picked on.

When word got around about him fishing with his dead father, his teacher, Mrs. Brown, took him aside and, with even more of the pity that he had grown tired of, told him that what he was saying wasn't true and that it wasn't healthy for him to go around telling these types of lies.

When he said he wasn't lying, Mrs. Brown smiled with a tinge of sadness in the corners of her lips and patted him on the head and took his hand and said, in almost a whisper, "I'm sorry this happened to you." That was the refrain people offered Soot these days. Apologies were as common as hellos and, even though a part of him knew that it would not last forever, he had simply grown bored with it. In fact, boredom was perhaps the best way to describe what he felt toward everything these days.

He was bored with the condolence letters and gifts. He was bored with the news crews that still came by a few times a week and asked more questions that made his mother break down into tears again and again. "How does it feel to know that your husband died at the hands of a police officer?" they asked. Or maybe they asked, "How does it feel to know that your son watched it happen?" Or maybe they asked, "How does it feel to know that your husband was killed simply for being Black?" Or maybe they asked, "How does it feel to know that your son will never see his father again?"

They asked the questions over and over again in different ways, and each time, Soot's mother answered their questions and seemed to promise herself that she would not cry again and, each time, she broke her promise.

The longer it went on, the more they came and asked their questions and she answered them and wept, the more she seemed to fade away. Each day she grew thinner, harder, more angled. Her softness seemed to be leached away from her bit by bit. She still cared enough to show love to her son, but the way she showed her love was hardened. She showed her love through discipline and structure. She showed her love through spanking and punishments. She showed her love through words of warning. She showed her love by teaching Soot that the world was danger, and, yet, she never told him why. She never said to him why the world was different for him.

It's the end of the night and I'm tired. Too much time in front of people isn't good for me. That's why I became a writer. Well, that and an imagination I can't seem to get a grip on.

I decide to take a walk because that's the kind of thing you do on nights like this. For me, it's all about getting away from people. And one thing I always forgot is just how much I love the quiet of small towns and the long roads that seem to lead nowhere and everywhere all at the same time. Only a fistful of buildings to speak of. Houses that pop up like memories along the side of pavement and gravel sometimes. It's a hell of a splendor.

The words I said back at the church, I can't really remember them. But they seemed to do whatever it was that people wanted them to do. They captured something. They were a voice for those who needed one. I just wish I could remember what they were. Sometimes, having the condition that I have, all of the daydreaming, all of the memory loss, all of the muddled thoughts, it makes me wonder what all I've forgotten in my life. It makes me wonder if there's some great and wonderful thing that I once knew that now eludes me.

But maybe it's a good thing that I can't remember everything the right way. I know what happened to my old man. But the old lady . . . something tells me not to think about that. It's like the thought of having lost them both is too much to fit in my head so it chooses not to know either way. But there's a catch to convincing yourself that you don't know a thing: yeah, it keeps your life on track, but for the thing or person you're choosing not to see or know, you're taking away their whole entirety. And ain't that something to do to a person? To a group of people? Ain't willful ignorance a hell of a thing?

Being back here in my hometown, I think I can feel that box opening . . . and it terrifies me.

So I walk the roads from sundown until my feet get tired and I have gone far enough out into the night that there is nothing left to do but come back. But, still, there are people out in their yards. People standing around in the dim glow of porch lights talking to one another about all of the things wrong with the world and all of the ways that things should be different and, more than anything, they talk about their anger and frustration. But the talk of anger and frustration is careful to avoid the conversation having to do with sadness. Because, ultimately, it's sadness that sits at the bedrock of all of the anger these people feel every day. Sadness at being left behind and left out of so much of what everyone else seems to have in this country, in this world.

To be these people is to be without a homeland, a lost tribe, a people whose only connection is each other and even that comes and goes. Sometimes all we're doing is waving at one another in the middle of the night and that's as close as we get to being together.

It's when I am walking back through town, passing beneath the shadow of the churches that stand so tall and silent in the moonlit sky, that I'm stopped by the man that I don't expect to stop me.

"Excuse me," the man says. His voice is weak and sheepish, as though he's trying to whisper and yet, at the same time, as though he needs very much to be heard.

"Good evening," I say, as brightly as I can manage. In my experience, when you come across a stranger in the later hours of the night on a lonely road the best thing you can do to keep yourself safe is try to be as bright and pleasant as you can be.

"Are you that writer guy?" the man says. He's a little over thirty. White. Dirty blonde hair with a vaguely familiar look about him. It's rare to run into White people in Bolton. For certain, Bolton has a few White residents. But first thought is that he's one of the news crews that have been hanging around since the shooting. There's no shortage of reporters floating around town these days. What began as a local and regional event caught wings on the national landscape pretty quickly and even though the news cycle wants desperately to move on to the next person who's been shot—and we all know that it's only a matter of time—for now, this little town of Bolton and what happened here is the main focus of the public eye.

The man looks nervous as he speaks. He fidgets a little and looks around. In the distance there are a few houses and now and again there comes the sound of conversation or the slamming of a pickup truck door followed by the rumble of an engine and tires on pavement. Whenever this happens, the man stands as still as a deer and listens, almost sniffing the air, as if he expects the truck to come for him like Death itself.

"Are you the writer guy?" he repeats. His tone is a little sharper, a little more hurried.

"I'm a writer guy," I say. "And, if I'm honest, I'm probably the writer guy that you're looking for. There aren't a whole lot of us around town."

"Good," he says, sighing a heavy sigh of relief. "Can we go somewhere and talk?"

I always get nervous when people ask me to go off in private and talk. I've seen movies that begin that way and they never end well for characters like me.

"What do you want to talk about?"

"Can we just talk?" he hisses. It's then that I'm able to finally recognize and understand exactly what it is I see written across his face: fear. Abject, undeniable, inescapable fear.

"Are you okay?" I ask.

"Please," he says. "Please."

WE WIND UP BACK AT THE FARMHOUSE. THIS PLACE REMINDS ME OF the house I grew up in. But if it was the same place, I'd know it, wouldn't I? I mean, I'm not that far gone, am I?

I'm not sure what time it is anymore. I smell like sweat and humidity and the late hours of the night. "Can I get you something to eat or drink? I'm not sure what all we've got in there, but my mama taught me to always do what I can to take care of people who come to visit."

"No," the man says. He stands at the threshold of the house like a vampire that cannot enter without being invited in.

"You want to come in?" I ask.

"No thank you," he says. The nervousness is thick in his voice. "I'd just rather stay out here. He takes a moment to turn and look back down the long road that leads out into the town of Bolton. "Do you mind if we sit out here and talk?"

"Okay," I say. "But you're starting to make me a little nervous."

He barks a laugh. "Why would you be nervous? If anybody's got cause to be nervous around here it's me." His southern drawl is as thick as The Kid's and twice as uneasy.

"Why's that?" I ask.

The man's face goes pale. "What? Are you fucking with me?"

"I don't think so," I say after taking a moment to check with myself and be sure that I'm not fucking with him. I've been known to fuck with people on occasion, but it looks like I'm not doing that right now. "So why are you so nervous?"

"Don't you know who I am?" the man asks, and I can tell from his tone and from the expression on his face that he can't decide if he should be happy or afraid that I don't know who he is. "Wait," he says, his eyes searching. "You really don't know who I am?"

"Not the slightest clue," I say. "And, to be honest, I'm not even sure whether or not you're real. I might be talking to myself right now for all I know."

"What the fuck are you talking about?"

"I've got a condition. That's all you really need to know."

While the man stands at the transom of the old farmhouse, I go fix myself a tall glass of over-sweet iced tea and come back out to the seat on the edge of the porch. "Well, can we get down to whatever this is?" I ask. "I've got a whole lot of things to get done, both real and imaginary. And I'd just like to get them over with and move on out of this town."

Finally, the man takes a seat beside me on the porch. He still looks fidgety, like an animal worried about predators.

"Maybe it's better if you don't know who I am," he says.

"I think that's true of everyone," I say. "Knowing people gets to be problematic eventually."

"I guess," the man says. I can tell he's having trouble getting a read on who I am. He's trying as hard as he can to understand me, but I guess I'm a bit of a mystery for him.

"First off, I guess you should know that I never read your book. It seems like the kind of thing that I should say. I don't want you to think I'm a fan or anything. I don't know much about you."

"Then we're on equal footing there, my friend," I say.

"We went to the same school, though," the man says.

"That a fact?"

"Yeah. I grew up here."

"In Bolton?"

"Just down the road in Freeman."

"A local boy for sure, huh?"

"Yeah," the man says. He grins a sheepish grin. Finally, he doesn't look as though he's being hunted by the night. "I was a few years behind you in school, though. So you wouldn't know me. Maybe you knew my brother, though. Harold Bordeaux?"

I think for a moment. "Nope, sorry. Can't say I remember him."

The man laughs. "I'm not surprised. He's a forgettable son of a bitch. He knows you, though. Always talking about how he and you went to school together. Swears up and down you two were the best of friends. He says you were a weird kid back then."

"That sounds about right."

"Said you used to spend all of your time sitting in the corner reading books. I guess it paid off, though. Don't think Harold's dumb ass ever read a book in his whole life."

"I know that type," I say. "But how many books you read don't make you a good or bad person. How many books you read is just how many books you read. My daddy didn't read a whole lot of books. My mama either. But they were damn good people."

"I guess you got a good point there," the man says. With each moment he relaxes more. His breath slows. All of the tightness that had been making him look so chased seems to have faded. "You got out, huh?"

"I guess so," I say. I take a long look at the star-filled sky. "But sometimes I wish I hadn't."

"Nah," he says. "You did the right thing. There ain't nothing good here."

"It can't be all bad," I say.

"No," he says, glancing up at the same sky. "It's not all bad. But that's not the same as it being good. And when you really sit and think about the past you realize that things have been pretty bad for a long time. Things were never really good. They just had flashes of things that weren't as bad."

He shakes his head.

"Not the most optimistic person, are you, friend?" I say. "But I think I can relate to that. I think I've been there and I know a few other people who've been there."

"My brother said you had a hard time in school," the man says. "Says you got picked on a lot after what happened."

"What happened?" I ask.

The man's face tightens. "Are . . . are you kidding?"

"I don't think so," I say. I try to contort my face into something that lets him know that I'm not mocking him, but I'm not sure if it's coming across or not. Mostly, I think I'm just confusing him.

"Are you fucking with me right now?" There's a tinge of anger in his voice all of a sudden.

"Why would I be fucking with you?"

"So you're telling me you don't remember what happened?"

"That's probably what I'm telling you. I still don't know what you're talking about so I can neither confirm nor deny whether or not I remember it. Plus, you should know, I've got a condition. I won't go into the details of it, but the bottom line is simply that I have an overactive imagination and it makes it difficult to tell what's real and what's not."

"You're a schizo?"

I laugh. "No. Nothing like that. I'm just imaginative."

The man looks at me with more than a little suspicion. Finally, he shakes his head. "I ain't got time for this," he says. He sits up straight, looking me in the eye. "Listen, you're a writer so I need you to write something for me."

"Sorry, I don't do ghostwriting."

"Shut up! I . . . I need you to tell people what happened." His voice is close to panic. It's full of pain, and despair, and something else that I can't quite understand.

"What happened?" I ask.

"I'm not a bad person," the man says.

"I believe you. You seem like a square enough Joe to me."

"That boy," the man says. His voice catches in his throat. "I can't let people think of me like that. I can't let them think of me as some sort of killer."

A shiver runs down my spine. I've run into my fair share of people asking me to write their life stories, but none of those stories have ever had anything to do with a dead body.

"I didn't kill that boy," the man says.

"Okay," I say.

"I mean . . ." The man swallows hard, as if his throat is attempting to betray him. "I mean, it was my finger that pulled the trigger, but it wasn't me. I'm not the kind of person to kill somebody. And nobody wants to hear my side of the story. Nobody wants to hear about what happened to me that night. Nobody wants to think that maybe I'm not some kind of goddamn mad-dog killer."

I think back to The Kid's corpse lying on that gurney, full of holes and lifeless. I think of his sobbing mother. I think of a thousand other dead bodies that looked like The Kid and a thousand other sobbing mothers and I want him to be able to see them the way I do. I want him to shut up and stop talking. But I'm still not even sure if he's real or not, and in case he's a figment of my imagination, I decide to let him keep talking. I'm speechless, anyway.

"The thing you got to understand is that this isn't about me. It's about everything. It's about everybody. I'm just a regular guy. Yeah, I'm a cop . . . or I was a cop . . . but that don't make me some kind of demon. I'm just a regular guy. I got a wife and a daughter." He spits. "Now the wife won't call me and she won't let me speak to my daughter. I tried telling my wife all of this. Tried to lay it all out for her the way I'm trying to lay it all out for you, but she wouldn't let me. Just up and walked out on me, crying like it was her kid that . . . well . . ."

"So you decided to come and look me up?"

"Something like that," the man says. "Been staying at a friend of my brother's since it happened. Have to sneak around. Can't hardly leave the house because I'm afraid of what might happen if I go out and somebody sees me. That's why I'm out here in the dark like this. You got any idea what'll happen if these people around here were to find me? If they walked up right now and caught me sitting out here in the open?"

"You think they'd hurt you?"

"They'd kill me," he says.

"How do you know?"

"Because . . . you know."

"No," I say. "I don't know. Why would they kill you?"

"Don't be like that," he says. "Don't pretend you don't know why. Don't pretend like you ain't never had the thought. Don't pretend like you don't sit around sometimes being angry, chewing your cud—like my daddy used to say—over everything that's been done in this country to people like you."

"People like me?"

"Black people. You're angry. And why shouldn't you be? But the thing about it is, I didn't do it. I didn't do any of it. I wasn't born when all of that slavery shit happened. I wasn't even a twinkle in somebody's eye. And you, you weren't never a slave. You weren't never nobody's property. Me and you, we went to the same school. Grew up just as broke. We lived the same life but I get to carry around all of the guilt. I get to be called an oppressor. I get to be told about how everything my ancestors did was terrible. Well how do I know? How do you know? Wasn't neither of us there. Not you nor me. So how you know that my folks owned slaves? How do you know that my folks had anything to do with hurting and harming your folks? And yet, you still want to blame me for it. You want to blame me just because you're angry about stuff that you can't control. I ain't gonna sit here and say that your people ain't had a bad shake. I won't say that. But they're all dead. All the ones that it happened to. They're all gone. And now everything's fair. Everybody's got a chance at things. Everybody in this country can have a fair chance. Hell! Just look at *you*!"

He points an angry finger at me and pokes me in the chest with it.

"Just look at you," he continues, "a goddamn fancy-ass writer. Been on TV. Sold more books than God only knows. And you did it all being Black. Made it a hell of a lot farther in this world than I have. You want to know the farthest I've ever been? Florida. That's the farthest I've ever been. Only time I ever even been on a plane. Went down there for a funeral. You ever stayed in a hotel?"

"What?"

"Have you ever stayed in a hotel?!"

"Yeah."

"A fancy one."

"Sure."

The man looks down at his hands as though they'd just betrayed him. "I ain't had no breaks. Not a single one. Don't that count for something? So, yeah, maybe I was a little mad when I came across that boy. I saw him and I saw people like you, people that got to have the things that were supposed to be promised to me." He shakes his head. "No, that's not true. Truth is I didn't know if he had a weapon on him. So I did what I did."

"You shot him."

The man purses his lips for a moment and turns away from me. I see a tremble run through his body like a goat that's swallowed lightning. He clears his throat and his hands turn to fists and his arms fold across his body and he buckles in half at the stomach and lets out a heavy, wet sob.

"I won't say that," he said.

"It's the truth."

"But I won't say it."

"And that's the whole problem."

Again he lets out a sob the size of Texas. He reaches into his pocket and pulls out a gun.

I manage to raise an eyebrow. I can't say I didn't see this particular development coming. Guns are like pets. Even if you don't own one, it's only a matter of time before your neighbor, friendly or unfriendly, brings one into your life and you have to cross your fingers and hope it's friendly.

"I need you to do something," the man says.

"Well," I say, "I suppose you've got a pretty good bargaining chip in your hand."

"You don't have to worry," he says. Finally, he sits up. He wipes the tears from his face in the near darkness of the night and takes a deep breath. "I doubt I'll really do anything with this."

"Then why'd you bring it?"

The man looks at the gun. His brow furrows as though he's only just realized he has it, as if his body had made the decision without him and only now was his mind catching up to the fact that he was carrying it. "I don't know," he says. "I guess because somebody had to."

"I'm not sure I understand that logic."

He chuckles. "Then you don't understand people."

"So what do you want from me?"

"I want you to help me figure this out."

"Figure what out?"

He waves his hand at the world. "This," he says. "All of it. I can't figure it out. I can only ever get pieces of it. And even those pieces are stuck inside of me. I can't get them out. If I could get them out, I could fix all of this. I could make it all better. People would understand who I am. They'd know that I'm not a bad person. They'd know that all I did was the only thing I could do in that situation."

"There are plenty of people who think otherwise."

"And that's exactly what I'm talking about," he says. He rests the gun on the porch between us. It's close enough that, if I was fast enough, I could probably reach out a hand and snatch it away before he could stop me. But I don't. If I did that, maybe he'd stop talking. Maybe he'd get up and leave. And, God help me, I want to hear what he has to say. I need to follow this thread out and see where he's going.

"I'm not a bad person," he says. "That's the thing that hurts the most. People think I'm evil. They don't know about how I'm a good father. They don't know about how good of an uncle I am. Do you know I've got a niece that I'm putting through school? Did you know that?"

"I didn't."

"Yeah," he says. He digs into his pocket and pulls out his phone. After a few fast swipes he shows me a picture of him being hugged by a brightly smiling blonde girl in a cap and gown. "Harold couldn't make the money and I had a little extra, so I'm helping her. Don't that make me a good person?"

"Sounds like a good thing to do," I say.

"But ain't nobody talking about that," he says. "All they want to hear about is me and what happened. All they want to do is whittle me down to just that one minute. Like I didn't have a whole life before that. Like I wasn't somebody's baby once. Don't the past matter?"

"It does," I say. "Not just three-fifths of it, but all of it."

A small movement in the field surrounding the property catches my attention. I look off and there, under the dim glow of the moonlight, is a man. His skin is dark and his hair is kinky. So dark is his skin that I cannot help but think of The Kid. The man has large lips and his hands are in shackles. His feet as well.

"The past matters," I say.

The man hears a change in my voice and his eyes follow mine.

Then there's another one standing in the edge of the field. A woman this time. Her hair is long and decorated with cowry shells. She wears kente cloth and, at her side, a young child stands naked. It too has the same dark skin that seems to glow blue in the moonlight. The woman and child, their hands and feet are shackled too.

The longer I stare the more of them there are, effervescing from the cornfield. Not all of them are shackled. Some stand in torn clothes with withered hands. Some of them with whip marks across their flesh. Severed hands and feet. Brands on their arms to identify their owners. They all stand and watch. They watch me. They watch the man.

Silent and eternal, they watch, and I do not know what to say to them.

"You see them too?" the man asks.

I don't know what to say to him.

He reaches, picks up the gun, and steps off of the porch. "I wish that boy were here," he says. Then he starts off toward the cornfield. As he walks, something stranger than usual in my life happens. With each step the man seems to fade away, little by little. Or, rather, he doesn't fade away, but he's replaced by something. A darkness. A blackness. Soon, after only a few steps, when he is still close enough for me to reach out and touch, he becomes nothing more than a silhouette of darkness. A shadow that walks. But it is not only darkness that forms the shape of him. There are stars there . . . I think. Inside The Shape that he has become, I can see twinkling, like that summer sky in the deep hours of the night. And yet, The Shape that was once a man continues onward, footfall by footfall, toward the cornfield and the figures that stand waiting for him.

"Why?" I ask The Shape. "Why do you wish that boy were here?"

But The Shape doesn't answer. He only offers a solemn wave goodbye and does not look back as he walks off into the cornfield that is dancing beneath the eternal Carolina night.

The figures in the cornfield watch him enter. It is as though they have been waiting for him, patient as a river.

Soon The Shape is gone.

Soon the figures are gone.

Soon there is only me, and me, and the lonely night.

I don't think he's well," Soot's mother said. The two of them sat side by side on a small couch in the psychiatrist's office, buried in the sound of ocean waves pumped out of a small CD player in the far corner. Posted around the room were various positive affirmations about inner strength and human resilience and the individual's responsibility to not be controlled by their past. Soot wasn't sure he believed any of it, but he tried to give it the benefit of the doubt.

"What do you think is wrong with him?" the psychiatrist asked. She was a thin, dark-haired woman who smiled whenever she looked at Soot. She gave him the same smile most people did now that his father was dead. It was a smile that tried to convey a message of sadness and empathy, but there was always an undercurrent of joy as well. It takes the misfortune of others to remind us of our own blessings.

Soot's life had become a walking reminder of other people's blessings.

"He sees things," Soot's mother said. Then she took Soot's hand and smiled at him. An apology danced in her eyes. "Lots of different things," she continued, turning back to the psychiatrist. "Animals, strange colors, all sorts of things. But, mostly, he sees his father."

The psychiatrist wrote something down on her notepad.

"He knows that his father's gone," Soot's mother continued. "We've talked about that. So it's not like he thinks his father's alive."

"He saw it happen, correct?" the psychiatrist asked.

"Yes," Soot's mother replied. Her body tensed for a moment, then relaxed again. "But he says that he's doing things with his father. He told people at school that he and his father went fishing the other weekend." Her hands wrestled with one another in her lap. "He's always had an imagination, and we always encouraged that. But this is something different. He believes it. He really believes it. And I don't know what to do with that."

The psychiatrist held up her hand. "Well, hold on a minute," she said. "Let me talk to him and find out what he really believes and what he doesn't. Okay?"

Soot's mother nodded. "Should I leave?"

"If you don't mind. It would make talking to him a little bit easier."

"Okay," Soot's mother said. Then she rubbed his back and kissed him gently on the forehead—her perfume smelling of vanilla and lavender. "I'll be right outside," she said.

"Yes, ma'am," Soot replied.

When she was gone the psychiatrist put away her notebook and threw Soot another warm smile. "Let's sit on the floor," she said. "I find that I always feel a little better when I'm sitting on the floor."

"Okay," Soot said.

The two of them settled onto a pair of beanbags and Soot

couldn't help but wonder how many other kids' mothers had brought them there and left them seated on these beanbags with this woman.

"So your mother says you're seeing things," she began. "Is that true?"

"Yes," Soot replied. He scratched the back of his hand to keep his mind off of the questions and to avoid looking at the tree that was growing in the corner of the psychiatrist's office. It was pitch-black with blazing white flowers and it had not been there when he came into the office. It had only sprung up in the corner a few moments ago but, already, it was two feet tall and its branches wove themselves into the flowered wallpaper, sprouting new white blossoms by the second.

"Do you see your father?"

"Sometimes," Soot said. In the corner, the sable tree continued to grow. Its branches consumed the corner of the office. Its flowers burst like stars.

"And what happens when you see your father?"

"What do you mean?"

"Does he talk to you?"

Soot smiled. "Why wouldn't he?"

The psychiatrist smiled back. "What does he talk about?"

"Just different things," Soot said.

"Does he ever ask you to do things?"

"Sometimes."

On the far wall behind the psychiatrist, the tree had sprouted tall and long. Its branches and flowers covered the wall and made their way onto the ceiling. Its roots dug through the carpeted floor, and broke into the concrete, and burrowed into the firm, black earth beneath it all. The branches broke the drywall and wrapped themselves around the core of the room, splitting two-by-fours and breaking windows. The tree's canopy, black and shimmering, melted across the ceiling and burst through and opened up the small, stuffy office to sunlight that fell through in a great, glowing swath of brilliance and warmth.

Soot smiled.

"What kind of things does he ask you to do?" the psychiatrist asked.

"He tells me to take care of myself," Soot said. Across the room the tree swayed back and forth like a song sung to a child. "He tells me not to be scared."

"Not to be scared of what?"

"I don't know," Soot replied. He struggled to keep his hands calm. More than anything he wanted to run across the room and climb that tree and have it take him away from the psychiatrist and all of her questions about his dead father. Where that tree could take him, his father would not be dead.

"You do know that your father is dead, don't you?" The psychiatrist asked the question as softly as she could, like handling something precious, and fragile, and destined to be broken at some point. But, more than anything, she wanted to keep it from being broken in her hands.

"I know," Soot said.

"And so you know that seeing him after he's dead means that what you're seeing is just a part of your imagination."

Above him, the tree danced and the black leaves filtered the light into black legs, and black arms, and black hands that cast themselves against the far wall and danced with the wind and seemed to call out Soot's name and, in those dancing shapes, he saw his father smiling back at him.

"I know," Soot replied. And he laughed and waved at his father and said, softly, "I miss you."

I MISS YOU.

Hell of a thing to say to someone.

My fingers type the words into my phone and then all ten of them give me a hard look, threatening to send those three words to Kelly. As much as my head might try to spend its existence anywhere but in the real world, my body seems to know what's up. Especially my fingers. They always know what my heart's up to.

And before you start in on me, I know that texting in all caps means that you're yelling but sometimes you need to yell "I miss you" to someone that's been on your mind more than they've been in your arms. It's a good thing I'm at thirty thousand feet again just now. Because at this height I can yell "I miss you" all I want but because my phone is in airplane mode it'll never be heard. I've always found that the best time to wax poetic about some dame that you've fallen head over heels for is to say it so that it can never be heard. That keeps you safe. Keeps your world rolling along on familiar tracks. I've found that to be the best thing to do with any upsetting information.

And I know she told me not to call her a Dollface, but that's the easiest way I can think of to pretend that she's not something special.

I MISS YOU.

Eight little letters with a whole hell of a lot to say. Seven letters that stick out like a sore thumb in a crazy fistful of life. I wonder if I sent those letters to her, what would she think? And, yeah, I know that ever since we beat the terrorists airplane mode ain't required anymore, but there's a safety in not being able to say a thing for a while. Not being able to send this text message feels like the heady moment when an idea is only in your head. That moment when it's untold and perfect. That moment before your fingers and hands get ahold of it and ruin it so that what comes out the other end is nothing like the thing you first fell in love with. I feel like that's the history of all stories and all relationships. Or maybe that's just me.

I MISS YOU.

Hell of a little mantra. How true can it be? I met her only once and got to hang out with her for fewer hours than I got on my hands and toes. Sometimes I can't even believe myself, even when I think I know what I'm doing or feeling. So is it any wonder that I question the realness of everything when that message that's still waiting to be sent—with that narrow thumb of mine hanging over the Send button—gets interrupted by an incoming message that reads: Do you miss me?

It's Kelly. In the flesh, digitally speaking.

Somehow airplane mode has been turned off on my phone. Somehow messages are getting through. Somehow I've been thrown out of hiding and into a conversation because no matter how much I might want to ignore this Call to Adventure, I know I can't. I have to answer it. I try not to question Divine Providence or major cell phone carriers when they team up and come knocking at my door.

I think so, I reply.

You don't know? she asks.

What's your favorite movie? I ask.

Don't change the subject, she replies. Are you scared?

Why would I be scared?

Because saying you miss someone feels like falling.

I'm at thirty thousand feet right now. I should be afraid of falling.

But it's only a fall if you think about the ending. Otherwise, it's called flying.

And then my fingers are sitting there, crippled, trying to find the right thing to say. But they're just fingers. They can't be expected to say the right thing to the person that's come along and made you feel things that you've been trying not to feel for far too long. That's not what fingers are supposed to do.

And I know what you're thinking: Aren't you a writer? Ain't that your whole *raison d'être*? That's a French word I learned from a Nigerian dame. I don't speak French but I speak existence. I speak fear. I speak insecurity. I speak it all when it's some unknown hour of the night and I'm flying through the skies and doing my best to figure out why some woman I met is stuck in my head at a time in my life when the thing in my head keeps spilling out into the real world. It's enough to make me wonder if she's even real. Like maybe she's just another thing I'm trying to distract myself with.

I'm real, the next message from her says. You're real. This is real.

Is she? Am I? Is any of it?

I HAVEN'T SEEN THE KID IN DAYS AND I MISS HIM. HE HASN'T BEEN around since Bolton. Not since I met with that guy who killed him. Maybe The Kid wanted me to do something. Maybe he wanted me to avenge his death like some billionaire superhero. Maybe he wanted me to be filled with rage. Maybe he wanted me to cry. Maybe he wanted me to scream.

And what did I do? I talked.

No wonder The Kid left me.

But he needs to learn some things. He needs to understand the way the world works. Maybe if he'd lived long enough, he would have come to understand that he's a part of all of this too. All of us are.

I mean, wasn't I somebody's baby once? Wasn't I a kid for at least eighteen years? So when did I change from being a victim of the world's cruelty to being a part of it? When did I become the thing that furthers the cycle of horrible things that crawl over the world each and every day?

Never, that's when. Just like everyone else, I'm not a part of the problem. It's not my responsibility to change anything any more than it's The Kid's responsibility. And if I had a responsibility, then so did he. I'm sure he could have done a thousand things differently. I'm sure he gave that guy a reason. He put his hands up too fast, or too slowly. He didn't get down when he was told to. There's no shortage of reasons for things like that to go wrong and people want to tell me that it's my job to do something?

Sharon has the nerve to tell me that I've got to say something about all of this? Renny tries to tell me that I've got a responsibility as a Black author to say something about the world? No. Not at all.

My responsibility is to sell books. My responsibility is to keep myself out of the poorhouse. My responsibility is to keep on doing what I'm doing without taking on any more than I have now. My mother and father would have wanted that. I'm a good person with pain all of my own. Why do I have to try to fix the world?

The best thing that I can do is keep my eyes on the prize. I've got to make this Denver interview matter. It needs to be the thing that sells enough books that the publisher knows they can't get rid of me. This is all about making sure that they keep me around. Keep paying me. Keep me touring. Keep me running. And if they do that, if I do that, I'll even find a way to call up Kelly and fall in love the way I was always supposed to.

Love cures all. Loves takes away pain. Love makes us forget, and each of us is deserving of a little forgetting. My dad told me that once.

I SHOW UP IN DENVER AND MY MEDIA ESCORT IS A LIVELY, OVERLY FIT woman named Bonnie. When I come up to baggage claim, she's holding a sign with my name on it. She's dressed in athletic gear the type of which I haven't seen since the Jane Fonda days. She looks like someone who is always in motion like she's sponsored by Energizer.

"———?" she asks.

"That's me," I say.

"I'm your handler, Bonnie."

"Nice to meet you, Bonnie."

"Let's grab your luggage."

We move over to the baggage carousel and, while we're waiting for the conveyor to start, Bonnie drops down into a few sets of squat thrusts. Her form is perfect.

"So how was your flight?" she asks without breaking rhythm.

"Swell," I say.

Oddly, no one is staring at her. They don't even seem to care. This must be normal for Denver.

"Ever been to Denver before?" Bonnie asks.

"I'm never really sure," I say.

Bonnie shifts from squat thrusts to wind sprints.

LATER, WE'RE IN BONNIE'S SUV, SLICING OUR WAY THROUGH DENVER freeway traffic. She's got some sort of apparatus set up between the driver's and passenger's seat that lets her get in a bicep and/or tricep workout while driving. Not the kind of feature I'd want in my car, but to each her own.

The bicep workout doesn't seem to interfere with Bonnie's ability to handle her five thousand pounds of steel and fiberglass. After a few miles, she reaches into the glove compartment and retrieves a sheet of paper.

"So, it says here we've got a few radio spots and one TV interview lined up."

"Sounds familiar," I say.

Bonnie tosses the itinerary into the back seat. Checks her watch. "We're good on time," she says. Then she reaches into the back seat and pulls out a Thighmaster. She sticks it between her knees and begins banging out a set. The SUV swerves a little to the rhythm of her repetitions. Everything in this universe is connected. Never forget that.

"So, you're from North Carolina," Bonnie says.

"Yep."

"Beautiful state. I love it."

"You've been there?"

"Nope," she says. "Never been out of Denver."

"Why not?"

"What will I find someplace else that's not already inside myself?"

"But I thought that travel was supposed to jar you loose inside. Help you find new parts of yourself."

"Only if you don't already know yourself. As for me," she says proudly, "I am who I am. I've met me." She reaches into the back seat and, after a few seconds of groping and swerving the car back and forth across a few lanes, she pulls out a copy of *Hell of a Book.* She tosses it into my lap. "Sign that for me?" Then she throws the Thighmaster into the back seat and returns to her bicep workout. "Hell of a book," she says.

I sign it.

"Thanks."

"Just a raging, brilliant, shitstorm of a book! So what's your next book about?"

I ignore Bonnie's question by looking out of the passenger window. I look out just in time to see a tow truck guy standing with a stranded motorist. The motorist is holding a wooden board—karate demonstration–style. The tow truck guy punches through the boards. The two high-five each other.

Denver's an interesting town full of interesting people. But that just makes me think of Kelly.

A few more miles down the congested freeway, there's another car parked on the shoulder. As we pass it by, I see Kelly sitting behind the wheel. She looks at me. A dialogue balloon appears next to her head: "YOU THERE?"

I don't tell her if I am or not.

WE GET TO THE TELEVISION STUDIO AND BONNIE POWER SLIDES THE car into a parking space. Tires squeal. Smoke rises. The whole five thousand pounds of domestic steel and imported rubber lurches to a stop perfectly between the lines.

She leads me inside the studio walking at the fastest pace I've ever walked. We're not even late. I think she just wants to be sure she's getting a proper workout in. I remember her saying something in the SUV about how people didn't know how to walk. Something about how we all use the wrong muscles to commit the act. I'm not exactly sure what she means, but she seems serious about it.

So be it.

"My author is here for his interview," she says to the receptionist. The receptionist is a thin man with close-cut hair and skinny jeans but he doesn't seem like one of those skinny-jean assholes. He seems like a decent guy. He tells us to take a seat and that we shouldn't have to wait long. Then he turns back to his dominoes.

The dominoes.

Oh, the dominoes.

I've never seen so many stacked so perfectly. Not outside of a television commercial. I can't say exactly how many there are, but the number's gotta be in the hundreds at least. Thousands, maybe. They come in all kinds of colors and they're everywhere. They sit on the desk and spill over onto the floor and the chair and along places on the wall where there were shelves.

It looks like it took eight lifetimes to set up this whole grab bag of fun. Maybe millennia.

As I sit there, fascinated by the dominoes, Bonnie signs the sign-in sheet and then drops down to the densely carpeted floor and bangs out a set of push-ups. She does the kind where she springs up and claps her hands at the top of the movement. Damned impressive stuff, if you ask me.

Time drags on in this place. Nothing ever seems to start on time when you're on tour and fighting demons inside your head. The last thing I want is to sit here with time to think. I've got to do something.

Without being asked, I walk over and start helping the receptionist with his project. Strange thing happens then: turns out helping is pretty easy. I seem to know what to do even before I touch my first domino. It's like I've been helping to build the domino thing my whole life. Like it's my project, my bag. I kinda feel like I'm creating something big and important. I kinda feel like I'm creating myself.

"So how long have you worked here?" I ask the receptionist.

"Worked where?" he replies, his focus never wavering from this big pile of awesome we're working on.

I make a gesture to the dominoes. "So what's it supposed to look like in the end?"

"What end?"

The exchange gets broken off early by the appearance of a TV producer who pokes her head out from behind the big, tall door at the end of the hallway. She calls my name.

"Yeah?"

"We're ready for you."

When I go over to the door, she shakes my hand like my uncle used to shake his tobacco pouch before he dipped. "Hell of a book, by the way."

"So I hear," I say.

I turn to take one final look back on what I'm leaving behind. Those dominoes. I feel like me and that receptionist were only a few pieces away from finishing it all up. And if I finished it all up, then the whole universe would be laid bare before us. Everything would be answered. The Kid might even come back!

But there's no time. The interview waits for me like the final chapter of a novel. Like some boss battle in a video game. Can't hide forever.

I enter the room. The door closes behind me.

I think I hear the dominoes fall.

THE LIGHTS ARE BRIGHT AND THE INTRO MUSIC ANNOYING. IT'S A typical three-camera setup with an elevated stage and a small studio audience. You know the type: the morning talk show where they give away free tickets to the Rotary Club and the Farmers Guild, and all the old people who don't have much else to do with themselves at this time of the morning come out to see what type of guest their local affiliate has managed to land.

Today it's me.

". . . So we're back," the interviewer says. She's a tall, thin White woman with sharp features and a smile like a mouthful of porcelain squares. She's nice and bubbly in that morning talk show way, so I guess she fits the bill for the job. "We're almost at the end of our hour-long interview with ———, the author of *Hell of a Book.*" She shows the book one final time and turns and looks at me with that toothy smile of hers. "I just wanted to thank you again for taking the time out to join us here on the *Morning Soup.*"

"It's been really great being here," I say in my best end-of-interview voice.

"Oh, we're just so glad we could have you here to talk about your book."

She smiles.

I smile.

The audience smiles.

"So," she says, "tell us what your book is about."

My smile fades just a little. I look up at the clock. It's just seconds before 10 a.m. We've been here for an hour already. Why does she want a recap in the closing ten seconds of the show?

I smile. "Excuse me?"

"Oh, c'mon. Don't be shy. Tell us about your book. That's why you're here, after all." She smiles at me, then smiles at the camera.

"You mean again?" I ask. "I'm not sure we've got time for me to do it again. After all, we've been doing it for the last hour." I smile at her, then I smile at the camera.

I take another quick glance up at the clock on the far wall of the studio. My stomach sinks. The clock says it's only two minutes after 9 a.m. But that can't be right. So I check my wristwatch. Somehow, it says the same thing. Tells the same lie. According to the two of these, the interview is only just beginning.

"I promise you," I say to the interviewer, "we just had this conversation. You and I have just spent an hour talking about my book."

"Nonsense," the host says, "we've only just begun, as the old song goes."

She laughs a little. The studio audience laughs stiffly. They're trying to figure out what's happening with the author in front of them. And the author in front of them is trying to figure out what's happening with the life in front of him.

I feel myself beginning to sweat.

"Now," the interviewer begins, "tell us—"

"We've already done enough of this," I bark. "We've already had this interview. Can we please not do it again? I don't want to talk about my book any more right now." My tie feels like it's choking me. It feels like some wrestler has taken a liking to my trachea. So I loosen it and wipe the sweat from my neck. I look up at the clock on the wall. Only 55 more minutes of interview to go.

"Well . . ." the interviewer says. She's being gentle. Kinder than she has to be.

"I don't understand why I have to keep telling this story again and again," I say. My breaths come fast and staggered. "I don't understand any of this whole process. The interviews, the hotels, the readings. Why can't I just write and go away? That's all I want to do. Why can't I just give one interview and be done with it? Why do I have to keep reliving this same day over and over again?"

"Because people want to hear it," the interviewer says. "Because you're an author and this is what you wanted."

I'm having trouble breathing but it seems as though I'm the only one who notices. I look around the room, hoping for something to happen, for someone to come, for anything that can get me through the next hour, the next interview that I've given a hundred times before already. I'm trapped by my own novel and no one will let me escape.

"So let's begin," the interviewer says. "Your book is all based on actual events."

"No," I say, correcting her. "It's fiction. It says so right there on the front cover. It says 'a novel.' That makes it fiction. I keep saying that and everyone keeps telling me something different. I've already told you, I've told everyone, it's fiction. It's all fiction. None of it is real. Nothing is real."

She looks at me and laughs. "Yeah, right!" she says. Then the audience laughs. "Now, tell us all the story. Tell us about how this novel came into being. Tell us the inspiration for it. The plot points. The pain you went through to write it. The self-doubt. The terror. The insecurity. We want it all. Tell it just like you've told it every time before."

I can barely breathe now. I keep rubbing my neck because I need to be sure that someone's hand isn't wrapped around it, closing off my airway. I scan the room again, looking for an exit, maybe. But the room doesn't seem to have any doors. It's just a box and I'm trapped in it, with the cameras, the host, and the audience.

The audience. I could have sworn there were only a few of them a moment ago. Fifteen or twenty at most. There's at least double that now. Maybe triple. All of their eyes aimed at me. I can feel the heat from their staring.

It's then that I see her.

She's seated in the front row, wearing her hospital gown. Watching me. I don't understand how I didn't see her sooner.

"So, let's go back over the basis for this book again," the interviewer says.

"I don't want to."

"But I'm afraid we have to."

"No," I say. "I want this to end."

"This will never end," she says.

I look out over the audience once more. I see Renny, somehow. I see Renny's wife, Martha. The TSA agent. My agent. My publicist. My editor. Sean. Every Kelly I've ever dated. The apparition of Nic Cage. The Culture Crew from Cubicle Hell. Bonnie. The receptionist with the dominoes. The receptionist with the Post-it notes. I see some kid in a well-cut suit that looks a lot like me. I see my old man. I see the woman in her hospital gown.

They all stare at me.

The studio lights are blindingly bright all of a sudden. I shade my eyes.

"So," the interviewer continues, "tell us what it was like to watch your mother die."

"What?"

The studio cameras push in closer to me.

"She died slowly, didn't she?" the interviewer says. She picks up her copy of *Hell of a Book* and begins reading from it. "It was a painful, protracted affair. A wasting away that bled from one sunrise to another."

"Stop that," I say.

"But these are your words."

"Are they? I don't remember."

That's the truth. I can't remember anything about my book. Haven't been able to since I wrote it. Writing it was like carving out a piece of myself. And once it was cut away, I left it there. I moved on, perhaps a little more incomplete than before, but at least able to ignore the pain of the emptiness more than I could bear the pain of memory.

"You don't remember?" she asks.

"No," I say.

"Of course you remember," she says. "And that's what scares you. You thought writing it all down would make you not remember, make you forget how badly it hurt. But now you have to retell it again and again, piece by piece. All of those little retellings adding up to reach the point where you're constantly reliving it. Pebbles become a mountain. It's called a *Hell of a Book.*"

"I know what it's called! I fucking wrote it! I wrote you! I wrote all of you! So don't you think I know what it's called?!"

A stunned pause.

"Excuse me?" the interviewer says. "What do you mean you wrote me?"

"You're not real," I sob. I'm not sure when the crying started. But it did. "None of you are real. You're just characters. Imaginings." I swallow. "Aren't you?"

Another look around the studio. Everyone I have ever known in my entire life is there now. Looking at me. Watching me crumble. But in front of them all is the woman in the hospital gown . . . my mother.

I realize now that every interview I have ever had about my book has been an interview about her death. It's why I don't remember them afterward.

"What's your book about?"

"It's about the death of my mother."

I see myself clearly, in all of the interviews, going over the story:

"It was Mother's Day weekend," I begin. "I was going away on a trip and she asked to come with me. She wanted to make it a mother-son expedition. Something that we would remember. But I told her no. She almost cried, I think. But it didn't matter. I left.

"On Mother's Day, as I was driving back home, I got the phone call. She'd been out working in the garden and collapsed. She was in the hospital. When I got to the hospital, they said she'd had a stroke. Said they didn't know how extensive the damage was, but they didn't want to set my expectations too high.

"She was in a coma for a week. When she came out of it, I was there—guilt had forged me into a responsible son, the type who would not leave her side. She looked up at me with bleary eyes and said 'Home.'

"The doctors called it aphasia. The mind says one thing. The mouth says another. You're trapped inside your own head. Much like being a writer. For six weeks, she saw me and she called me 'Home.' Over, and over, and over again she said it. Everything was 'Home.' If she was thirsty, she asked for 'home.' If she was hungry, she asked for 'home.' When I kissed her on the brow and told her good night, the last thing she said to me before falling asleep was 'home.'

"Then, she died. And I can't decide if it was because she finally went home, or if it was because I could never take her out of the hospital, could never actually take her away, back to the glorious place in her memory where she raised her only son. I failed at that. I failed her."

. . . beep . . . beep . . . beep . . .

"And then, one day, I wrote a book about it. It made me successful. I took her love and turned it into profit because I wanted to get away from her, wanted to write her out of my mind."

. . . beep . . . beep . . . beep . . .

I looked up at the audience. I saw only her.

"Didn't work."

The sound of that heart monitor rings in my ears, coming from everywhere all at once.

I'm sweating and gasping for air now. I don't know when it started, but I can't breathe.

"Are you okay?" the interviewer asks. "Maybe we should take a question from our audience. How about that?" The interviewer smiles and aims a finger at the studio audience where a woman is waiting. Her skin is the color of mahogany. She wears her hair in a ponytail. A flowered skirt hangs from her waist crowned by a red blouse. She looks so much like my mother I can hardly breathe. All the lines of my life are blurring together. "You there," the interviewer says. "We've been waiting for you."

"May I come up there?" the woman asks. It's about this time that I recognize her.

"Of course you can," the interviewer replies, flashing a mouthful of glowing white teeth. "You can have my seat, actually."

"Don't," I protest.

But she walks up onstage. Somehow, she is two things at once, the way a memory is both alive and dead. She is my dead mother and she is The Kid's mother. She is the dead mother of all the dead sons, dead daughters. My heart can't believe my eyes and so, because it is ruined in disbelief, my heart hurts.

"My boy is dead," The Kid's mother says. "He was shot and killed a few weeks back. Maybe you heard about it." Her voice trembles as she speaks. Her hands struggle with each other in her lap.

"Yes," I say. I want to reach out and take her hands in mine, settle down the conflict between them, the same conflict I've seen in my own extremities. It's the battle between wanting to accept life, and feeling powerless to change it. "I heard about your son," I say, catching my breath as I look into my mother's eyes even as I look into the eyes of a stranger. "I tried to feel something for him when I heard, but when I dug down, there was nothing there. Nothing in my belly, you know? Been that way ever since my mother died, I think. Something got miswired after that. It hurt to feel, so I stopped doing it."

The woman who both is and is not my mother nods gently. "I know," she says as the tears begin to fall. "But mothers are supposed to die. Not their children. And their children aren't supposed to give up when their parents die."

I know this woman is not my mother. She is memory and imagination gone too far, no matter what her visage might tell my heart. I don't know how she got here. I don't know where she came from or what she wants from me and, most of all, I don't know if she's real. But it doesn't matter. Her stare, her tear-streaked face, they're the only thing I really need to see and know about right now.

"What did my boy do?" she asks. "What did he do to deserve to die like that?"

"In my experience, life doesn't care much about what we deserve."

"But what about God? Why did God let this happen?"

"Don't ask me questions like that. I'm just a writer. We've already got enough of a God complex and I can't pretend to know the hows and whys of whatever God people happen to believe in at this time."

I look out to the studio audience, but they are all gone. Empty chairs. Unmanned cameras. The terror of disappearing lives.

There's just her and me, buried in our grief in the empty studio.

"I don't know what to do with it," the mother says.

"Neither do I."

"It's not supposed to happen."

"I guess death isn't supposed to happen, but it's the only thing that we can ever really depend on. It makes time for each and every one of us."

"What kind of answer is that? My son is dead!"

"I know," I say. "And I'm sorry about that. Even though I don't know you and have only just met you, I'm sorry about that. Believe it or not, the death of your son keeps me up at night. It makes me uneasy. It tightens me up inside because I know that I should stop everything I'm doing in my life in order to mourn with you, in order to let you know that you are not alone, in order to let you know that your son truly mattered and that his death was a tragedy that cannot happen again in this world. I want all of that." I want to say something more, but can't find the courage on account of how I know what she'll ask. I know that she'll keep me talking and the more I talk the more I'll feel. It's as inevitable as a fucking freight train bearing down on your head. I wish that she would go away. I wish I could change the channel, close the window, open a new tab, swipe her away from my reality.

I wish that I could become invisible like The Kid, but I can't.

So I sit and wait for what is coming.

"If you believe all that you say you do, then why don't you do something?"

The question hits me square in the teeth.

"You know why," I manage, half mumbling, doing the best I can to say nothing at all. "You know how it is. It . . . it just gets too big. All of it. Stacks up every fucking day and none of us can make a dent in it, so we just sorta move through it without ever letting it get its hooks in. It's survival. It's how you stay sane. It's how you stay alive. And there ain't no way to change that."

The woman who is and is not my mother shakes her head.

The woman who is, and is not, The Kid's mother wipes the tears from her face.

"I want my boy back," she says.

"I know."

"I suppose you want your parents back."

"I do."

"But they can't come back."

"I know. And neither can your son."

"I know."

"But that doesn't make it hurt any less," I say. "Knowing that something can't be changed, it still hurts. That serenity prayer people are always chirping . . . I always knew it was bullshit."

"This isn't the way it was supposed to happen," she says. "We were supposed to be a family. I get so tired of this. I get tired of the news. I get tired of waking up tired. I get tired of being afraid for people that look like him, for people that look like me, for people that look like you. I just get stretched out and worn down by it all." Her voice quivers, the way my mother's used to. "Over and over again, each and every day, it wears me down. It hangs over my head, just like it hangs over your head. And it hangs over the heads of everybody else like us."

I reach out and take her unsteady hands in mine. For the first time, they relax.

The oldest memory I have is of my mother's hands. It's a disjointed recollection, like a flash of light in the back of my heart. Her hands are large in my memory, large enough to hold all of me. Her hands radiate warmth. They smell of raw earth dug up from her vegetable garden.

Memory and death are countries that know no geography.

Somehow, they have both taken up residence in the hands of the woman who is, and is not, my mother. As I hold her hands in mine, calming them, for the first time in decades, I can feel something other than fear.

"That boy of yours," I say, "he seems like a good kid."

"You say that like you know him?"

"Only in my imagination," I say. Then: "Can I ask you something?"

She nods.

"Why me?" I ask. "Why come to me with your story?"

"Because you're the voice," she says. "This time."

"'This time'?"

And then she does not speak. For what seems like hours, the two of us sit in silence. And then, as if they had always been there, we are surrounded by the audience again. I'm onstage again, staring at the camera. The audience is just as shocked and awed as they were before both my mother and The Kid's mother left.

Of course, she was never really there.

"I should go," I say to the morning show host, my words catching in my throat.

Since starting the medication, every day was a daze for Soot. The world was always far away. Sometimes, he sat on the edge of his bed looking down at his feet and trying to understand how the floor had gotten so far away from them. His feet hung there, feeling as though they belonged to someone else. His whole body felt like it belonged to someone else.

He didn't laugh. He didn't cry. He didn't get angry—which wasn't a thing he did much before the medicine, but that wasn't the point. When he rode the school bus in the mornings and Tyrone Greene came over and began asking him why he was so black—the brief reprieve he had been given after the death of his father couldn't last forever—Soot didn't feel any dread, or worry, or shame anymore. He only sat quietly and let Tyrone ask his question over, and over, and over again. He only heard the words calling him "so black" and he let the thoughts about what it meant to him come and go.

The medicine was supposed to take away the things that he saw, but that was hardly the case. He still saw creatures in the sunset. He still saw black trees sprout from nothing and blossom into everything. He still saw his dead father come and talk to him. The only difference was that now he could hardly hear what his father said to him. His father became little more than an image, a moving picture that came and sat beside him sometimes and tried to talk to him about life and the world and, perhaps, tried to tell his son that he loved him even after death and that all he wanted was for the boy to be safe in this world.

But Soot no longer heard his father's words or felt the love that the dead man was trying to give. His father was just a ghost now, in the way that ghosts existed in stories. He was just an apparition, a shadow of the man that once was, that came now to haunt those who were left behind.

The psychiatrist told Soot that this was the best way. She said that, eventually, even the ghosts would fade away into nothing. "All you have to do is trust the medicine. Trust that it will work." And Soot did trust in it. He trusted in it for as long as he could, but he couldn't feel his mother's love anymore and he could not feel his own. Love, much like the dead father who used to be so real to him, was nothing more than an idea. He knew that he loved his mother and that she loved him, but he did not feel it.

When he woke up to the sound of her crying alone in her bedroom, he knew he wanted to care about it. He wanted to be sad for her. He wanted to get up and go and sit beside her and hold her and let her cry into him, losing himself in the cool of her body the only way that melting into a mother's love can happen.

But night after night she wept, and night after night he lay awake listening, and he searched for compassion for her pain, and he searched himself for sorrow for her tears, and he searched himself for love enough to go to her, but he found nothing. The medicine took it all away.

So he stopped taking the medicine and, soon, everything that was not real came rushing back to him along with everything that was. They seemed glad to be with him again, the impossibilities that only he saw. The creatures loved him again and the sunsets sparkled again and he could hear his father's voice again when the man appeared out of nothing and said, "I love you, son."

This was when Soot found writing. It was a way to capture his father's love, a way to keep the man alive, page after page, story after story. It was the means by which he could see his father and not get caught up in it so much that the doctor realized he was off of his medicine.

I'm sitting in the luster and glow of pale sunlight funneled in by the faux open-air design of the Denver International Airport and, thanks to a credit card that my publisher hasn't had a chance to deactivate yet, I'm well on my way to a good, self-flagellating drunk. The kind of bender we all deserve when our lives have come crumbling down around our ankles. I'm at a small bar fiddling with the brim of my hat—trying to pick together the threads of my sanity—and staring up at a screen where I can see myself and, for once, I think I'm not just imagining it. There's the image of me on-screen yelling at the camera, screaming, "I wrote you!"

The caption beneath the video reads "AUTHOR MELT-DOWN ENDS BURGEONING CAREER."

The world works fast.

You wouldn't think everything a person chased after and fawned over for the whole of his life could come crashing down around the brim of their hat so quickly, all on account of a little ol' semi-psychotic break on local television that went viral. I mean, don't it seem like life could just take something like that in stride?

I feel like I've been living in this airport. I couldn't tell you how long I been here. Few hours? Few years? Who the hell knows? I just know that the Illuminati did a real good job designing this place. The swastika-shaped runaways, the creepy murals of blue swords and red savagery, the blue mustang with the laser eyes. This is the kind of place that disrupts an unsettled mind and answers questions only a shattered brain can ask. Maybe that's why I feel so at home here.

I could live here if somebody gave me half a chance. And why shouldn't I? People have lived in airports before. Just ask that guy who used to live in the Charles de Gaulle. Eighteen years of living in the space between destinations, the world between worlds. He did it because he had no country, and I figure that's a sentiment people like me can relate to. They tell me I have a country but, hell, try telling my country that. Try telling my world that.

Is it any wonder I lost my shit like I did?

I keep trying not to check my phone, but, let's face it, who can ever get by without keeping up with that little rectangular soul-killer? What am I looking for when I compulsively pull it out of my pocket more times than an OCD exhibitionist with a penchant for pocket jobs?

I'm looking for her, of course. The Alpha Kelly. The one that got away.

I tell myself that I need her.

A text. A call. Anything.

I love her . . .

. . . I think.

Love's a hard thing to nail down, even after you get it backed into a corner. All I know for sure is that it's easiest to call it love. It's easiest to pull that word up from the soles of your feet—where you've been trampling it beneath your heels for years—and stuff it into your head and decide that it's really what you need to be okay.

I wonder if Kelly's still there. I wonder if she's still waiting for me to get back to her, still willing to believe me when I tell her that I'm looking for a love story. I need to be believed when I say that. I need everyone to believe me when I say that, even if it isn't true.

I like to think that if I called her up she could solve the problem of me. But what if she's just another fantasy? Just another person who isn't really there? Just a phantasm pumped out by the mind of another Mad Kid grown old.

I check my phone yet again. And, this time, much to my surprise, I catch the incoming call. The caller ID says "Alpha Kelly."

"HELLO?"

"Hey," she says, her voice sounding like a dream. "You still there?"

"I guess," I say.

I'm more than a little thankful for the fact that this is all happening over the airwaves and fiber-optic signals rather than face-to-face. I'm not fully sure that I could handle facing her right now.

"So, I saw your interview," she says.

"Yeah," I reply, swirling the bourbon in my glass, watching the copper-colored sea invite me to take a dive. "Was a hell of a show, wasn't it? I wonder what the Nielsen ratings people are gonna have to say about it. 'Viral,' that's the term, right? I've officially gone viral. Hell of a thing to accomplish."

"Why do you keep doing this to yourself?"

"Excuse me?"

"Why do you keep running away from everything until you fall apart?"

"I don't know what you're talking about, Toots."

"Don't fucking call me Toots. Be a person. A real goddamn person."

I take a long drink of the bourbon. I empty the glass down my gullet and, already, I can feel her voice beginning to fade away. The sunlight spilling in through those Mason-designed Illuminati windows seems to grow five shades less golden. This is the start of running away again. And, this time, it'll be permanent. I know it, and I think that she knows it. "I don't know what a real person is anymore," I say. "That's my whole problem. Haven't you been paying attention to anything at all? Why don't you just get on with it?"

"Get on with what?" she asks, and I can hear the frustration in her voice. She sounds like she's reached the end of her waiting with me, and who can blame her?

"Get on with the fixing, Dollface."

"I told you not to call me that."

"I need to be put right," I say. "I need to be squared away, and that's your role in all of this. You're the love interest, have been since the very beginning. I've made promises about you and me, promises to people you don't even know. Promises to people all over the place. This is how it's supposed to be. This is how it's supposed to go. You're supposed to teach me about all the failings within myself, you know? Heal me with the power of love."

"Heal you with the power of love?" she says, and it sounds like she wants to laugh. Or maybe she wants to cry. It's always hard to tell the difference. But it's never hard to tell when you've missed your chance to change who you are. That moment, even if we deny it, is impossible not to recognize.

It was always going to fail, so let's get on with the failing.

"Don't act so surprised," I say, adding a few sharp edges to my tone. "Your role is one of the great traditions of not only American storytelling but Western storytelling as a whole. The woman is the oracle through which men like me find redemption and self-correction. You're the mirror in which I'm able to see myself for who I really am and, in doing so, correct the flaws that have been plaguing me from my earliest days."

"Fuck you," she says. Each word is an anvil slammed across my spine.

I tell myself that her resentment is misplaced. I mean, who doesn't mind being the tool by which somebody heals themselves? It's like the redshirt who sacrifices himself at the beginning of a *Star Trek* episode so that the viewer knows the monster isn't foolin' around. People like me have been redshirts for generations of storytelling.

"Just play your part," I tell her. "I mean, when you really stop to look back on it, you've been a great secondary character in this narrative of mine. But the thing is, I misunderstood your role. I thought you were the unachievable trophy. But you're not the Trophy, you're the Healer. So . . . you know . . . go ahead and get to healing. Sort me out. Sort me out and send me home. Make me a better man like all the Hallmark cards and Lifetime movies say you're supposed to do."

The sunlight's all but gone now. Something gray and impenetrable has moved in and covered up the clear blue skies behind the airport glass. And to make matters worse, the entire airport is empty. Every single schmuck has gone away. There's just me, the bar, and the blackness beyond the windows.

No, that's not all. There's one more thing: the silence. The long void of two people dangling in the space between the life that might have been and the life one of them condemned them both to.

I've always lived in that silence. Always found comfort there. As cruel as it can be, it's easier than saying something. Saying something sounds a lot like change, and change isn't something I've ever been particularly invested in.

And maybe the same can be said for her. Who can say? I never treated her like a real person so there's no way I know her. I just wanted to know someone other than myself.

So I could say something, and keep her in my world, or I can let her go, and see if I'm able to really figure out what my world is. Maybe actually get to know her some other time, if those three Greek ladies that guide us all cut us some slack.

After thinking it all through, I've got only one choice.

I hang up. I let go.

As soon as the call's over, the black void around the airport disappears. Sunlight blooms in the heavens again. Only . . . it doesn't look the same as it used to. It's not as warm, and I don't know that it ever will be again. Some decisions are irrevocable, even for imaginations like mine.

The people repopulate the airport, shuffling about their lives. I'm even back on TV again, still having my meltdown in front of the world. Proof of irrevocability.

Just then, my cell phone buzzes and, right on cue, my heart sinks. If it's her calling back I don't know what to do about it. Luckily, or unluckily, depending on what version of life you're rooting for, it's not Kelly, it's Sharon: "I'll be brief. And after today's scene . . . well . . . I just don't think you and I will be able to keep working togeth—"

I end the call. Nothing more to see here. Move along.

More drinks.

More time passes.

"I'm sorry," The Kid says.

I turn in my chair to find him sitting next to me. I knew he would come.

"What for?"

"For what happened to your mama."

"You shouldn't apologize for things you didn't do. And unless you ruptured the blood vessel in her brain and made me write a whole book about it, it wasn't your fault."

The Kid thinks about this for a moment. "Just because I didn't do it doesn't mean I can't be sorry that something happened to you."

"Sorry is pity. And I don't want pity."

"I think you do," says The Kid. He keeps staring at me, like he's waiting for something. It's a gentle type of demand. He sits there with that apology of his hanging in the air between us, promising that maybe somebody in this world really does care about me and all of the things that I've been through. I know he's just a figment of my imagination, but maybe that's the best way that the mind can take care of itself.

"I'm not imaginary," The Kid says.

"I don't feel like arguing this point with you, Kid. I'm too tired. I've lost too much. I just want to be here and to wallow in all of this without feeling bad about it. And that's all you really do, Kid. You make me feel bad about things. You make me feel bad about the world."

The Kid finally looks away and I hate myself for making him do it. I hate myself for not having room enough in my head for him and all the other kids like him. I hate myself for scrolling past news articles about dead kids, and dead mothers, and dead fathers. I hate myself for ignoring everything that has to do with people in pain, for spending all this time running. But what can I do? It's the only way that I know to live.

"Will you do it?" The Kid asks. For the first time in a long time, there's an edge of sharpness in his voice.

"Do what?" I say, pretending that I don't know what he wants. Even though the truth of the matter is, I've known what this kid wanted from the moment I met him. It was always there, no matter how hard I tried to deny it.

"I want you to talk about me."

I cluck a laugh. "You want me to tell your story."

"Yeah," The Kid says. "That's what everybody wants."

"But you're not everybody. You're a cop-killed Black kid who's become a figment of my imagination."

"No," The Kid says. "I'm the person next to you. And I just want you to talk about me. I want you to stop ignoring me. It's like I told you in the beginning: I just want you to see me."

"I see you, Kid. Now go away. Leave me alone."

"No, to *see* me. To know me, to not push me away. To tell my story."

"I don't know how to tell your story. It's too big. It's too much. What happened to you—what happened to people like you—it's too big for anybody to ever really get behind. It's too big of a story to tell. It hurts too fucking much. Haven't you seen what you've done to me? Haven't you already done enough? I can't sleep. I can't even mourn my own pain because I'm worried about yours. Pain makes people selfish. We only have so much so I can't take yours too. I can't carry your water, Kid."

"I'm not asking you to carry it," The Kid says. "I just want you to see it. I just want you to see it the way it really is. Just stop ignoring it and look at it. Stop pretending I don't exist. No more jokes. No more looking the other way. No avoidance. See me!"

"Okay," I say. "Okay."

Somewhere, a Black boy walks along a street alone at night. Perhaps it is a country road. Perhaps beneath the glaring light of a bustling city. Perhaps in a small suburban village where most people do not look like him and he has been aware of that for all of his life.

He walks along this road for no reason other than he wants to. Perhaps he has been bullied at school that day about the dark nature of his skin. Perhaps he walks because it helps him clear his head when the worry that has followed him through his life begins to get too big and clouds over everything that he sees and feels. Perhaps the late hours of the night are the time when he is finally able to be free. Perhaps crowds of people make him nervous because he has been picked on or simply felt like an outsider for all of his life and being alone takes away those feelings.

Or, perhaps, his father was killed in front of his home years ago and he does not remember that anymore because it is simpler to not remember than to live with that memory each and every day, so he has created a world in which his father is not dead. He has created a world in which he has no father. He has created a world in which his father has simply moved away. He has created a world in which his father is simply in prison. He has created a world in which his father is off adventuring. His father is off chasing dragons and outsmarting sirens. His father is climbing great mountains, defying death again and again. His father is living on a beach in the Caribbean, basking in sunlight and sleeping until noon. His father is in Wakanda, surrounded by people who look like him and the son that has been left behind, and, one day, that father will come back for him. One day, his father will come to take him home. One day, his father will return and take away all of the pain. One day, his father will come and take him to a place where he is not afraid, a place where he does not feel like an outsider, a place where his skin is not a curse or an affliction . . . a place where no one calls him "Soot."

He has created a world in which, one day, his father will come and take him to a place where he has a name.

He has created a world in which his father has died of cancer. The boy has created all of those worlds because they are easier than the world in which his father was shot and killed in front of him by the long arms of a system that he is powerless to overcome.

So this boy, who lives in all of these imaginary worlds solely because the real world around him is more than he can bear, goes out for a walk one evening. In one iteration of this, he is a boy who goes on to become a writer who tours and drinks and dreams. In another iteration, he is a child who dies and, yet, somehow finds a way to go on. In another still, he is a child who goes on to become a writer who hides so deeply in his characters that the stories he tells of them become muddled in the story he fears to tell of himself, so he throws in dashes of truth among the lies, until even he cannot tell which is which.

This child, he is in the country and the sky above him is littered with stars. He stares upward as he walks, like all children should, dreaming of life on those stars and imagining the stories that could occur between them. He imagines spaceships and aliens, fantastic worlds where the ills of this one do not apply. In one moment, he imagines traveling the expanse of space alone, only the hum of the meager electronics of some small spaceship to keep him company. In another moment, he imagines all of humanity surrounding him on his journey. Millions of people cluster together beneath a great window aboard the ship and they all stare out at a gas cloud being pulled into a star. The swirling trail of glimmering particles are pulled downward into the gravity of a glowing star, and everyone stands aboard the ship watching in awe. And in this particular world, on this ship, Soot stands above the crowd, watching them and watching the spectacle of the star at the same time, and he feels as though he is part of them. He feels no fear. He feels no shame. He does not feel as though he does not belong. He feels as though he is mired in with them as they make the journey through this life, even as he stands outside of the masses, watching and hoping that they will all come to love and care about him the way that, as a child, he cannot help but love and care about them.

All of these visions and dreams go through the boy's head as he walks alone and stares up at the stars. He is wearing a pair of old, familiar jeans and a hoodie because it is the early arm of fall that has come and wrapped itself around the earth and he loves the feeling that it has given him.

As he walks, the world around him sings. There are night owls and crickets, a peacock, and somewhere off in the distance, the low hum of traffic as people make their way through this world. The boy imagines that the sound of traffic is the sound of a great ocean that lies just beyond the length of his vision. The ocean glimmers in the dim starlight, reflecting the universe upon its glassy surface. The ocean stretches out and reaches every place in this world and Soot dreams, briefly, of sailing across that ocean.

Travel, the boy always dreams of travel. And why wouldn't he? Somewhere else in this world, there has to be a better place than the one in which he finds himself. Somewhere else in this world, he cannot be afraid. Somewhere else in this world, he cannot be sad. Somewhere else in this world, he is accepted and loved and his father is not dead. It is only a matter of finding that place. It is only a matter of going out far enough into the length and breadth of the earth and that place will appear. All of the things that he wants will be made manifest if he can simply go out far enough. If he can walk long enough. If he can jump in a car or board a plane and disappear into the horizon, there will be the place where all of these fears no longer live. The place where his mother is happy.

Again, and again, and again he imagines happiness. And it is because he is so deep in his imagination that he does not see the man standing in the street ahead of him. It is because of his imagination that he does not see the blue lights flashing. It is because of his imagination that he believes that he will be okay.

"Hands in the air." The words go up like fireworks, and so do his hands. He has been taught this since before he can remember. "Hands in the air," his father would tell him when he was so young that he still had to learn how to get dressed. It was a game that the two of them would play. "Hands in the air," his father would say. And Soot—who had not yet been named "Soot" by the world—

would raise his hands over his head and smile as his father pulled his shirt off. "Good job," his father would say.

"Hands in the air." The words rise up like rockets. The blue lights blot out the night, blinding Soot, and, instinctively, before he knows what is happening, he looks up to see his hands in the air. His body knows how to keep him safe better than his mind does. Perhaps his father was not just dressing him on those days. Perhaps it was training.

"What did I do?" Soot says. Again his body tries to keep him safe. His body says to him: *Be quiet. Silence keeps you safe. Just do what you're told.* But as his body speaks to him, his mind says, *Silence has never kept us safe. So what do we do?*

"What are you doing out here?" the figure ahead of him calls out.

"N-nothing," Soot says, his heart beating in his ears. "Just out for a walk."

"Where you walking to?"

"Nowhere," Soot says. "Just . . . just walking. Not really going anywhere. Just walking, that's all."

"Let me see some ID."

"I don't have any," Soot says. He can feel the fear in his body as it tells him to run. It tells him to run and it tells him to hide. It tells him to fall down on his knees and beg not to be killed like his father was killed. It tells him to beg not to have a gun put in his back like his uncle had. It begs him not to be shot down like so many other boys and men that looked like him and then went on in life to become nothing more than hashtags and names on shirts instead of living out the lives that they were on course to live. All Soot wanted right then and there was to disappear. To disappear utterly and completely. Disappearing was a way out of everything in his life.

Disappearing was a way out of the cycle of violence. Disappearing was a way to not hate himself when he saw that skin of his in the mirror. Disappearing was a way for him not to hate everyone else that had skin like his. Disappearing was a way out of everything and he knew that was the reason his mother had taught it to him. It was the reason she and his father had tried so hard to teach him how to disappear. If he could disappear, he could be free from fear. If he could disappear, he would not have to worry about bullies. He would not have to worry about cops. He would not have to worry about legislation aimed at his skin. He would not have to worry about the history of slavery that led him to here. He would not have to worry about feeling inferior. He would not have to worry about being angry, and afraid, and never sure which was better to feel because they both hurt in different ways but they seemed to be all that he had left. He would not have to worry about not knowing what to feel when he watched video footage of people that looked like him being sprayed with fire hoses. He would not have to worry when he saw old, grainy footage of a man standing on the steps of a school shouting "Segregation now! Segregation forever!" He would not have to worry when he saw men with torches marching in Virginia. He would not have to worry when a boy about his age in South Carolina was found hanging from a tree. He would not have to worry about watching movies and TV shows in which people who looked like him always died or, if they lived, were good only for dancing and talking about prison life and the lack of fathers. He would not have to worry about a world in which those were the only boxes he could live in. He would not have to worry about all of the kids who didn't think he was Black enough. He would not have to worry about liking hip-hop and Dungeons & Dragons at the same time. He would not have to worry about his skin being too dark or too light. He would not have to worry about his hair being the wrong texture. He would not have to worry about his lips being too big. He would not have to worry about all of the things his mother and father had both been afraid of.

No. He could be free of all of those things. That was the reason his parents had taught him to be invisible. That was the reason for the gift they gave him.

Soot closed his eyes.

"What are you doing?" the voice called out from the darkness.

Soot said nothing. He only focused on disappearing. He took in a deep breath and held it and focused on slipping away into that other place where he was safe and unseen.

"Answer me!" the cop yelled.

Soot heard what sounded like a gun being drawn. It was a sound he'd heard a thousand times before in movies and on television. That slip of steel against leather. A shudder of fear ran through him, and broke his concentration briefly. He opened his eyes and, sure enough, there was the barrel of the gun aimed at him. The cop holding the gun took a step forward and, finally, Soot could see his face. He was young-looking, with thin, brown hair and a square face. Even though his face was tight, Soot could imagine him being a kind man. If he had a family, he was the type of dad who made shadow puppets in the late hours of the night. He was the type of dad who was hard on the outside but gentle on the inside. The type of dad who lectured you about doing something wrong and then, moments later, tried to think of a prank that the two of you could do on Mom.

He was not the type of person who would shoot a boy.

Soot closed his eyes again. He could hear the music that came with his invisibility. He could feel the warmth of that place. The freedom. The safety.

"Hands up!" came the command, then came the gunshots.

Soot felt nothing before the darkness swept over him. No pain, no fear. He only heard the voices of his parents, each of them calling his name, each of them screaming out for him, moaning and wailing, trying to save his life, just as they had been trying to do every day since he was born.

But, in the end, as it is with all of us, he could not be protected from the world.

This was supposed to be a love story. The kind of story that started off serious and mixed in some funny and stayed both ways from beginning to end. The typical format: boy meets girl, boy loses girl, boy gets girl back. But here we are. It's all fallen apart and I don't know what to do with it.

"Man . . . so what?"

You don't get it, Kid. This is bigger than all of that. This isn't just about the fact that I didn't find anybody to love. It's not about the fact that I didn't get my new novel written in time. It's not even about the way that my mother died.

I know why your mom taught you to be invisible. She wanted to protect you. Being who we are . . . it's hard. We get shot or put in jail. It's all we see. It's all we know. Our whole story is about pain and loss, slavery and oppression. It defines us. It seeps into our skin. We bleed it even as we're covered by it. All we want is to be something other than the pain that we have been born into. All we want is to be known for something else. We want the great history we see in others. And all we're ever given is the story of being in pain and being forced to overcome.

Your mama, she wanted to protect you. Protect you from bullets. Protect you from cops. Protect you from judges. Protect you from mirrors that you would look into and see something less than beautiful. She wanted to protect you from the black skin that you should adore and be proud of, but that you're going to spend your whole life trying not to hate. You'll hate it in yourself and in anyone who looks like you. You'll secretly see other Black people and hate them for not solving the riddle of the self-loathing you've been taught. It'll follow you through everything in your life. You'll be angry and not know why. And the anger won't ever go away, not really. It'll hang in the back of your mind. It'll hang in the back of your world, haunting you, guiding all of your decisions. And when you get tired of being angry, it still won't go away. It'll just change into something even worse. You'll take that anger and turn it on yourself and it'll call itself depression. And, just like anger, it'll take over your life. It'll live with you every day. You'll look in the mirror and hate what you see. You'll tell that person in the mirror—with that skin that looks so dark—that it's broken. You'll tell that person that they deserve less. You'll tell that person that the good things in this world are not for them.

And then, rarely, you'll try to break out of that. The pendulum will swing in the other direction. Maybe you'll take a stab at being an optimist. You'll say that race doesn't matter. You'll say that everyone is treated equally and you'll try to live that life. You might even say that you don't see color. You'll hide in not being as Black as some other Black people. You'll look at Black people who don't behave the way you do as doing it wrong. You'll divide yourself up. You'll make fun of the way they talk, the way they dress.

But all you'll really be doing is making fun of yourself.

But, for a little while, it'll feel good.

And then, when you've been optimistic for long enough, you'll turn on the news and someone who looks just like you will have been shot and killed. And maybe the optimism will hold for a while. Maybe you'll be able to say to yourself, "Well, that's just one case. A freak accident. It doesn't mean that the world is like that."

And then—and this part won't take long—you'll see another case. You'll see another person who looks like you that's been shot. And then you'll see another. And another. And another. And maybe you'll stop reading the news. You'll retreat into books or movies. But then you won't see anyone who looks like you. Or, if they do, they don't act like you. They act like those stereotypes. They act like those Black people that you always thought you were better than, those people who use the language you don't. Those people that dress the way you don't.

And then, eventually, you'll come to understand that you're all the same person. You'll finally come to understand that you're a part of it all. That they're you. And that'll break your heart and make you proud at the same time. And the anger and depression will cycle back through again and again and the only way to escape them is to pretend that you don't see how broken the world is. It'll be that way every single day of your life.

And then, you'll have kids one day, and you'll want desperately to protect them from all of that.

That's what your mama wanted. She wanted to protect you. She wanted to have a son that she could keep safe from all of this.

She wanted to have a child that could exist beyond it all. She wanted a child that could be free from it. A child that could never get shot. A child that didn't have to be afraid. A child that she didn't have to be afraid for because, at any moment, they could just disappear.

They could hide from the gun. From the cops. From the judges. From the mirror.

That's all she wanted for you.

And she made it happen. She gave that to you. She made you able to be free . . . but it didn't work forever. It never does. You still died. You still got shot because the truth is that we can never get away from this. None of us.

And I don't know what to do with that. I don't know what to do with what happened to you, with what happened to all the other kids like you, with what happened to me. To all the kids like you who got shot and maybe even lived through it and grew up to be people like me: Black and broken and trying to remember that they are beautiful.

Trying and trying and trying, day in and day out. Through song, through dance, through pants hung low and bass beats. But we're all fractured and I'm not sure if we'll ever be made whole. I know I won't. I don't know if I'll ever really be okay.

God knows we're all trying. But maybe you can be a little better than I was.

"CAN I ASK YOU SOMETHING?"

After all we've been through, Kid? You can ask me anything.

"Am I real?"

You're as real as I am, Soot.

"I never told you my name."

I know. And I never told you mine. But that's what they used to call me back when I was a kid. So that's what they called you.

"Did your daddy get shot like my daddy did?"

What you're really asking is whether or not you and I are the same person. And I'm not really sure that it matters. No. What matters here with me and you, Kid, is what we do with it all. What matters is how we feel about it, about one another, about ourselves. What matters is the fact that if it wasn't my dad that got shot and killed it was somebody else's dad. What matters is that if it wasn't you or me that got shot and killed, it was another kid.

And it's always been someone in this world. That's the catch.

I know I told you that people weren't real, but at some point, a person can't just keep getting by like that. At some point, a person has to be seen. You told me that. You asked me for that. At some point, we have to turn on the news and see people and have them follow us home. We have to be able to sit around in our house and see them there. We have to be able to talk to them just the same as we would if they were sitting right in front of us.

"Is that what I am?"

I guess. And that's what I am too. I'm not real to anybody. I'm just someone they see on the dust jacket of a book. Or maybe they see my face on my website, but not likely. Sharon used to tell me how few people visited author websites. Mostly, I'm just as unreal as you are. And yet, if you asked me, I'd say that I was totally and completely real. I'd say that the story I've told you about my life was a real one. I'd say that it all happened to me just the way I described it, just like you'd say that the things that happened to you happened just the way you described them.

You and me, Kid, we're the same person in that sense. And

maybe in a bigger sense than that. You know how I told you that this was going to be a love story?

"Yeah."

Maybe that's still true, just not in the way that I expected. Maybe the love story here is more reflective, you know? Like maybe Narcissus had spent his whole life hating himself before that one day when he saw his own beauty, his own worth.

"Ha ha! Geez, that's lame."

Laugh all you want, but I think learning to love yourself in a country where you're told that you're a plague on the economy, that you're nothing but a prisoner in the making, that your life can be taken away from you at any moment and there's nothing you can do about it—learning to love yourself in the middle of all that? Hell, that's a goddamn miracle.

I WALK OVER TO THE KID AND OPEN MY ARMS AND HE LOOKS FRIGHTened for a second, like he doesn't know what I'm doing. But he knows exactly what I'm doing and he's afraid of it. Hell, so am I. But I'm also tired of being afraid. My whole life I've lived afraid. My whole life I've been afraid. I've been running. I can't remember anything else. Same goes for him. And I know it because he and I are the same. Me and everyone who looks like me are the same. We all carry that same weight. We all live lives under the hanging sword of fear. We're buried under the terror that our children will come into all of the same burden and be trapped, just like we were. So we stay put, running in place. Most of all, people like me fear that we can't do anything to break the cycle.

And I don't know if we can or not. I just know that we have to try.

That *I* have to try.

The Kid knows it too. I can see it in his eyes. Finally, he wraps his arms around me and I hug him tighter than I've ever hugged anyone in my life. Hugging him is hugging myself. Finally, after a lifetime, I am the unseen and the undeniable all at once.

I'm sorry, I tell The Kid.

"Are we gonna be okay?" The Kid asks.

Quick as a whip and honest as a dollar, I say to him: Never can tell, Kid. But we're gonna damn sure take a shot at it.

"So that's it. Everything's fixed now, right?"

*". . . But isn't that what we all want?
To believe that everything's fixed?"*

"Well, that's anticlimactic."

*". . . What if it doesn't help? None of it.
What if I screamed and shook my fists
at the heavens, only to have my voice
swallowed up? Only to still be invisible."*

". . ."

"Maybe next time."

*"Names would just make it true.
All of it. Not just true, but real.
I'm not sure we can let it be real.
I'm not sure we could face that reality."*

"That's a dangerous word."

"What if it wasn't 'fixed'?
What if you could only hope to help?"

"But it's real. And reality
is something you continue to struggle with."

"Then at least you said something.
Even if you had to use someone else's
voice to do it."

"Have you noticed that, throughout
all of this, you still haven't used
his name? His real name,
I mean. Or your own, for that matter."

"Why?"

"'. . . We?' What else could we do?"

ACKNOWLEDGMENTS

Thank you to all those who picked me up each time I fell down. My family: Sonya, Sweetie, Angela Jeter, Justin, Jeremy, Diamond, Aja, Zion, and the infinity of aunts, uncles, and cousins who made me. To my friends: Cara, Justin, Randy, Dan, Carrie, Maurice, Zach, Bill, Ramm, Will Dean (I still hope Chun breaks an ankle), Shannon, Kiki, Kristen, Paul, Terah and Aiden, Michelle White (strongest person I know), Natasha Nunez, Michelle Brower, and Sean Daily. Every day I am indebted to you all. I apologize that there is not enough space for me to list everyone. That fact is perhaps the greatest blessing of my life.

Thank you to everyone who has ever learned to sing in a world that does not want to hear your voice.

Lastly, a message to the Black boy that was: You are beautiful. Be kind to yourself, even when this country is not.